old brother, has plans for stowing away to China...

FLIGHT OF THE MANDARINS

Daughter of the manse Isabel Monrose had always wanted to become a missionary, so she was thrilled to leave 1920s Edinburgh for a post in Shanghai, accompanied by Gordon Campbell, a member of her father's church. Settling into her new home in China, she makes friends with Yen Chen and Mei Lu, the daughter of a local tea merchant, and with Adam Butler, the Chens' American accountant. Meanwhile at home, her sister Mary has a suitor she must keep secret, and Robbie, their fourteen-year-old brother, has plans to escape Scotland for China...

FLIGHT OF THE MANDARINS

by

Shirley Worrall

Dales Large Print Books
Long Preston, North Yorkshire,
BD23 4ND, England.

British Library Cataloguing in Publication Data.

Worrall, Shirley
    Flight of the mandarins.

    A catalogue record of this book is
    available from the British Library

    ISBN   1-84262-458-X pbk
    ISBN   978-1-84262-458-6 pbk

First published in Great Britain by D C Thomson

Copyright © Shirley Worrall

Cover illustration © Mark Viney by arrangement with
P.W.A. International Ltd.

The moral right of the author has been asserted

Published in Large Print 2006 by arrangement with
Shirley Worrall, care of Dorian Literary Agency

Dales Large Print is an imprint of Library Magna Books Ltd.

Printed and bound in Great Britain by
T.J. (International) Ltd., Cornwall, PL28 8RW

Chapter One

Rumour had it that spring had arrived, but Ishbel Montrose saw no evidence of that. Edinburgh steadfastly refused to release its grip on winter.

She was bent almost double against a biting wind that carried icy needles of rain. Water trickled down her neck as she walked faster. She could have found Gran's house blindfolded.

As always, the door was unlocked, and Ishbel quickly shut out the wind and rain.

'It's only me, Gran!'

The warmth was welcome, and Ishbel felt better already. She took off her coat and hung it in the hall to dry.

'Get by this fire, Ishbel love, before you catch your death,' her grandmother called back. 'The Lord alone knows what we've done to deserve such weather!'

At seventy-five, Moira Kerr was still an impressive figure. Ishbel had to smile at the expression on her grandmother's face. She was standing at the window, scowling at the weather outside as if she could bully the sun into shining.

'But there!' She returned to her chair.

'What can't be cured must be endured. And we can't change this weather.'

For years, Ishbel had called on her grandmother on her way home to the manse, and for years they had aired their views over oatcakes, Madeira cake, scones – and Gran's jam, which Ishbel thought the best in all Edinburgh.

This was to be one of her last visits. Ishbel found herself blinking away tears.

Of all the things she would miss when she left, Gran would top the list. Oh, she looked as if she would go on for ever and outlive them all, but that was fanciful...

The tears were still dangerously close, so she busied herself making tea.

It didn't help. Her grandmother, usually talkative, wasn't saying a word. Ishbel looked up to see Gran gazing straight at her.

'Is there anything wrong, Gran?'

'That would be for you to tell me, wouldn't it?'

'There's nothing wrong with me,' Ishbel said immediately. 'Except I'm starving.'

She helped herself to a scone – anything to stop her bottom lip quivering – and filled it with jam.

'As good as ever,' she approved, her mouth full.

Moira didn't reply. Instead, she rose to her feet.

'I've something for you, Ishbel.'

6

She left the room, giving Ishbel a welcome few moments in which to compose herself. Heavens, it was another four weeks before she left Scotland! If she was on the verge of tears now, what would she be like when she had to say her goodbyes?

'Here.' Moira handed Ishbel a package, and returned to her seat beside the fire.

Curious, Ishbel carefully removed the cardboard casing.

'Oh, Gran! It's beautiful!' She ran her fingers over the soft, red leather and opened the diary. What would she write on the first page?

'You must have read my mind. I've often thought of keeping a diary. Thank you. Thank you so much.' Again, the tears were close.

'You were born at the turn of the century, lass, and you'll see plenty of changes in your lifetime. When you get to my age and look back – well, it's often good to be able to remember.' Moira's eyes softened. 'Aye, the bad times as well as the good. We all fear change at some point in our lives, love, and yet, years later, we can look back and laugh at our worries.'

If it had been anyone else, Ishbel would have denied having a single worry. But Gran knew her better than anyone.

'I don't have worries, exactly,' she murmured. 'It's just–'

Just what? She was doing what she'd wanted to do for as long as she could remember. So why was she so – frightened?

'I know, lass.' Moira sipped her tea. 'It's fear of the unknown. It's the thought of leaving home, leaving your family, leaving Edinburgh – and even leaving this confounded weather behind, I shouldn't wonder.'

'I suppose that's it. The thought of saying goodbye to everyone and everything I know.'

'That's only natural.' Moira nibbled a biscuit. 'What would you do if you were told tomorrow that it had all been cancelled? That you wouldn't be going to China after all?'

'Well, I don't know.' The question surprised Ishbel. 'I haven't thought about it.'

'Think about it now, love.'

Ishbel did, and she knew exactly.

'I'd be disappointed.' The first smile of the day curved her lips. 'I'd be upset – and bitterly disappointed. I'd be furiously angry, too!'

Moira nodded her understanding.

'It's what I've always wanted,' Ishbel went on. 'For as long as I can remember, I've wanted to be a missionary. And China – oh, it's a dream come true! I can hardly believe it even now.

'The people have so many problems – and I know I can make a difference. I'd hate to think I'd gone through life without having done something worthwhile – without having made some impression, no matter how small.'

She hugged the diary to her chest.

'My first entry in this will be when I reach Shanghai.' She grinned suddenly. 'No! I've heard so many awful tales about the journey. I might never make it to Shanghai. I'll start it as soon as we're on the ship. It will give me something to do while we're at sea.'

'Good idea.' Her gran nodded. 'It's easy to forget things if you don't write them down. And I shall be expecting some really long letters, Ishbel, love, with nothing left out.'

'You'll get them.' Ishbel jumped up from her chair to hug her. 'Thanks, Gran. Not just for this, but for everything. For always making me see life more clearly...'

Moira stood at the window, watching Ishbel race along the pavement on her way home to the manse. She was having to lean into the wind to keep her balance, but even that couldn't disguise the fact that she was a tall, striking lass.

From the moment she was born, everyone had remarked on Ishbel's likeness to her grandmother. It was something that never failed to fill Moira with pride.

They shared the same way of thinking, too. Always had.

'I'm going to miss you, lass,' she murmured. Moira was unspeakably proud of her granddaughter, they all were, but it was a poor life that had no fun in it...

9

She returned to her chair. Her eyes grew heavy watching the dancing flames, but she wasn't in the mood to sleep.

Perhaps it was Ishbel's imminent departure that was leading her mind back to the past.

What would John have thought of Ishbel setting off for China? Knowing him, he'd probably have wanted to go with her – if only to feel the sea rolling beneath his feet once more!

When they'd first met, John had worked, like so many others, on the whaling boats. Only after Veronica was born did he leave the boats to begin working in the offices.

Moira smiled, thinking of their baby. The birth hadn't been easy. Even before John arrived to see his daughter for the first time – he'd been away at sea – Moira had been told there would be no more children.

'This one's so beautiful,' John had said, holding the tiny girl in his strong arms. 'We'll not want for more, love.'

He'd taken his daughter's small hand in his. 'We'll call her Veronica!'

Moira chuckled at the memory, but at the time she had been horrified. Veronica was – well, it simply wasn't a name folk in Leith gave their children.

'It was the *Veronica* brought me home safe to you both,' John said softly.

So Veronica it was.

It was funny how things turned out...

Veronica was said to have wiped the face of Jesus on His way to the Cross. And now, there was her Veronica, hers and John's, mopping the brow of her Presbyterian minister–

The door opened and closed, and a familiar voice called out.

'It's only me, Mum!'

'Another one soaked to the skin?' Moira laughed.

'The kettle's on the boil,' she added. 'Bring in two cups, love.'

The advantage of growing old! The family came to her; all she had to do was sit back and provide the tea.

'I've brought you cake,' Veronica said as she came in. 'Don's parishioners have been generous again. I don't know why I bother baking.'

'The way to a minister's heart!' Moira chuckled. 'Here – sit yourself down and dry off. You've just missed your elder daughter.'

'Oh? How did she seem?' Veronica asked anxiously.

'She's fine. Why shouldn't she be? She's about to embark on the adventure of a lifetime. I envy her.'

'It's not an *adventure*, Mum!'

Moira had to smile at the disapproval in her daughter's voice. It was true, though: Moira *did* envy Ishbel. There she was, twenty years of age, with her whole life ahead of her. If Moira had been twenty, and

11

about to leave for China – well, she'd have her cases packed already!

And Shanghai, of all places! She would have chosen somewhere a little quieter for Ishbel, but then, the more she heard about the city, the more it fascinated her. Shanghai seemed to have everything.

'I'm not so sure about Ishbel.' Veronica's voice softened. 'She won't admit it for the world, but I think she's beginning to have second thoughts.'

'It wouldn't be natural if she didn't,' Moira said calmly. 'It's a big step, and the lass is leaving a lot behind.'

'I know, Mum, but I think it's more than that. You don't think she's going through with it just to please us, do you? Her dad and me?

'Donald's almost speechless with pride, of course, but I'd hate to think she was going just to please him.'

'Of course she's not!'

Moira was quite confident about that. If Ishbel had wanted to change her mind about going to China, she would.

From the moment she was born, Ishbel had known her own mind. She was going for herself, and she was going because she believed God was sending her.

If anyone had the power to influence her decision, it would be young Gordon Campbell. Not that Moira would dream of mentioning such a thing to her daughter...

12

Veronica would be sure to find something else to worry about.

A couple of weeks ago, in church, Moira had seen the way Ishbel had looked at Gordon. Unless she was very much mistaken, Ishbel was already a little in love with Gordon Campbell.

'China's such a long way away, though,' Veronica said, and Moira had to smile.

'And you hear such tales about it!' Veronica went on. 'If anyone mentions China – well, it's the revolution, or opium dens or–' Words failed her.

'And that's at best.' Her lips set in a thin line of disapproval.

'There's good and bad everywhere, love, and we can't keep Ishbel to ourselves for ever. We have to let her go.'

'But it's such a – *strange* place. What if she's unhappy out there, Mum? It's so far away from us all...'

That thought had given Moira a few sleepless nights, too, but she wasn't going to tell her daughter that.

'Ishbel isn't the type to be unhappy, love. She has great faith in herself, and in her work. And you know she makes friends wherever she goes. She always has.'

'I suppose you're right, and at least she'll have company. Gordon's a lovely man, isn't he? Mary works with his sister. Did you know?'

'So I believe.'

When she'd heard he and Ishbel were off to China together, Moira had made it her business to find out all she could about Gordon Campbell. It had been surprisingly easy.

One afternoon, she'd decided to meet Ishbel's sister, Mary, outside the printing company where she'd recently started work as a clerk.

When Mary emerged from the building, she'd been so engrossed in conversation with her friend, she'd almost walked straight past.

Moira soon realised that the gregarious friend was none other than Gordon's twin sister. So chatty was Flora that Moira soon had Gordon's life story...

But that wouldn't stop Veronica worrying – her daughter loved those bairns to distraction.

She herself was a worry to her daughter, Moira knew.

When John died four years ago, their daughter had immediately assumed Moira would leave her home of almost fifty years, to live at the manse. Moira had been appalled by the idea.

She loved her family dearly, and she appreciated the offer, but she valued her independence far too highly. God willing, she would die in this house.

'How's Don?' she asked, moving to an easier subject.

14

'As busy as ever,' Donald's wife said with a smile.

'What are you looking for, Don?' Veronica tried not to sound exasperated, but it wasn't easy. He was a dab hand at pulling things out of cupboards, but not so keen on putting them back.

'My jacket – I thought it was in the shed, but it isn't.'

'That old gardening jacket? What are you wanting with that?'

'I was going to look at the garden in the morning!' He straightened from the wardrobe and shook his head. 'It can't just have vanished, can it?'

'I'll have a look for it later,' she promised. 'Now – come downstairs and eat before it gets cold.'

'Is everyone waiting for me?'

He looked bemused, and Veronica had to smile.

Her husband was an excellent minister, one of the best. He worked long and hard for his parishioners, understood their problems, and was always where he said he would be. In fact, he was noted for his punctuality.

But when he was at home, things were very different. At home, he lost all sense of time. He would forget to eat at all if Veronica didn't nag him.

'They are,' she said. 'Rob's wearing a face

like thunder, so I expect he's in trouble again; Mary's vowing she'll die of starvation if we don't eat within the next two minutes, and Ishbel's in a rush to get off to her meeting.'

'Then we'd better eat!'

Donald's smile never failed to touch her – it was calm, yet warm. She'd always loved that smile of his, as she loved the man behind it – even more than she had on their wedding day.

He hadn't changed much since then, apart from his hair. Mind you, her own hair was showing a disturbing amount of grey…

Theirs was a good marriage; it was all Veronica had ever dreamed of – and more. And their three wonderful children were something she never failed to thank God for.

Ishbel, her first-born, was the image of her grandmother. No parents could wish for a better girl, but Ishbel also had strong ideals and an unwavering strength of character – just like Moira.

Given the same opportunities, Moira would have thought nothing about going to China.

Veronica was proud of Ishbel, but the thought of her little girl – it was easy to forget her 'little girl' was twenty years old! – going so far away, to a country that was as different from Scotland as it was possible to be, was terrifying.

Shanghai, of all places! Of course, there was

no point sending missionaries to quiet, God-fearing civilised places – but Shanghai…

Mary, born three years after Ishbel, was a good, sensible girl who gave them little worry. She was hardworking and conscientious, and her employers at the printing business thought highly of her.

Robbie, just fourteen, was the baby of the family, born with a rebellious streak. He was sensitive, gentle and loving. And then there was the other side to him…

'Well, then,' Donald said mildly, and they all bowed their heads for grace.

Ishbel looked as if she was miles away, and Veronica supposed she was.

Mary was, as usual, twisting her hair round her finger in the hope that it might curl. It wouldn't. Poor Mary had been born with straight hair and nothing would coax it into even a wave.

Rob looked a picture – sullen, as he often was, and yet angelic, thanks to his huge, doe-like brown eyes. His dark hair, newly cut, was too short…

Talk was general, if a little subdued. They had almost finished when Donald's mind returned to his garden.

'Has anyone seen my jacket?' he asked.

Ishbel and Robbie immediately said they hadn't, but Mary coloured, and Veronica knew exactly what must have happened to Donald's jacket.

17

'Mary?' he prompted. 'Have you seen it?'

'Which jacket?' The colour was still high in Mary's cheeks.

'The one I use for gardening.' He smiled. 'Believe it or not, spring has arrived. I thought I'd spend an hour in the garden tomorrow. Anyway, I'm sure I left my jacket in the shed.'

'You haven't worn that old thing for ages,' his daughter pointed out.

'I haven't had a chance to go into the garden for ages.'

'What time's your meeting, Ishbel?' Veronica said, trying desperately to change the subject.

'I've another half hour yet,' Ishbel said, oblivious.

Donald wouldn't give up.

'*Have* you seen it, Mary?'

There was a pause long enough for Veronica to offer up a silent prayer.

If Mary told her father what had happened to the jacket, she would be in trouble. If she lied and denied all knowledge, she would be in even more trouble.

'I didn't think you wanted it,' Mary said at last. 'It had been in the shed for months. You'd left it on the floor – it was damp and horrible.'

'So you *have* seen it?'

'Yes.' Mary's eyes were fixed on her empty plate.

18

'And?' Donald was frowning.

'I gave it away.'

Before her father could utter a sound, the words came pouring out.

'It's all very well Ishbel dashing off to China, and you standing in your pulpit – but in case no-one's noticed, there are people living here, in Edinburgh, right under our own noses, who have no clothes on their backs, no boots on their feet–'

'You gave *my* jacket away?'

'Yes.' Mary met his angry gaze. 'We have clothes, Father. We're lucky. I gave your jacket to a man who had *nothing* – no coat, no shoes – nothing.'

'You asked permission from no-one? Am I right?' Donald's voice was cold.

'Yes.' Mary's voice shook slightly.

'Perhaps you would like to tell us all your definition of theft, Mary?'

She looked up at that.

'I don't consider it theft.'

'Go to your room!' His voice was still soft, but no-one would have argued with him.

'Go to your room this instant and read your Bible. Then, when you know exactly what the Bible has to say on the subject, you may share your knowledge with us. Go!'

'I'll go.' Mary rose from the table, head held high and proud. 'I'll go, Father, but I stand by what I did. I can't sit back and watch people go without food or clothes – not people from our own city. You may be able to, but I can't.'

To Veronica's horror, she paused at the door.

'While I'm at it, I'll see what the Bible has to say about giving to the needy.' And she closed the door quietly behind her.

Mary threw herself down on her bed and lay staring at the ceiling.

Once Ishbel left, she would have this room to herself. The thought didn't cheer her as much as she'd thought it would. She would miss her sister too much.

Mary liked to talk through her own thoughts. She rarely took any advice Ishbel might give, but she always felt better for having talked it over.

They'd argued a lot lately, and Mary regretted that. She knew she usually started most of their squabbles.

Why on earth did Ishbel have to go rushing off to do good in China? There was more than enough to do in Edinburgh, just after the War to end all wars. Charity surely began here at home!

Mary realised she'd be glad when all the fuss died down. People in Father's congregation were beginning to look upon Ishbel as some sort of saint.

Typical – Ishbel sets off to China to read the Bible to people, and everyone marvels at her. I give an old jacket to someone far more deserving, and all I get is trouble! Where's the justice in that?

Not that Mary would want to go to Shanghai. Her sister spoke of the city with great excitement, but the thought of it – and all those people crammed inside it – frightened Mary.

Just then, she heard her sister's light step on the stairs, and Ishbel dashed in.

'Has he calmed down?' Mary asked.

'Still furious.' Ishbel was hunting through her drawers. 'And little wonder, Mary. You shouldn't have taken his jacket without asking.'

'I didn't think he wanted it,' Mary muttered.

Smiling, Ishbel nodded at the Bible beside Mary's bed.

'Have you looked at it?'

'There's no point! I know exactly what it says on the subject of theft, and on giving to those less fortunate.' She grinned. 'I expect it has plenty to say on the subject of being impertinent to one's father, too.'

'Sure to.' Chuckling, Ishbel stopped rummaging. 'You haven't given my gloves away, have you?'

'No!'

And the two of them were helpless with laughter.

'You left them by the fire to dry off,' Mary

reminded her sister when they recovered.

'So I did. Right, I must dash.'

'Is Gordon going to this meeting?' Mary couldn't resist asking.

'Gordon?' Ishbel stared at her. 'Yes. Why?'

'Oh, just wondered.'

'What a strange thing to wonder! I'll see you later, Mary. Oh, and I'd give Father a wide berth this evening.'

'I will.'

Alone again, Mary's thoughts returned to Gordon Campbell.

Being friendly with Flora, his twin sister, Mary knew all there was to know about Gordon Campbell – except his views on Ishbel.

'He's got a mind above girls,' Flora had told her. 'He doesn't even notice them.'

Mary wondered if that was true. Unless she was very much mistaken, Ishbel had noticed Gordon. More than noticed.

The two of them were friendly, and because they were going to China together, they were even more closely involved, but Ishbel's views on Gordon went much further than missionary business. Mary was sure of it.

Ishbel, as usual, was tight lipped on the subject, but her wee sister had noticed how two bright spots of colour appeared in her face if his name was mentioned.

Flora worshipped the air her twin breathed, but Mary had only met Gordon Campbell twice. He seemed polite, easy to get along with, but nothing out of the ordinary.

With light brown hair and a moustache that never looked tidy, he wasn't handsome or dashing – not the type that would make a girl's heart beat faster.

Unlike Jack Keller…

The thought came from nowhere, but it had the power to make Mary blush. Jack Keller – tall, dark hair, neatly-trimmed moustache, laughing brown eyes–

Jack Keller was well known in Edinburgh. There were dark rumours of where his family's wealth had come from. But on his father's death, Jack Keller inherited the lot.

There were rumours, too, about Jack Keller's integrity as a businessman…

Jack set out to buy property. Indeed, it sometimes seemed that he owned half of Edinburgh. By all accounts, the high rents he charged put those properties out of the reach of ordinary folk.

He wasn't, she felt sure, the type of person she would like. If reports were true, his only concern was accumulating more wealth. Mary knew there was good and bad in everyone, however…

She'd known Jack by sight for years, everyone did, but she'd only spoken to him once, in passing. He'd called at McIntyre's offices just as she'd been rushing inside, fearful of being late.

He'd heard her dashing along the corridor,

and waited to hold open the door for her.

'Thank you very much.' Her breathlessness wasn't entirely due to exertion.

'My pleasure.'

That had been it, except for the smile he gave her.

That smile of his came instantly to mind whenever she thought about him, which was far more often than she should. Sometimes she couldn't seem to *stop* thinking about him!

'I don't know what's got into Mary these days,' Don muttered. 'I'm used to Ishbel speaking her mind; she's too much like your mother. But Mary–'

The bairns were in bed, which was where Veronica longed to be, though not until Donald had calmed down a little.

'We have to make allowances for her, Don,' she pointed out quietly. 'It can't be easy for her.'

'What can't?'

'The way people are making such a fuss about Ishbel going to China, and the way Mary is being left out. She's always enjoyed being the centre of attention–'

Veronica knew as soon as the words were out that they hadn't been chosen wisely.

'She's a good girl, Don, you know she is,' she added. 'It's just that when she feels strongly about something – well, she feels strongly.'

'It's not the jacket so much.' The deep frown still marred his face. 'Although she should know better than to take it without asking. It's the way she can stand there and say–' But words failed him. 'Have we – I – been too soft on her? Is that it?'

'No.' Veronica poked the fire, but there was no life left in it.

'Mary's a good girl with her heart in the right place. She might have seemed a little disrespectful, but she respects you. She loves you dearly, Donald Montrose, as well you know.'

His face softened, and Veronica felt herself sag with relief.

Donald would die before admitting it, but his bond with Mary was deeper than that of most fathers and daughters.

He loved Robert as every father should love his son, and he loved Ishbel as every father loves his firstborn, but even if he didn't know it, Mary held a special place in his heart.

And, almost from the moment she was born, Mary had idolised her father.

'Is she jealous of Ishbel, of all the fuss, do you think?' he asked.

'Of course not, but she's going to miss her dreadfully. We all are, Don.'

'Aye.' He was silent for a long time, lost in thought.

'Let's go to bed and get some sleep,' Veronica suggested. But an hour later Donald was still tossing and turning beside her.

'I suppose,' he said into the darkness, 'we'll have to let the matter rest. I thought I should deal with Mary, but, well – under the circumstances–'

'Yes, do let it rest, love,' Veronica murmured, and Donald put out his arm and pulled her close against him.

'What was that she said? "I'll see what the Bible has to say about giving to the needy"?'

It was too dark to see his face, but Veronica caught the amusement in his voice. She kissed his cheek.

Donald wouldn't admit it, but he was proud of the spirit his children had...

'Whit is it you're awa tae dae in China, Mr Campbell?'

Ishbel smiled as she watched Gordon trying to explain to young Tom exactly what missionaries did in China. The other bairns, always keen to escape Sunday school, had left, but Tom was full of questions.

'Missionaries do all sorts of things, Tom. They help the local churches, they teach–'

'About Jesus and things?'

'Yes.' Gordon smiled. 'About Jesus and things. About everything.'

'And that's it?'

'Everything's quite a lot, Tom.'

'Don't you get tae dae anything interesting?' Tom sounded disappointed.

'But it is interesting!' Gordon protested. 'Don't you find Sunday school interesting?'

'Sometimes, I suppose.' Tom shrugged. 'But when I grow up, I want to work on a big ship, or maybe build some bridges.'

Bored with the subject, Tom quickly said his goodbyes and rushed out of the church to catch up with his pals.

Gordon moved more slowly than usual as they tidied up. He handled every book, turning it over and over, before putting it on the pile.

'That's it, then.' He put the last one down, and looked around at the familiar old church. He looked as sad as Ishbel felt.

'I suppose we should feel relieved that we can leave the little horrors to someone else,' he said lightly, and she smiled.

'I suppose so.'

But she didn't feel relieved, and she suspected he didn't either.

'I'll walk you home,' he offered, as he always did.

'Thank you.'

Ishbel took her time putting on her coat and gloves. She was fine with Gordon when they were busy, but as soon as the time came to walk home, she always needed a few moments to compose herself.

'I think it's warmer outside than in today,' she remarked as they stepped out of the church.

He nodded, but didn't reply. Ishbel wished she could think of something interesting to say.

It seemed that Gordon wasn't in the mood for talking either, because they were almost at the manse before he spoke.

'How are your family taking it, now that we're on the verge of leaving?'

'Oh, we're all putting on brave faces,' she said lightly. 'What about you? How does your mother feel about it now?'

Life would be very different now for Gordon's mother. Mrs Campbell had lost her husband early in the war. When Gordon left for China, she would only have Flora for company.

'I think she's accepted it.' He pulled the collar of his coat up against the raw wind. 'She rarely mentions it. I sometimes wonder if she's really accepted that I'll soon be gone. Perhaps it's just me feeling guilty about going – about leaving them. Mum can cope – she's had to. But it won't be easy for her.'

She could understand the guilt, but she knew it was something he felt he had to do, and Gordon's mother would know it, too. She might not like it, but she would know.

'I'm lucky, I suppose,' she said. 'My family will hardly notice I've gone.'

'You know that's not true, Ishbel!' Gordon laughed softly, then turned to look at her. 'How are *you* feeling about it?'

'Excited. Nervous.'

'Yes. I'm the same.'

'Do you worry that you're making a mistake?' she asked curiously.

'No.' He was clearly surprised by the question, but spoke with a confidence she envied. 'Do you?'

'Not really. I just wish I knew what the future held in store.'

'Mm. It's strange, but I feel China is – right. I would have gone anywhere, of course, but there's something about China… Does that sound fanciful?'

'I don't think so,' Ishbel said. 'Everyone has such terrible tales to tell of China, though. If only half the rumours are true–'

'I doubt even half are.' He cut her off. 'The only news we get to hear is the bad news.'

'I'm sure you're right.' She glanced up at him. 'Will you be taking your fiddle?'

'I certainly will!'

She laughed at his outrage. She should have known that he wouldn't go anywhere without that precious instrument, and that pleased her. It would be good to hear him playing; the tunes would be a reminder of home.

Here they were, outside the manse. She wished – oh, she wished he would say something, or do something. Anything!

He never did, though. He often walked her home. Did he even notice, she wondered suddenly, that they always ended up to-gether?

'I'll see you on Wednesday evening,' he said. 'I'll call for you on my way, if you like.'

'Thanks, Gordon.' The unexpected offer had her blushing.

'About six?'

'Yes. Fine. Thanks. See you then.'

Glad to hide her face, she turned and walked up the steps to the manse. She could feel him watching, as he always did, and when she had the door open, she turned and gave him a cheery wave.

He raised his hand, as he always did, then carried on walking.

Robbie stood in the doorway of Ishbel's and Mary's bedroom, too shocked to utter a sound. His big sister was crying!

He'd gone along to see Ishbel, but now he didn't know what to do. She *never* cried. She wasn't making a sound, but even though she had her back to him, he could see her hands were wiping tears from her face and her shoulders were shaking.

Not knowing what else to do, he turned and walked silently back to his room. When he got there, there were tears in his own eyes.

He blinked them back and stared moodily out of the window. He hated everything. And he couldn't even begin to imagine how awful life would be without Ishbel.

He hated China, too. His pal at school, John McIntyre, said people kept getting killed out there. He wished Ishbel had never heard of it.

As for being a son of the manse, you could keep it. Even John kept daring him to do things to prove he wasn't a goody-goody. He always accepted the dares, which was why he was always in trouble.

Not for much longer, though, Rob vowed. As soon as he could, he was going to run away.

He'd leave the manse, and Edinburgh, far behind him. He'd find work on a ship and sail the seas. Perhaps–

He stopped tracing patterns on the window-pane. That was it!

He'd work on a ship bound for China. When he reached Shanghai, he'd jump ship and find Ishbel. He'd live with Ishbel and keep her safe!

With this new idea to mull over, he felt better than he had for ages.

He wouldn't tell Ishbel about it, though. She'd only try to change his mind, remind him that he should be studying for the future, and assure him that she'd be fine in China.

No, the first Ishbel would know of it was when he turned up in Shanghai... He wouldn't tell anyone. He'd make his plans and keep them to himself.

Feeling much better, he drew a ship on the

pane, then smeared his hand across it to hide it from prying eyes…

By the following day, his plan didn't have quite as much allure. For one thing, it wasn't going to be easy getting work on a ship. He could start from Leith, but he knew it wouldn't be easy. And, for another thing, Ishbel's departure was so close. This time tomorrow, she would be gone!

He'd been trying to catch her on her own all morning, but it had been impossible. It seemed to Rob as if everyone in Edinburgh had called to say goodbye to her.

She was trying to appear calm and polite, but Rob could tell she was far from calm, and if she was feeling anything like him, none too polite, either.

He felt like telling everyone to go away and leave her alone.

Ishbel must have felt the same. That afternoon, he caught her putting on her hat and coat.

'Where are you going?' he wailed, despairing of ever getting her to himself.

'Just for a walk.' She was almost at the door. 'Would you like to come with me?'

Would he? He pulled on his coat before she had a chance to change her mind.

The wind nearly knocked them off their feet, but he didn't care.

'Where are we going, Izzie?'

He'd forgotten his vow to call her Ishbel.

As a baby, he'd called her Izzie instead, and the name had stuck. Now he was fourteen though, he thought it made him sound babyish.

Not that Ishbel seemed to care what he called her.

'Anywhere,' she said. 'I just want to look at familiar streets and buildings.'

And so they walked. On and on. Rob followed where she led.

'Will you miss me?' he asked suddenly.

'Oh, Robbie!' She stopped walking, and hugged him so fiercely he listened for the sound of his ribs cracking. 'I'm going to miss you more than you can imagine.'

'I'll miss you, too.' He sniffed against the cold, damp fabric of her coat.

He wouldn't think about it. He'd think, instead, of the way she'd called him Robbie, just as she always had.

In any case, she wouldn't miss him for long. Rob felt a warm glow inside at the thought. As soon as he was able, he'd be on his way to China.

'You must be good, Robbie,' she said urgently. 'If you'd a mind to, you could do well for yourself. You could make Mum and Dad proud. There's no need to keep getting into trouble – real friends won't think any more highly of you. And look, when you *do* get into trouble, talk to Gran. You can tell her anything, Robbie. Anything at all.'

But Robbie didn't want to talk to Gran; her only wanted to talk to Ishbel.

'Will you promise me, Robbie?'

He nodded, but his mind was far away, sailing the high seas to China...

Ishbel felt sick. If it hadn't been for Gordon standing beside her, she'd jump overboard and swim the half-mile or so back to shore. The grey water beneath them didn't frighten her half as much as the disappearing Scottish coastline.

She'd coped with the goodbyes fairly well. Although her throat had been painfully tight, and her eyes had stung with hot, unshed tears, she had coped. But now–

Now, the panic was raging inside her like a tornado.

'I've been dreading this moment for weeks.' Gordon's voice startled her, but his words and his tone comforted her. At least he felt the same.

'So have I,' she admitted. 'And it's far, far worse than I imagined.'

'Yes.' He gave her a rueful smile. 'For me, too.'

Ishbel suspected they both gained a great deal of comfort from the other's presence as they watched Scotland drop over the horizon.

'We must look forward now, Ishbel, not back.'

Gordon was right, of course. But still Ishbel couldn't drag her gaze away...

Gordon left the railings to find one of the crew and, standing on the deck with only the circling gulls for company, loneliness almost overwhelmed Ishbel.

'Faint not for fear, for He is near...' She murmured the words from one of her favourite hymns.

'Dear God,' she whispered fervently, 'I fear I'll be calling on You for help a lot in the future. I'm sorry I'm not as strong as You'd like me to be.

'If I ever waver, please remind me why You're sending me to Shanghai. Remind me of all the people who need me, of all the people who need to know You.'

She relaxed. She wasn't alone; she was never alone.

When she'd stood on the quayside, saying those painful goodbyes, Ishbel had been so intent on being brave that her father's words had washed straight over her. Now, she could hear his voice as clearly as if he was standing next to her.

'You'll never be alone, Ishbel.' He must have guessed how she would feel. 'Never forget, God's aye by your side. The work will be hard and – aye – there will be times you'll feel helpless, even times when you'll doubt yourself. But if you help just one lost soul to find God, it will all be worthwhile.'

He had taken her in his arms then, and crushed her to him.

'I am more proud of you than I can say.' His voice had almost broken. 'God bless you, Ishbel...'

The loneliness had gone now, replaced by an inner strength and determination. She was going where she was needed. She could make a difference; she *would* make a difference.

Ishbel left the side of the ship which faced Scotland and crossed to the opposite rail. Gordon was already there, looking outward. He greeted her with a smile.

'Well, Ishbel, we're on our way. No stopping us now!'

Chapter Two

The journey from Leith was fine, enjoyable even, but since leaving Southampton on the biggest ship I've ever seen, it's become monotonous. All around is sea – as far as the eye can see. At this moment, I would give all I had to be in my own room—

Ishbel put down her pen, thoroughly ashamed of herself. There was no use wallowing in self-pity.

She'd known from the start how long the

journey would be. And, after all, although the sea conditions had been severe enough to send passengers to their bunks, so far, she and Gordon had suffered no ill effects.

There was no privacy on the ship, but then she hadn't expected any. Only those who could afford to pay for it had that. The vast majority of passengers, like Ishbel, were travelling steerage.

Looking around the cabin, she tried to see it in a good light. It was difficult.

Perhaps she'd been spoiled by all the space at the manse, but she still found it hard to believe that eight women could sleep in such a confined space. At times, it seemed so cramped and airless, she thought she would faint…

Jane, one of her travelling companions, came into the cabin just then, holding her six-month-old baby in her arms.

'How are you feeling now?' Ishbel asked. 'Any better?'

'Not really.' Jane's face, tired and grey, told its own story. The poor girl had been seasick before they were even out of sight of Southampton. 'You're so lucky, Ishbel.'

'I know.' She must remember that. 'Here–' She held out her arms. 'You lie down and rest. I'll look after wee Ted for a while.'

'Would you? Oh, thanks.' Jane was grateful to transfer her baby to Ishbel's capable arms before dropping on to the mattress opposite.

Ishbel gazed down at the bairn sleeping in her arms. Teddy had cried throughout several long nights and kept them all awake, but it was impossible not to love him. At that moment, he looked angelic.

Just as Rob had at that age! A pang shot through her. Against all odds, Robbie, too, still managed to look angelic in sleep.

Once they finally reached China, Ishbel would be fine, she knew. Until then, though – well, she was far more homesick than she would have believed.

She constantly seemed to be asking God for His help, and she felt dreadful for being so weak. Father would be ashamed of her!

Jane was soon asleep, she was pleased to see. What with coping with Teddy and feeling ill, the poor girl had suffered too many sleepless nights.

What would happen to her new friend when they reached Shanghai? Jane's was a worrying story, one that Ishbel had discussed – and argued about – with Gordon.

He hadn't been able to offer any constructive advice, but then, she hadn't expected him to. He was very disapproving, more so than she'd expected. But she'd felt better for sharing her worries with him, and she knew he'd do all he could to help.

For Jane, the aim of her voyage was simple. She was going to track down the father of her child.

The fact that she didn't even know the name of the tea company for which Edward Clements worked didn't seem to perturb her at all.

Neither did the fact that he had visited his family in England, enjoyed a brief fling with her, and returned to China without a second thought.

Jane was already thinking of marriage, but Ishbel was doubtful.

If, and it seemed a big if, they found Edward, would he want to know Jane? Would he accept the child? Would he believe he was Teddy's father?

'For all we know, Ishbel, he may even be married and have a family in Shanghai,' Gordon had pointed out.

Ishbel fiercely hoped not. Jane might be immature, foolish and easily impressed, but Ishbel liked her enormously and would love to help her. Pray God they could find a way!

At least worrying about Jane and young Teddy helped to take her mind off all the dear people she missed so dreadfully...

'I don't see nearly enough of you, Robbie,' Moira Kerr told her grandson. 'You're just in time for tea! Let's see what we fancy.'

Robbie might have been more silent than usual lately, but his appetite certainly hadn't abandoned him. Scones, Madeira cake – he didn't leave a crumb.

'This is just like old times!' Moira sank back into her chair. 'Ishbel often used to join me for tea. Perhaps you'll keep me company in future, Robbie? When you can spare the time, of course.'

'I could,' Robbie agreed slowly.

Moira had always got on well with her grandson. Despite that rebellious streak, he was a gentle, sensitive boy. How she wished that she could get close to him now, when he clearly needed a friend.

'I miss Ishbel dreadfully,' she began, assuming that was at the root of the boy's obvious unhappiness. 'You must miss her, too, Rob.'

'I suppose so.' There was a long silence. 'She said I could talk to you if I got into trouble, Gran. She said I could talk to you about anything.'

'And she's quite right. That's what grans are for, aren't they?' Moira hardly dared to ask. 'Are you in trouble, sonny?'

'No.' The immediate denial had her breathing a sigh of relief.

'Not yet,' he added, and she wasn't quite sure what to make of that.

'Are you expecting to be in trouble? Are you planning something?'

He'd been gazing at the fire, but he looked up sharply at that.

'No!' And he looked away again.

Robbie was one of those boys who'd always found it difficult being a child of the manse. His friends, Moira knew, were typical boys – fun loving, if a little wild at times – but for all that, they got themselves into far more scrapes than Donald liked.

Yes, Robbie would miss his big sister. People could say or do anything, but they would never shock Ishbel.

If she didn't understand people's actions, she would never judge, but would put herself in the other person's shoes until she *could* understand. Ishbel had been born with the admirable ability to see both sides of a quarrel.

'Do you like Gordon Campbell, Gran?'

The unexpected question caught her unawares.

'He's a fine man,' she said automatically, and then thought about it.

The truth was, she didn't know him well enough to reach any conclusions. She assumed, as everyone else did, that a Bachelor of Divinity was, by definition, a fine man.

'Ishbel likes him,' she added, 'so he must be a nice man, mustn't he?'

'He'd better look after Ishbel until I–' He stopped, reddening slightly. 'He'd better look after her, that's all!'

Until when? What had Rob been about to say?

She would probably never know. Robbie went quiet, and only began talking about trivial matters once he had another slice of

Madeira cake in his hands.

Moira didn't consider herself the type to worry for worry's sake, but she was concerned about her grandson. She wouldn't voice her worries to his mother, though. Veronica was a right mother hen where her bairns were concerned.

No, Moira would keep a very close eye on Master Rob...

Mary turned into her home street, walking slowly. Despite the chill wind in her face, it was a pleasure to be out in the sunshine.

She was in a world of her own when she heard her name being called, impatiently. Chuckling, she crossed the road to her mother.

'Sorry, Mum, I was miles away.'

'I was hoping I'd catch you. Get on home and feed your father, will you, love? He's finishing his sermon, and I promised the Women's Guild I'd be at the hall.'

'I will. I'm hungry myself.'

It was Ivy's day off, but as Mary finished work at one o'clock on Saturdays, there was no danger of her father starving.

After a quick chat, Mary walked smartly on to the manse. Father would either be engrossed in his sermon, or he would be wanting his lunch...

She hadn't been inside for more than five minutes when there was a knock on the scullery door.

Standing outside were a woman and two young children.

'I'm looking for work, miss,' the woman explained. 'Is there anything I can do here? I'm hard working and honest.'

The wee boy was about seven, Mary supposed. He looked hungry and frightened. His sister, a couple of years younger, was clinging to the woman's skirt.

Despite the rags they wore, the children looked clean – but oh, so hungry! So did their mother.

'I'm sure there's something that needs doing.' Mary was sure of no such thing – their maid always had everything done before she took her day off. 'Come inside.'

They followed her into the kitchen, where the smell of the simmering broth made the children's eyes widen.

'You'll be wanting some dinner before I set you to work.'

The children looked at their mother, eyes pleading.

'I won't take charity,' the woman said, her neck stiff with pride.

'And I won't offer it,' Mary answered briskly. 'I'm Mary, by the way, Mary Montrose. My father's the minister.'

'Ruth, miss, Ruth McKinlay. This here's John, and his sister, Bella.'

They were sitting at the kitchen table, but

Mary was dismayed to see that although the children ate heartily, Ruth only managed a couple of mouthfuls.

'Come with me, children.' She turned to Ruth. 'I'll be back in a minute to show you what needs doing.'

She took the children into the hallway, opened the door to the cupboard beneath the stairs and found the box of Robbie's old toys that had been put ready for the church sale.

'You can play with these,' she told them, 'while I talk to your mother. Oh – and quietly.'

John and Bella were already delving into the box and, smiling, Mary left them to it. Her smile faded when she saw Ruth. The poor woman looked on the point of collapse.

'Sit down,' Mary said at once. 'Perhaps you'd tell me what sort of work you're wanting? To be honest, you don't look strong enough for anything too heavy.'

'I'm as strong as the next woman!' Then, seeing Mary's disbelieving expression, Ruth went on with a sigh.

'I haven't been well, that's all. I'm over it now, but it's left me without much of an appetite.'

'Is the children's father in work?'

'He died last year,' Ruth said quietly. 'He was a good man. A hard worker – worked on the boats, he did.'

'I'm so sorry.'

From the moment she'd seen the family at the door, Mary had felt drawn to Ruth. The feeling was even stronger now.

'I had a job, cleaning at Drake's,' Ruth explained, 'but when I got ill, that was that.

'I managed to pay the rent and feed the bairns with a bit I'd put by, but it wasn't much, and it couldn't last for ever.

'Yesterday, when I couldn't pay the rent–' She shrugged, and said no more.

Mary noted that 'feed the bairns' – Ruth had gone without.

'What happened yesterday?'

'We were turned out.'

'You were thrown out on the street? Just because you couldn't find a week's rent?' Mary couldn't believe it.

'With no work, there was no hope of finding next week's rent, either. Jack Keller's a businessman, not a charity. Not that I'd take charity from him – or from anyone else!' She flushed. 'That's not to say I don't appreciate what you've done for us, Mary. I do. We all do. The bairns needed a hot meal.'

Mary dismissed the gratitude with a shake of her head. She was far too busy thinking of Jack Keller!

And this time she wasn't thinking of their one and only meeting, or the memory of his smile. None of that mattered now.

What did matter was that he'd thrown a good, decent woman and her two young bairns on to the street to fend for themselves!

'He can't just throw you out,' she said furiously.

'Of course he can.' Ruth's voice was matter of fact. 'What does he care? All he wants is his money. He can do exactly as he pleases.'

'Can he? We'll soon see about that!' Mary muttered.

Donald Montrose admired ministers who could deliver a sermon with little or no planning at all. He couldn't.

He needed to gather his thoughts, put them in order, and then write the whole thing out. Every sermon he'd delivered over the years had been written in his neat hand and stored in his desk.

He needed to plan, and he needed peace in which to do it.

Everyone knew that, and respected it. Even Robbie managed to keep quiet – usually.

So who was making such an infernal din? Sighing, he put down his pen and went to investigate.

He'd taken two steps out of his study when a young urchin cannoned into him. Donald had never seen the child before in his life.

'What the–? Who are you?'

'Mary said we could play here,' the boy said. There was a girl, too, at the end of the hall.

'Did she indeed!' He might have known

Mary was involved.

Donald clamped a hand on the boy's shoulder, caught the girl by the hand, and frog-marched them to the kitchen.

'Mary– 'He nodded curtly at the strange woman sitting at his kitchen table. 'Would you like to tell me what's going on? I can't hear myself think!'

'Certainly, Father.' Mary got to her feet, and the woman did likewise. 'This is Ruth McKinlay, her son, John, and daughter, Bella. Ruth is going to clean the scullery for us.'

'Clean the–?' But Mary's expression stopped Donald asking why an already spotless scullery was going to be cleaned.

'Your lunch is ready,' Mary went on. 'If you've finished your sermon, I'll serve it.'

'I haven't!'

Looking more closely at Ruth McKinlay, Donald saw despair in her eyes. He looked at the children, and saw fear in theirs.

He hadn't a clue what was happening, but he guessed it would be best to leave Mary to it. She clearly didn't need his help.

'Aye, well. Play a bit more quietly, bairns, eh? I'm working on my sermon.'

Back in his study, he had all the peace he wanted, but he couldn't concentrate. His mind was full of Mary.

Lately, they seemed to do nothing but clash.

'It's because the two of you are so alike,' Veronica told him.

Donald wasn't so sure. There had always been a special bond between them, but surely he had never been so stubborn, or so determined to change the world single-handed...

It was a fair distance to Jack Keller's house, but Mary needed to walk. It might calm her down.

Only once she was standing on the steps by his front door, breathless from temper and exertion, did it cross her mind that he might not even be there.

The front door swung open, and she found herself face to face with a plump, kindly-looking woman.

'Mr Keller, please.'

'I'm sorry, lass, but he has company. If he's not expecting you...'

Good. He was there.

'It's a matter of great urgency,' Mary said. 'I'll only keep him for a couple of minutes, but–' she smiled '–I'd be grateful if you'd tell him I won't budge from his door until I've spoken with him.'

The woman's eyes widened.

'In that case, you'd better step inside.'

Mary walked into a wide hallway, full of the smell of beeswax. There wasn't a speck of dust to be seen, but the furnishings seemed to shout 'money'. Mary wasn't impressed.

'Wait here, lass.'

Mary waited. Only when the woman emerged from a door followed by Jack Keller did she realise she'd been holding her breath.

'Sorry to keep you waiting.' He gave her that heart-stopping smile, but Mary wasn't about to be taken in.

'Please–' He pushed open another door. 'We can talk in here.'

He didn't even recognise her, Mary realised.

The room was surprisingly warm and cosy. She would have loved to curl up in the armchair by the fire with a good book...

'I don't have much time, Mr Keller, and I know you're eager to return to–'

'Please, call me Jack.'

Mary felt her face turn crimson, and couldn't utter a word. Whatever would Gran say to that!

'And you are? We didn't get round to introductions at our previous meeting, did we?'

So he did recognise her – not that it mattered.

'Mary Montrose,' she said crisply, then jumped as her hand was swamped in his.

'So, Mary – please, sit down and tell me what I can do for you.'

Mary sat in the armchair beside the fire. She would have preferred to stand, but he'd got her into such a state...

'Mr Keller–' She couldn't – wouldn't – call

him Jack. 'Mr Keller, I've come here about Ruth McKinlay.'

She could see the name meant nothing.

'She's one of your tenants. Or rather, she was, until you threw her and her two children on to the street to starve.'

'Ah.'

Mary waited.

'Is that it?' she demanded in amazement. 'You throw honest, decent people on to the street, and all you can say is "Ah"?'

'Let's get this straight, Mary.' He spoke calmly. 'In Mrs McKinlay's lease, it stated quite clearly that in the event of–'

'She was ill! She lost her job!'

'And I sympathise. However, I can't afford to keep my properties–'

'Can't *afford?*' She glanced around the room.

'That's right. The property I own has to provide me with an income.'

'So you'll happily allow a woman and two bairns to starve? They've nowhere to go, no money, no food – can you sleep with that on your conscience? I know I couldn't.'

Jack Keller looked at her for so long that she thought he wasn't going to answer her. It was a strange look, one she couldn't analyse. It was impossible to tell what he was thinking.

'How old are the children?' he asked suddenly. 'I've never met the family.'

He wouldn't, Mary thought. He'd employ other people to do his dirty work.

'The boy's seven, the girl just five.'

He nodded, walked to the fireplace and gazed at the glowing coals.

'I should have another property available on Monday,' he said abruptly. 'I can't guarantee anything, and *if* it's available, it will be much smaller. I'm prepared to let Mrs McKinlay have it on the understanding that by the end of the month, she's able to pay the full rent.'

'What about tonight, and tomorrow night? Where can she go?'

'That, I'm afraid, is her problem. Tell her to be at my office at ten o'clock on Monday morning. She'll need to speak to me.' He glanced at the clock on the mantelpiece. 'I'm sorry, but I shouldn't keep my guests waiting any longer.'

All his smiling charm had gone now.

'Of course. I'm sorry I've taken up so much of your time.' She was out of her chair and by the door.

'I'll tell Mrs McKinlay to see you at ten on Monday. No need to show me out...'

The cool air was welcome after the warmth and richness of his house.

Mary marched along the street, wishing she could stop trembling.

'Let's get those hands washed,' Veronica

51

said briskly.

It had been a shock to find Ruth and her two bairns at the manse last Friday, but Veronica had taken to them immediately.

It was a joy to have John and Bella in the house, and Ruth was lovely. She was one of the proudest women Veronica had ever known, yet over the weekend she had shown them a warm, loving personality.

'There we are.' She dried the children's hands and marched them to the table. 'Breakfast now.'

She'd been pleased, but not particularly surprised to see that John and Bella waited for grace to be said before eating.

She knew Donald was pleased, too. She could see he didn't quite know what to make of it all – or what to make of Mary. He wasn't sure whether he should reprimand their daughter for, once again, taking the law into her own hands, or commend her thoughtfulness.

Robbie was in his element, happy not to be the youngest for once. He chatted away to young John about school, ships, and a hundred other things, as if he'd known the boy for years.

It would do Robbie good, Veronica thought. He'd been too quiet since Ishbel had left. She suspected he missed his big sister more than he was prepared to admit.

They all missed her, though. If they could

just have word that she was safe…

'I'll have to dash.' Mary rose to her feet. 'It won't do if I'm late for work.

'Make sure you're at Mr Keller's office good and early,' she warned Ruth. 'He doesn't strike me as a man prepared to wait.'

'We'll be there,' Ruth promised. 'And thank you, Mary. Thank you – all of you.'

The sparkle of grateful tears in her eyes brought a huge lump to Veronica's throat.

'You keep in touch,' Veronica said gruffly.

'I will. I promise.'

It seemed a lifetime ago that Ishbel had sat on the edge of Robbie's bed, spun his globe round on its wobbling axis, and shown him where Bombay was.

'That's where we change steamers,' she'd told him.

'What will it look like, Izzy? Will it be hot? What will the people be like?'

Ishbel had answered his questions to the best of her ability, but she had known very little about the place then.

'I'll write,' she promised, 'and tell you all about it.'

'I wish I could go with you…'

There would certainly be plenty to tell him, she thought now. The changeover had been chaotic.

When the coaling began, the air was soon black. Everything was black.

It was a sight Ishbel would never forget – the huge coal barges floating up to the ship, the hundreds of dirty-looking men sitting on the coal – and then the sight of those men, in one continuous stream, walking up the side of the ship on a plank of wood, huge baskets of coal on their shoulders.

They had left Bombay now, and Ishbel was both pleased and relieved to find herself sharing a cabin with Jane once again. It was virtually identical to the previous one, with thick grey blankets covering each of the eight mattresses.

The dining saloon on this ship was smaller, but it still had rows of long, spartan tables and those endless rows of swivel seats, weighted to prevent them moving in rough seas.

The whole ship was smaller, but Ishbel preferred it.

As the days passed, she saw more of Gordon, too, and that lifted her spirits immensely. He was her one link with home, but, more than that, her tower of strength. He was everything Ishbel was determined to be.

Unlike her, Gordon wasn't calling on God's help every five minutes because of homesickness. Gordon was unwavering in his calling; a true soldier.

Instead of feeling sorry for himself, or complaining about life in his diary, Gordon was soon conducting Bible reading classes.

Once again, Ishbel was thoroughly ashamed of herself. She'd been so eager to reach Shanghai that she hadn't thought of the work they might be doing on the journey.

Back home, she'd met every day as a challenge, an opportunity to do God's work, but here on the ship, she had been lost.

Thanks to Gordon, all that had changed. Once more, her purpose in life was clear.

People from all walks of life attended the classes – businessmen, diplomats, civil servants, military and naval personnel. Even Jane went along.

Sure of herself now, Ishbel found the days passing quickly, and before long, it was their last night aboard ship.

'Dry land tomorrow,' Gordon remarked, with a wry smile.

She hadn't expected to see him before morning. This chance meeting, out on the deck, was an unexpected pleasure.

As they leaned on the ship's rail, his shoulder was against hers. Ishbel hadn't believed it possible to gain such comfort from someone's touch.

'It will seem strange after life on the ship,' she answered. 'It's like a separate world, isn't it?'

He seemed to understand.

'Thank you, Gordon.' She looked up at him.

'For what?'

'Oh, for putting me back on the right path – reminding me what I'm to do with my life. For some reason, I lost all sense of direction. All I could do was miss my family–'

'That's all too easy. But don't put yourself down, Ishbel. You've cared for Jane and her baby, you've helped countless other people.

'All I've done is preach, but you–' He gazed at her for a long moment. 'You're so *good* with people. You spread God's word in a more practical way than I ever could. Take Jane – you, and the person you are, brought her to our classes. I couldn't have done that.'

Ishbel knew Gordon well, and knew he didn't speak lightly. His praise touched her heart.

'Wait here.' He smiled at her, and went of along the deck.

Ishbel gazed ahead. Still no sight of land! They'd enjoyed some wonderful, clear nights on the voyage, but unfortunately, this wasn't one of them. There wasn't a star to be seen.

On the upper decks, she could hear people talking and laughing – then she heard the soft, lilting strains of a fiddle. She turned around with a smile in place, but she couldn't see Gordon for a sudden blur of tears.

She'd heard him play many times before, but this was special. The notes, clear and pure, floated away on the breeze.

As usual, he played the traditional favourites, tunes that brought a tear to any Scotsman's eye. Soon, several other passengers, including a Welsh missionary and two Scots, had gathered round, and the singing started in earnest...

Ishbel drifted off to sleep that night with Gordon's music still in her head and in her heart. Mingled with that was the memory of his shoulder against hers, the smile in his eyes as he'd played his fiddle...

She awoke to a great commotion, and went up on deck as soon as possible. And there it was, Shanghai!

There was little space to be had on the deck, but she and Gordon squeezed into a tight spot against the railings. Neither spoke.

Aboard ship, they had heard too many stories about Shanghai – about the gangsters operating from night clubs that never closed, the spy rings, the international arms dealers. It was too soon to judge the city that lay before them.

But it was vast. The task of finding Teddy's father struck Ishbel as more daunting than ever.

'We have a lot of hard work ahead of us, Ishbel,' Gordon said quietly.

'Yes.'

And she knew they could cope with it. She had never felt more confident of anything in her life.

Shanghai had many problems, but she

knew, without any doubt whatsoever, that together they could make a difference.

She closed her eyes and offered a silent prayer of thanks for bringing them here, and giving her the strength and courage she needed.

The crush was increasing, and Gordon had to put his arm around her waist to prevent them being pushed apart. His touch gave such comfort, and more than comfort. Her whole body was tingling…

'We make a good team, Ishbel,' he said in his calm voice. 'We may not win the war, but, with God's help, we'll win a great many battles together.'

'Yes. Yes, we will.'

'I'm so glad you're with me.' The sincerity behind those words was in his eyes for all the world to see.

'So am I, Gordon.' Her voice broke slightly.

She couldn't imagine the day when she wouldn't be by Gordon's side – didn't want to imagine it, she realised. She needed him – needed his unwavering courage, his strength.

An inner voice suggested other things she needed from Gordon but the future was too uncertain to complicate things with matters of the heart.

They had finally arrived in Shanghai, and there was work to be done. Only God knew what the future held.

Chapter Three

Ishbel gazed round the room, her eyes shining. When she and Gordon had received invitations to this luncheon party from Mr Sun Chen's wife, Ishbel had vowed to write and tell her grandmother all about it.

She wouldn't even know where to begin!

Gordon, she noticed, was on the far side of the room, talking to Mr Chen. Ishbel tried not to stare, but Sun Chen fascinated her.

'Ishbel – you're all alone!' Helen Chen appeared at her side.

'I was just admiring your home.' Ishbel turned to her. 'It's very beautiful. And so warm,' she added with a smile.

'Ah.' Helen's eyes misted with memories. 'I remember arriving in Shanghai all those years ago and thinking that, if nothing else did, the weather would send me scurrying back to England! Stifling hot in summer, and unbelievably cold in winter.'

Helen Chen was a great supporter of the mission. From the moment she had learned Helen was married to a Chinese man, Ishbel had been curious.

'The weather must have been the least of your concerns,' she remarked. 'After Scotland – well, Shanghai is so very different from anything I've ever known.'

'Yes.' Helen smiled.

'When I met Mr Chen–' her eyes strayed to her husband, still talking to Gordon '–he told me I would fall in love with Shanghai.'

She laughed softly.

'I spent months longing for home!'

'Where was home?' Ishbel asked.

'In Devon – my parents have a farm.' She was silent for several moments.

'Mr Chen was lucky enough to travel to Europe to study when he was thirteen years old,' she explained.

'The students were warned in no uncertain terms to disregard both Christianity and European women–' She smiled, and again that fond gaze rested on her husband.

'We fell in love. I was twenty-three when Mr Chen brought me to Shanghai as his bride. Forgive me, Ishbel. I'm boring you.'

'Oh, no. Not at all!'

Quite the reverse. Ishbel was fascinated by the story, and would have loved to hear more.

Mr Chen was a softly spoken man, wearing the long, traditional Chinese gown. Yet, behind those gentle, Oriental eyes, she thought, there must lie a very strong-willed man. It must have taken a great deal of courage to defy tradition all those years ago.

'Let me introduce you to our Mr Butler,' Helen was saying. 'He's one of the most entertaining young men I know. American,' she added, as if that explained everything, and Ishbel had to smile.

Mr Butler was a tall, fair-haired man, only a couple of years older than Ishbel, who looked totally at ease in his surroundings.

'Excuse me.' Helen left them alone while she went to attend to another guest.

'What a lovely woman,' Ishbel murmured. And very beautiful, too, she thought. No wonder Sun Chen had fallen in love with her.

'Do you know Mr and Mrs Chen well, Mr Butler?'

'Yes, I do.' His voice was warm, the American accent slight. 'They're a very sociable couple, and I've been lucky enough to be invited to their home many times. I studied at the American university in Peking,' he explained, 'and now I work as an accountant for Sun Chen and Company.'

'Goodness,' Ishbel said, impressed. 'I'm sorry, you must think me terribly ignorant, but I've no idea what Mr Chen actually does!'

'He's in the tea business – import and export. As you can see–' he gestured to their surroundings '–he's a very successful businessman.'

'Indeed.'

Even from the outside, with black lacquer gates, stone lions and courtyards, the Chens' home was impressive.

Inside, it quite took the breath away. The tasteful furnishings were an intriguing mix of East and West, rather like the Chens themselves, Ishbel thought.

'Mr Chen started with a very small office and two customers,' Mr Butler explained. 'Now he has one of the largest import and export businesses in China. He's a good employer – honest and fair. I like him – I like the family. Mrs Chen, as you probably know, does at lot of good work in the city.'

'Yes, we're grateful to her.'

It was through her good work that Gordon and Ishbel had met Helen.

Like them, Helen was appalled by the poverty, the cheap labour and the dozens of other problems that were part of Shanghai, and had shown an interest in the teaching work they were doing.

She had given the mission a more than generous donation.

'And what about you, Miss Montrose? Mrs Chen said you'd been in Shanghai for – what? Six months?'

'Almost to the day.' She nodded.

'And what do you think of the place?'

'Gosh!' She laughed. 'I'm still not sure. For as long as I live, I will never forget the day I stepped ashore for the first time. Dozens of different languages being shouted. And the smell – expensive scent mingling with garlic, fish – and a host of other things.'

She could see he knew exactly what she meant.

'And you, Mr Butler? Do you like Shanghai?'

'I love it.' He didn't hesitate. 'I love the noise, the energy, the smells, the mix of East and West – it's unique to Shanghai.'

'I know just what you mean. I saw my first wedding procession yesterday.'

He nodded.

'It's quite a spectacle, isn't it?'

The bride, wearing a red silk gown and with her face covered by red silk, had been carried in a red and gold sedan chair painted with a phoenix and dragon. The procession had been a colourful, noisy affair – red lanterns, banners, trumpet blowing, the clanging of gongs...

'And I love the sense of expectancy,' Adam Butler went on.

'What do you mean?' she asked curiously.

'This China of ours.' He shook his head. 'There are so many problems. It's a mix of great wealth and terrible poverty.

'At times, it seems as if the country will race out of control – if it hasn't already – but I believe great changes are on the way. It sometimes feels as if the whole country's holding its breath – waiting for–'

He broke off suddenly.

'Uh-huh?' she encouraged him.

'You're from Scotland!' he exclaimed.

'Yes.'

Helen had been right, Ishbel thought with amusement, Mr Butler was an entertaining young man.

'I'd been wondering about your accent,' he explained. 'Now I've placed it. There was another missionary here – she's moved up country now, but I knew her quite well. Lizzie McKie – she's a Scot, she did her missionary training in Edinburgh at a place called–'

'St Colm's!' Ishbel said, startled.

'That's right.'

'Oh, I wish she were still here – St Colm's is where I trained!'

Ishbel felt light-headed for a moment. The sudden mention of the college had brought with it a vision of grey skies, and a sudden, painfully strong longing for home.

'Do you still keep in touch with her?' she asked, doing her best to ignore the home-sickness.

'I promised I would,' he admitted sheepishly, and she laughed. 'When you get to know me better, Miss Montrose, you'll discover that I'm a great talker and a hopeless letter writer. I have her address at home, though, and I'll look it out for you. She'd love to hear from you, and chat about life at St Colm's.'

'I'd like that, too. Thank you, Mr Butler.'

'Please – call me Adam.' He held out a

strong hand, and she shook it.

'Ishbel.' Oh, she did like him. She liked him enormously and would like to know him better. She loved his friendly, open, easy ways.

At home in Edinburgh, she'd never have asked a young man to use her Christian name. It was different here.

'Ishbel – it suits you. It's a very pretty name.'

'Thank you.'

To her embarrassment, Ishbel found she was blushing furiously. She had to look across the room.

'Helen's a very popular hostess, isn't she?' she murmured, changing the subject.

'She is.' He grinned suddenly. 'Popular with everyone but her youngest daughter.' He nodded towards the corner where a girl of about fifteen years old was clearly sulking.

'That's Mei Li. She's a clever girl, and is determined to persuade her parents to allow her to go abroad and study to become a doctor.

'Unfortunately,' he added, amused, 'she hasn't yet learned that her tantrums and sulking win her no favours with either parent.'

Ishbel was amazed at the way Adam Butler spoke about the Chen family. It sounded almost disrespectful, but it was clear he had enormous respect for them – and a great fondness.

'Do you know who that is over there?' She nodded at the Chinese girl in question. 'The very beautiful one with that exquisitely embroidered coat?'

'That's Liang,' he said at once, 'Mei's older sister. Come – I'll introduce you. I'm sure you'll like her.'

From the moment Adam made the introductions, Ishbel felt drawn to the shy girl who had inherited her father's gentle Oriental complexion and her mother's graceful beauty.

'Ishbel – Miss Montrose – was admiring the embroidery on your coat, Liang,' Adam explained.

So he called Liang by her first name, too, and seemed perfectly at ease with her.

Liang, though, was a picture of respectability. Ishbel knew that Chinese women were expected to hold themselves sedately, lower their eyes in response to men's stares, smile without showing their teeth, make no hand gestures–

She and Liang must be about the same age, but their lives couldn't have been more different.

Adam was called in to join Mr Chen just then, and left them alone.

'I was admiring the embroidery on your sleeve,' Ishbel told Liang. 'Is it your own work?'

'Of course. The butterfly – in China, it is a

symbol of joy and summer.' She pointed to the two birds on her sleeve band. 'These are my favourites – the mandarin ducks.'

'They're beautiful.' And they were.

'Shall we sit down?' Liang suggested, and Ishbel agreed, intrigued both by the embroidery and by the girl.

They sat on two ornate, but not particularly comfortable, chairs. Expensive though they undoubtedly were, Ishbel knew that her mother wouldn't have given them floor space at the manse.

'What do the mandarin ducks mean?' she asked.

'Fidelity,' Liang replied softly. 'If they're separated, they pine away and die.'

'Gosh. How touching. You're very fond of them.' Smiling, Ishbel pointed to another pair of embroidered ducks.

'Yes. My grandmother – Father's mother – often embroidered them. She was very skilled. Sadly, she died four years ago.'

'I'm sorry. You must miss her.'

Liang simply nodded.

Always more of a listener than a talker, Ishbel was surprised to find herself telling Liang about her own family.

She spoke of her parents at the manse, her sister and her wee brother, and just how much she missed them all.

Then she talked of the love she had for her own grandmother. She hoped that by talking so frankly, she would encourage Liang to speak about her own life.

And it worked.

'My grandmother was a very strong-minded woman, too.' Liang smiled fondly at the memories.

'When my father brought an English-woman home to Shanghai as his wife, she disapproved strongly – the whole family did. She stood by them, though, which took great courage.'

'It must have.' Ishbel glanced across the room at Helen. 'Your mother must have found it very difficult at first.'

'She did.' Liang was looking far more relaxed now. 'But she and Grandmother were soon the best of friends. It was Grandmother who stood by my mother when she refused to have my feet bound.'

Ishbel instinctively glanced down at Liang's feet, and the toes of the embroidered slippers wiggled in response.

'Grandmother's feet were bound when she was three years old, you see, and they caused her nothing but pain. She refused to inflict such suffering on me.'

Ishbel was glad. She hated to see Chinese women shuffling along with their tiny, deformed feet. It seemed to sum up for her how different this country was – how different her expectations of life were from Liang's.

'Adam – that is, Mr Butler – was telling

me your sister wants to train to become a doctor,' Ishbel remarked.

'Yes. It is impossible, of course,' Liang said flatly. 'It is said in China that uneducated women make better wives, but our father made sure we received a good education. Unfortunately, he won't allow us to use it.

'I would very much love to work with him in the business, but Chinese society doesn't allow such things. Mei and I will have our husbands chosen for us, and–'

She shrugged, and said no more.

'But surely, your father – he married for love,' Ishbel protested.

'And the treatment he received has made him more determined to arrange good marriages for his daughters.'

It seemed a very empty future, Ishbel thought, for a bright girl like Liang...

'My grandmother's feet were bound as a symbol of her subservience. But Grandmother wasn't subservient.' Liang smiled at Ishbel. 'Neither am I.'

Ishbel's eyebrows rose at the steely determination in that gentle voice.

'Good for you!' She knew instinctively that she and Liang were going to be good friends.

They went on to discuss Shanghai's weather, and Ishbel's work.

'I didn't realise until I was talking to Mr Butler that your father was in the tea business. I'm looking for someone, on behalf of a girl I met on the journey here – he works in the tea business in Shanghai. A Mr Edward Clements. I wish now that I'd asked–'

'Mr Clements?' Liang repeated, frowning, and Ishbel's heart began to beat faster.

'Does the name mean something to you, Liang?'

'Do you think I'm worrying unnecessarily, Gran?' Mary asked. 'Rob can be the biggest nuisance born, but I hate to see him so low. He seems to have lost all enthusiasm for life.'

His sister knew the reason for it. Robbie had always looked up to Ishbel, and he clearly missed his sister dreadfully.

Sadly, there was little Mary could do about it – she and Robbie had never shared that bond, that closeness.

'No. No, I don't, love.' Moira sighed. 'He calls on me quite often, but I can't get anything out of him. He obviously misses Ishbel, but if I start talking about her, he clams up on me.'

'I'll see if I can get through to him,' Mary murmured. 'We might not share that special bond, but we're still brother and sister.'

'You are, and don't ever forget that, lass. Yes, see if you can get him to talk.'

'I will,' Mary promised. 'I must go, Gran. I promised I'd call on Ruth and the bairns...'

It was a cold, damp afternoon, but Mary's welcome from Ruth McKinlay and her children was as warm as ever. The house was always spotless.

Today, though, Mary couldn't help noticing that it was tidier than usual. There were no toys lying around, and no sign of Ruth's fabrics and threads.

'We're expecting a visitor,' Ruth explained. 'Our landlord's calling on us.'

'Oh?' Mary was immediately suspicious. 'And what does Jack Keller want?'

'I've no idea.' Ruth smiled at her. 'He'll be delighted to see you, though.'

'Me? Why on earth?'

'You tell me. All I know is that he seems to have taken a personal interest in this property. He's for ever calling – to see if I'm looking after the place, I suppose – and he always asks after you.'

'He does not!' Mary scoffed as her face grew hot with colour.

She disliked Jack Keller intensely! She'd never forgive him for putting Ruth and the children on the street.

Things had turned out well for Ruth, though. With a little help from Mary, who'd had a little help from Gran, she'd set herself up as a seamstress and was starting to get some work.

The children, John and Bella, were happy in their new home, too. They'd settled in well and had made friends already.

'Jack Keller asks after you every time I see

him,' Ruth insisted. 'Without fail.'

'I don't know why,' Mary murmured. 'Bella! Come and tell me what you've been doing...'

Unfortunately, not even Bella's chatter could shift Mary's mind from Jack Keller. Since the day she'd visited his home, full of anger at the way he'd evicted Ruth and the bairns, she'd only seen him once.

Shortly before Christmas, they'd passed each other in Princes Street. Mary had given him a quick 'Hello' without even slowing her pace.

Funnily enough, she'd thought at the time that he would have stopped to chat if she'd given him the chance...

He arrived at four-thirty – prompt.

Strangely, despite the fact that he was used to more opulent surroundings, he managed not to look too out of place. He was polite, only taking a seat when Ruth offered him one.

He even had a friendly word for the children, not that it did him much good with John, Mary couldn't help noticing.

John might be young, but he knew full well who'd put him, his mother and his sister out of their house.

'You're looking well, Mary,' Jack Keller remarked.

'Thank you, Mr Keller.' She began to blush, and had to turn to Ruth. 'I'll take the children out for a walk while you talk.'

Mary had the bairns bundled into coats, gloves, hats and scarves before anyone could argue.

'We'll see you in an hour,' she told them.

'I hope we meet again, Mary.' Jack Keller rose to his feet – an impressive figure. 'Soon.'

'Yes. Well, goodbye, Mr Keller.'

'Is "Jack" really so difficult to remember?' His face was a picture of polite enquiry, but his eyes were laughing at her.

'Not at all. Goodbye…'

Of course, the rain started as soon as they stepped outside, so Mary marched the children round the corner to the tearooms.

John and Bella were more than happy to chatter their way through lemonade, scones and cakes, and it was worth the expense to escape from Jack Keller.

What was it about the man that unsettled her so?

True, he was handsome, and he had a certain flirtatious charm, but Mary had never been the type to fall for good looks and a silver tongue.

And he had the nerve to use her Christian name in front of everyone, and worse, ask her to use his! The cheek of the man.

No, Jack Keller was everything she disliked – ruthless, selfish, thoughtless, arrogant…

When they returned an hour later, he'd gone, but Ruth was looking agitated. Her eyes were shining, but her face was pale.

'Is something wrong?' Mary said quietly.

'No – nothing.' Ruth hugged the children and nodded at their chattering, but she was in a different world.

'Ruth?'

'Go and tidy my button box,' she told the children.

That was a treat, and the children ran upstairs.

'Whatever's happened?' Mary was worried now.

'Mr Keller has recommended me – well, my work – to a friend of his, a Mrs Kensington. Mary, her father's a member of parliament, and her husband – oh, I can't remember what he does, but we're talking posh. She lives in London, but she was born here and she's just bought herself a house.' Ruth looked around.

'I've scribbled down her address.' But she couldn't find it. 'Anyway, she wants to talk to me about doing new curtains and cushions all through the house. Can you imagine that? It's sure to be a huge place, and she'll only want the best.'

By now, Mary was as excited as Ruth. They'd stuck neatly-written cards in shop windows to advertise Ruth's skill with a needle, but they hadn't expected anything on such a large scale.

'You can't have lost her address!'

'No – it'll be here somewhere, but it doesn't matter. She's sending her car for me.' Ruth dropped into a chair.

'Her car! Oh, Mary, I've never been in a car. Horrible, dirty, noisy things – they frighten me to death!' she exclaimed.

Mary spluttered with laughter.

'That's the least of your worries. Oh, Ruth, I'm thrilled for you. When are you to go and see her?'

'Monday afternoon.'

'Then I'll call in on Monday evening and you can tell me all about it. Gosh, I can't wait!'

'I can't either.' Ruth grinned suddenly. 'But I'd rather walk – or take a cab.'

'Nonsense!'

'So you see,' Ruth added, eyes brimming with laughter, 'your Jack Keller isn't all bad.'

Mary wasn't so sure about that, but she didn't argue. In fact, it was only when she was lying in bed that night that she realised what Ruth had said.

'He's not my Jack Keller,' she muttered into the darkness.

'What a day!' Ishbel said. 'I don't feel as if my feet have touched the ground. Jane, I want to catch Gordon before he goes out, but then I'd like a word with you if you've got a minute.'

'Have I done something wrong?'

'Of course not! Nothing like that.' She was surprised at the concern in Jane's voice. 'Jane, most nights I climb into bed wondering what we'd have done without your help! Give me ten minutes, and then we'll have a cup of tea.'

As it turned out, Gordon had already set off for his meeting, so she'd have to catch him when he got back. At the end of the day, they usually talked over everything that had happened.

It was Ishbel's favourite time. She loved the way they shared their concerns, their hopes, their small successes...

But as she walked back to the kitchen, her mind was on Jane and how she would take this news.

The cups were set out, and Jane was boiling water for their tea.

'Where's Ted?' Ishbel was surprised not to see the bairn dangling off Jane's hip.

'I've just put him down.' The anxiety returned. 'Is it Gordon? Does he have a complaint about me?'

'No! Quite the reverse. Gordon can't praise you highly enough for all you do here, Jane. Why, only this morning he told you how good you were at settling the children. I heard him!'

Jane turned slightly pink. How they all craved compliments from Gordon, Ishbel thought with an inner smile.

It was true, though. Jane was good with the children. While Ishbel and Gordon tried to teach them, Jane's gentle ways and endless patience won their love.

How they loved to teach her new Chinese words, and how quickly she learned!

Once they were sitting at the table, Ishbel came straight to the point.

'We have some news of Edward Clements,' she explained, and Jane gasped.

'What sort of news?' Her hands were shaking so much that she had to put down her cup and saucer.

'We've discovered that he works for Sun Chen and Company, which has offices on Nanking Road. Unfortunately, however, he's not in Shanghai at the moment.' Ishbel took a deep breath. 'He's in England, Jane.'

'England?' Jane stared at her. 'You mean I've come all the way to Shanghai to find him, and he's in England?'

Ishbel nodded.

'Oh, Ishbel – do you think he's gone to look for me?'

Ishbel hated to kill the bright sparkle in those pretty blue eyes, but she didn't think so for a second.

She didn't know the man, of course, but from what Jane had told her, Edward Clements didn't sound as if he'd care too much about anyone other than himself.

'No.' Jane answered her own question. 'I

77

don't suppose he has.'

'I gather he's combining business with visiting his family,' Ishbel said cautiously.

'But he's returning to Shanghai?'

'He's expected back in nine weeks, I was told.'

Jane was silent while she took this in.

'Nine weeks isn't so long,' Ishbel said encouragingly. 'And at least we know where to find him now.'

'Yes, of course. Thank you, Ishbel – I really appreciate your help, more than you'll know.

'I appreciate your friendship, too, and your loyalty. I'll never forget the way you've stood by me. I'm not proud of what I've done, and I know you must think of me as a–'

'I think of you as a good friend,' Ishbel said sharply. 'I don't have the right to judge anyone, Jane.'

'Before I left England, my head was full of romantic dreams,' Jane said shakily. 'Now – well, I'm under no illusions. I'd like to speak to Edward, and I'd like to think he'll accept responsibility for me and his son. If he does, I'll do all I can to make our marriage a good one – but I'm not expecting miracles.'

Ishbel was surprised. She hadn't expected Jane to be so calm.

Perhaps she shouldn't have been surprised; the girl had certainly grown up a lot over the last six months.

'Ishbel? What will I do if Edward isn't prepared to accept Teddy as his son?'

Ishbel caught the tremor in her voice, and wished there was something positive she could say.

'We'll cross that bridge if we come to it, Jane…'

'Mary!' Veronica was pleased to see her daughter walk into the kitchen.

'Mary – it's Rob. He's crept out of the house before breakfast again, and your father – well, you can imagine the mood it's put him in.

'Run round to young Tom's and see if he's there, will you, love? And perhaps check at Jimmy's? I'll keep your breakfast hot.'

'Oh, isn't he the limit!' Mary groaned. 'It's not properly light yet, and hark at that wind rattling the windows. I'll go, but I bet the young devil's out skating on the loch again.'

'Your father will have a few words to say to him if he is!'

'He's not the only one,' Mary retorted, going to the hall for her coat.

In a way, Veronica hoped Robbie *was* having fun at the loch. He hadn't been his normal self since Ishbel left – but, there, none of them had. The manse felt dreadfully quiet without her.

'Never worry, Mother – I'll drag the little

devil home by his ear!' Mary poked her head round the door, wrapped her scarf about her neck and left.

Donald came into the kitchen, and gave Veronica an absent-minded kiss.

'No sign of him yet?'

Veronica shook her head.

'The young rascal,' Donald muttered. 'I'll scalp him when I finally get my hands on him. He knows fine he's not allowed out before breakfast.'

Veronica had no answer to that one.

'And where's Mary?' he asked impatiently.

'I've just sent her to look for Rob.'

They heard the door open and close.

'At least we can rely on the young devil's stomach to bring him home,' Donald said. 'But I intend to have a few words with that lad. It's high time he learned–'

But it wasn't Robbie who walked into the kitchen. As soon as Veronica saw her mother, icy fingers of dread clutched at her heart.

A dozen fears raced through her mind, but she couldn't utter a word. The fact that her mother was at the manse so early, the anxious expression on her face–

'I woke up to find this note pushed under my door.' Moira looked from Donald to her daughter and back to Donald. 'I came straight here.'

As she handed the note to Donald, Veronica snatched it from his fingers.

Dear Gran,
Will you please tell Mum that I'm going to
China to find Ishbel. Thank you.
Your loving grandson, Robert.

Chapter Four

Newcastle-upon-Tyne was an impressive city – there was no doubt in Robbie's mind about that.

He had just admired the swing bridge that swivelled about its centre on huge roller-bearings, and now he was gazing at the High Level Bridge, the world's first road and railway bridge.

Impressive, yes, but Robbie wished he was gazing from Cramond at the familiar outline of the Forth Bridge. This was a different world.

Even the people were different. Their clothes were different, and Robbie struggled to understand half of what they said.

Mind you, he'd understood the skipper of the *Linden* all too well. The threat of fetching the police came through forcefully in any language.

He turned away and walked smartly on. He had no intention of staying here long, and it didn't much matter what the city looked like.

Robbie was tired, cold and hungry, and he had just enough money to solve two of those problems. Only once he'd found somewhere warm that would serve him hot food would he worry about where to sleep.

Warm cafés seemed few and far between, but he came across a man selling hot tatties. The smell was impossible to resist and Robbie bought two.

He was eating his way through the first, heading back towards the river, when a lad raced round the corner, cannoned into him and sent the tatties flying into the gutter.

Robbie had never been so hungry in his life, and he felt the sting of tears in his eyes. He hated Newcastle, and he hated the stupid boy who'd sent his food into the rain-soaked gutter even more.

Robbie had to look up to the lad, he was so much taller, but that didn't stop him grabbing the lapels of his jacket.

'You owe me for two tatties!' he roared.

'Wasn't my fault. You should look where you're going.'

'I was! You're the clumsy idiot who ran into me.'

'You talk funny,' the boy said.

'I do not. I'm a Scot!' That statement added another couple of inches to Robbie's height. 'You're the one who talks funny. Everyone round here does.'

'We're Geordies,' the lad said. 'There's nothing funny about Geordies.'

Robbie released the grip he had on the boy's jacket, but he wasn't giving in.

'I don't care what you are! You still owe me.'

There was a long silence. For a moment, Robbie half expected the lad to hand over a coin, but he shrugged.

'I haven't got any money, but you can come home with me, if you like. Me mam'll have me dinner ready, and you can share that.'

Robbie was torn. What would the boy's mother say? And a dinner – even half a dinner – was perhaps a bit much in return for one-and-a-half baked tatties.

On the other hand, Robbie was still hungry. And cold.

'OK,' he replied casually, not sure about a 'Thank you' just yet.

'So why do you talk like that?' the boy asked as they set off down a maze of streets.

'I told you. I'm from Scotland.'

'Whereabouts?'

'Leith.'

'Never heard of it. Where's that?' The boy looked blank.

'Edinburgh. Don't you know anything? What's your name, anyway?'

'Victor, but you can call me Vic, if you like. What's yours?'

'Robbie Montrose.' If Victor was expecting

more, he was going to be disappointed. Robbie never told anyone he lived at a manse if he could help it.

'So if you live in Edinburgh, what are you doing here?'

'It's a long story.' Robbie guessed it would all come out sooner or later. 'My sister's gone to work in China...'

'By gum!' That impressed Victor. 'What sort of work?'

'She's a missionary.'

Victor groaned, and Robbie had to leap to his sister's defence.

'Ishbel's all right. I'm going there to find her – live with her.'

'You're going to *China?*' Vic's eyes were wide. 'How?'

'Well–' Robbie only wished he knew. 'All I need to do is get to Southampton, and then I'll either work a passage or stow away on a ship for Shanghai.'

'You can't stow away!' Victor scoffed.

'Why not? It got me here.'

'Did it? By gum!' Victor said again. He might be a year or so older, and definitely bigger, but Robbie knew he was impressed.

'Yes. There was a ship in Leith – the *Linden* – that was coming here for repair work. I hid on that. Mind you,' he admitted, 'the skipper found me when we docked. At least, I reckon it was the skipper. He was threatening to fetch the police so I got out.'

He gave Victor a sideways glance.

'Your dad's not police, is he?'

'No!' Victor grinned. 'He does work in shipbuilding, though. What does your dad do then?'

'He's a minister,' Robbie answered quietly. He always said it quietly, hoping that people wouldn't hear properly.

'That's tough luck,' Victor said, and Robbie was so surprised that he laughed.

'Aye. It is.'

He might hate the fact that his father was the minister, but Robbie still loved him – and his mother – very much. He was a little ashamed of that brief note he'd left at Gran's now, because he knew his parents would be worried.

As soon as he knew when he could get a ship to Shanghai, he would write and let them know he was safe.

They walked into another road, lined by terraced houses, and through a narrow alley.

'Not far now.'

Robbie was pleased. He was almost asleep on his feet.

'Where are you going to sleep tonight, Rob?'

'I don't know,' Robbie admitted. 'I don't have much money.'

'Me mam'll let you stay with us. Why don't you bide for a bit? Get work at the yard and save your money–'

'It would take ages!' Robbie protested.

'Better than ending up in the jail. It's easy to hide on a boat from Edinburgh to New-castle, but China's a long way away.'

'I know.'

'Oh, well, suit yourself. Here we are.'

The house was identical to all the others lining the narrow street. Robbie wished with all his heart that his mother could be inside, waiting for him.

He wished his father worked down the shipyard, and he wished his big sister was back at home, just like everyone else's sister was...

Once again, Ishbel was struck by the sheer elegance of Mr and Mrs Chen's home. She herself would have aimed for more in the way of comfort, but the furnishings showed style and taste.

'Forgive me for calling unannounced, but I was passing and wanted to thank you for the party,' she told Helen. 'Mr Campbell and I enjoyed it very much indeed. It was so kind of you to invite us.'

'It was my pleasure, dear. I'm only glad you could come. Hopefully, we'll see a lot more of each other in the future. Tell me,' Helen said, smiling, 'what did you think of Mr Butler, our American friend?'

'Oh, I like him immensely,' Ishbel told her at once.

'Good. So do I. He cheers up the place with his humour and his – well, somewhat brash ways.'

Ishbel had to laugh. Adam Butler was indeed a little brash.

'I prefer to think of them as American ways,' she said, and Helen smiled knowingly.

'Either way, he's a truly fascinating guest. He never fails to cheer me up.'

'Do you need cheering up?' Ishbel was surprised.

'Not really, no,' Helen admitted. 'Sometimes, though, Miss Montrose, I despair of this city. I think of all those children begging on the streets, or worse–'

'Yes.' Ishbel knew exactly what she meant. 'There's certainly a great deal of work to be done. One of the rickshaw men reduced me to tears yesterday. How they survive, I really don't know. The competition is so fierce, and how they manage to pull rickshaws all day on a diet so lacking in nourishment is beyond me.'

'I know. But at least you're here, and doing such a lot for the children. You must be feeling very proud.'

'We're very pleased with the way the school is going,' Ishbel admitted.

'And you're not homesick?' Helen asked.

'Not *too* homesick.'

Helen smiled her understanding.

They chatted for a while about Edinburgh

and Devon, and then Helen had to leave for an appointment, just as her elder daughter came home.

'Would you like to drink tea with me, Ishbel?' Liang asked.

'I'd love to, if you're not too busy.'

'No.' Liang smiled. 'I was only going to do some needlework.'

'Don't let me stop you. Can you sew and talk at the same time? Perhaps I'll learn something.'

Again, Ishbel felt drawn to the beautiful girl with the gentle eyes and shy gestures.

Tea was brought to them, and Liang soon settled herself with her silks.

Ishbel knew the tea they were drinking must be one of the finest in the world, but it didn't taste right. There were times when she would give all she had for a cup of tea from her grandmother's pot...

'No mandarin ducks?' She nodded at Liang's work.

'Not today. This is a tiger collar for my friend's son. In China, tiger clothing is made to ensure a boy's future success and good health.'

Liang was an expert with a needle, and quite put Ishbel to shame. But then, Ishbel used to do her sewing curled up in the armchair at the manse, whereas Liang sat upright on an equally upright chair. Her perfect posture was quite natural.

'Why the tiger?' Ishbel asked.

'The tiger is said to protect against evil and disease,' Liang explained in her soft voice. 'A child will wear tiger shoes, too. Because tigers can see in the dark, it's said that the animal will guide the child's steps.'

She glanced up shyly.

'You must think this is foolish?'

Ishbel knew that only God could protect against evil, but then, her own dear mother came close to hysterics if anyone dared to put shoes on the table!

'No. Not at all,' she protested, and Liang nodded, satisfied.

'In China, it is always better to have a son than a daughter. A son will carry on the family line and provide for his parents. A mother will do anything to protect her son. Also, his birth will have given her a high standing in her husband's family.'

Ishbel wondered about Sun Chen. Had he wanted sons? Had he been disappointed to be presented with two daughters?

Surely not. Surely he was proud of Mei Li and Liang? They were both bright, intelligent girls.

'If my father had a son,' Liang remarked softly, making Ishbel feel guilty, 'he would have someone to carry on at Sun Chen and Company. He is disappointed.'

Ishbel's heart ached for the young girl who, in a different culture, could have made her father so proud.

'He loves you both very much,' she said. 'That's clear to see.'

'Yes.'

They fell silent for a few moments, but Ishbel had to ask.

'Do you think you could succeed in your father's business?' At Liang's enquiring gaze, she added, 'I, for one, don't even know how tea is made.'

Liang smiled.

'It is not difficult. The top leaves of the tea plant are picked in April and May, and then they are dried. A bamboo brush is used to toss the leaves in a drying pan before they're put on tables. There, the workers gather bundles together and mould them, to twist and condense the leaves. The leaves are then dried – over a slow fire if the tea is to remain green, but if it so be black, the leaves are tossed over a charcoal fire until they turn black.'

'Gosh. And that's it?' Ishbel was impressed.

'The sorting process is next,' Liang explained. 'The leaves are sorted for quality before being loaded into boxes.'

'I drink tea,' Ishbel admitted sheepishly, 'but I had no idea how it was made.'

'I believe the British like the Indian teas now,' Liang remarked. 'Perhaps because you have a different diet and like to add milk to your tea.'

'Yes, our diets are very different.' But it wasn't only their diets; their lives were very different, too.

'Mr Butler has promised to give me a tour of your father's business,' Ishbel went on. 'Will you be able to come with us, Liang?'

'I'll ask my father.' She smiled. 'I'm sure he will agree.'

'I hope so. I'm looking forward to the tour, and I enjoy your company.'

'Will you tell me about life in Edinburgh?' Liang asked.

'Gosh!' Ishbel laughed. 'Where do I begin?'

Once she started, however, the problem was knowing where to stop. Her home town was as different from Shanghai as it was possible to be.

She spoke about the people, too, whose lives were so very different from Liang's.

'My sister is in the office at a printing works – she's a clerk.'

Liang didn't answer that directly.

'Do you know of the St Andrew Society?' she asked instead. 'My mother has told me they celebrate St Andrew's Day in style. A special race meeting – horse racing – is held and whoever comes last is presented with a huge wooden spoon that must be filled with whisky!'

'I thought whisky would come into it,' Ishbel replied with a chuckle.

'They have a ball in the evening with dancing,' Liang added, and Ishbel's heart gave a familiar lurch. She could picture it; kilts and sporrans, tartan sashes. She could almost hear the sound of the Scottish reels...

'Gordon – Mr Campbell – plays the fiddle.' Ishbel's smile was at odds with the moisture that suddenly glistened in her eyes. 'Only last night, my friend Jane and I danced as he played for us. It was great fun.'

'I'm very sad for you,' Liang said softly. 'You long for your home.'

Ishbel couldn't deny it, but she didn't want Liang's sympathy.

'I came to China because I wanted to, because I felt I had to,' she tried to explain. 'I don't regret my decision, Liang – I'm proud of the work we're doing here. I miss my parents and my grandmother. And I miss Mary, and my wee brother, Rob, but this is where I belong. In any case, I have friends in Shanghai now. I'd like to think *we* could be good friends, Liang.'

'I thought we were,' Liang said, surprised.

'Yes, but what I meant was really close friends.'

'So did I, Ishbel.'

The sincerity behind Liang's words touched Ishbel. On an impulse, she reached across and hugged her.

Together, they would help each other. Liang would help Ishbel fight the dreadful homesickness that threatened to overwhelm her at times, and Ishbel would help Liang towards that bright future she longed for.

How she would do that, Ishbel had no idea. All she knew was that she refused to sit back and watch Liang waste that quick brain by ending up in a lonely, loveless marriage arranged by her father...

It was early when Gordon reached the schoolroom, but Ishbel was already there. He couldn't see her; all he could hear was her voice.

He didn't recognise the song she was singing, but it lifted his spirits. Ishbel always lifted his spirits.

'Good morning, Ishbel,' he called out. 'You're early.'

She emerged from the walk-in cupboard.

'Good morning, Gordon. How are you today?'

'Better for seeing you.'

And he was. More and more Ishbel was intruding on his thoughts. He was beginning to miss her when she wasn't with him.

She looked especially lovely today, too. It wasn't so much what she was wearing, although her white blouse with its tiny lace edging on the collar and cuffs was pretty enough, and her skirt was as neat as ever.

It was more the freshness of her skin, the sparkle in her eyes, the warmth of her open smile, the way the light caught her hair...

She came forward, smiling, and Gordon couldn't resist reaching for her hand. As he held it in his, he could feel her pulse racing. Or was it his own?

'Ishbel, you look–'

There was a brief, sharp knock on the door, and then that American from Chen's, Adam Butler, was in the schoolroom.

Confound the man! Not that he'd done anything wrong – in fact, Gordon liked him – but he could have timed his entrance a little better.

He'd only been going to tell Ishbel how lovely she looked, but it could wait; it would have to. She had snatched back her hand, and the moment had gone. The only hint of it was the heightened colour in her face.

'I'm on my way to the office,' Adam explained, 'but I wanted to stop by and give you Lizzie McKie's address, Ishbel.'

'Oh, thank you.' She took the piece of paper from him and turned to Gordon. 'Lizzie McKie is the woman I was telling you about, who trained at St Colm's.'

'I've dropped her a quick note telling her to expect a letter from you,' Adam said.

'I'll write to her this evening,' Ishbel said. 'Thank you, Adam.'

Why on earth was Ishbel using this American's Christian name? Gordon wasn't sure he approved, bearing in mind that Ishbel had only met the chap once before.

'I visited Helen and Liang yesterday,' Ishbel went on, 'and Liang told me about the St Andrew Society. I wonder if Lizzie McKie knows about it? According to Liang, they have horse racing and a ball to celebrate St Andrew's Day. It sounds wonderful!'

Gordon was surprised by her enthusiasm.

'Are you sure, Ishbel?' he asked. 'I suspect horse racing translates as gambling, and the ball as drinking far too much whisky.'

'Oh, Gordon!'

He'd heard that 'Oh, Gordon' from Ishbel before. Their aims were the same, but their methods differed occasionally.

Ishbel could do God's work at a party, a ball, a race meeting – anywhere. She liked nothing better than seeing people having fun. Gordon preferred, and needed, more formal surroundings.

'It sounds terrific,' Adam put in.

'I think so.' She looked up at Gordon. 'I'm sure it's all very proper and correct.'

'And I'm sure it's no such thing!' But her earnest expression made him smile.

'I'd better be on my way,' Adam said. 'Ishbel, if you write to Lizzie this evening, would you send her my best regards, please?'

'I will, Adam. And thank you again.'

'Be seeing you both.'

He left a suddenly tense silence behind him.

'What were you about to say before Adam

arrived, Gordon?'

Gordon knew exactly what he'd wanted to say, but the moment was lost.

'Oh, nothing. It wasn't important.'

'Right.' She gave him a tight little smile. 'I'd better get back to sorting out those books, then.'

He watched her walk away, her back straight and her head held high, and he wondered at the disappointment he'd seen flicker in her eyes.

Could it be that she'd guessed what he was going to say? Had she wanted him to speak?

'Ishbel?'

She stopped and turned to look at him.

'Yes?'

He went to her and, again, took her small hand in his.

'I was going to say that you look especially lovely this morning. That was all.'

'Thank you.' He felt her hand tremble in his. 'That's quite a lot, actually, Gordon. Something every girl likes to hear.'

'Then I must tell you more often.'

Reluctantly, he let her hand go. But how she looked had nothing to do with how he was beginning to feel about her. It was the fact that they worked so well together, shared the same hopes and fears, strove for the same things...

Looking at Ishbel's questioning eyes, he wondered if perhaps their partnership might grow into something deeper. A partnership for life, even...

With every step away from the office, Mary told herself she had finally taken leave of her senses. Yet still she walked on.

It was the helplessness about Robbie she hated the most. She had to do something!

Unfortunately, the only thing she could think of was asking Jack Keller for his help.

Once again, she found herself standing on the steps by his front door. Once again, she was shown into his sitting-room by the friendly-looking, plump woman.

On her last visit, Mary had been struck by the warm and cosy feel of the room, but this time she barely noticed her surroundings.

Jack was far too handsome for his own good, she decided, as he shook her hand.

'We'll have tea now, Mabel, if you'd be good enough to bring it.'

Mabel. Yes, she looked like a Mabel. She also looked as if she'd walk across hot coals for this man.

'This is a rare pleasure, Miss Montrose.'

Miss Montrose? Perhaps he was beginning to take the hint.

'Thank you.' Mary didn't want tea, but as she was asking for his help, she decided it would be difficult to refuse the kindness.

'Here – sit closer to the fire.' He pulled a leather armchair nearer to the hearth. 'It's a dreary day.'

'Yes.' Mary sank into the chair. 'Thank you, Mr Keller.'

It was difficult to hold an intelligent conversation with someone when you struggled even to look at them...

The tea, when it came, did Mabel proud. Jack Keller was obviously trying to impress, but it didn't work. All it did was remind Mary of how Robbie's mouth would have watered at the sight of the cakes.

And didn't the social niceties take an age, she thought impatiently...

'I've come to ask for your help,' she was able to say at last.

'I guessed as much.' Jack was eating a scone, very slowly. 'Sadly, I didn't think for a moment that this was a social call. I assume you mean financial help?'

'I certainly do not!' Did he honestly believe she would ask him for money? She would starve first!

'I'm terribly sorry,' he said quickly. 'I've offended you.' He returned his plate to the tray and sat back in his chair.

'Perhaps you'd like to tell me what the problem is? It's obviously serious, to bring you to me.'

'It is.' Mary took a deep breath. 'It's about Robbie – my brother. My sister, as you may know, is working in Shanghai as a missionary.'

'Good heavens!' Was that amusement in his eyes? No, it was gone now... 'I had no idea, Miss Montrose.'

'Well – since she left, Rob, my brother, has been quite low in spirits. The two of them were very close, you see.'

'How old is your brother?'

'Coming up to fifteen. He's always been one for getting into trouble,' Mary went on, 'so that's nothing new, but now he's vanished. He left a note at our grandmother's, saying he was going to Shanghai to find Ishbel – since then, we've heard nothing.'

Dark eyebrows rose as she told her tale, but Jack didn't comment. It was impossible to know what was going through his mind.

'We've no idea where he is,' Mary said, 'but someone must know. Fourteen-year-olds don't just vanish. And he has no money to get him anywhere near Shanghai.'

'I don't see what it is you want me to do.' Jack was frowning.

'You have contacts,' Mary pointed out. 'Good heavens, you own half the city–'

'Not quite! I have many business contacts, and a wide circle of friends, yes, but I honestly can't see that I can help. Presumably if your brother intends to get to China, he'll have taken a boat, a train or–'

'But he has no money,' Mary reminded him.

'Then perhaps he managed to get a free

99

ride. Almost fifteen – he's old enough to take care of himself, you know.'

'You don't know Robbie,' Mary said flatly. 'Other fourteen-year-olds might be, but not Robbie. So you're not prepared to help?'

Jack sipped his tea reflectively.

'It's not that simple. I can certainly ask around, but–'

'Would you?' Mary was almost begging.

'Of course, but I'm not at all hopeful.'

'I'd be very grateful. Really – you can't imagine what it's like. My mother is worrying herself to death. She can't sleep, she won't eat. If we could just have word about him!'

'All I can do is ask around.'

'The police can't help,' Mary told him, 'but you know people. You must be able to pull a few strings.'

He sat up in his chair.

'You'll need to give me all the details – exactly when he left, what he looks like, what he would have been wearing, his friends' names – things like that.'

Mary spent the next five minutes giving Jack all the information she could. Strangely, she felt better for simply having talked about it...

'I warn you now, Mary, it will cost you.'

Well! She might have known. The Jack Kellers of this world did nothing for nothing.

What on earth had possessed her even to ask for his help? Desperation, an inner voice answered. Seeing her mother look more beaten every day...

'How much?' Her voice was distinctly cool.

'I hadn't thought about it.' His voice, on the other hand, was like honey. 'Shall we say an evening out together? Dinner, and then dancing?'

Mary stared at him for so long that he was almost laughing aloud. All the while, she could feel her face burning.

'An evening out?' She found her voice. 'You and me?'

'Yes.'

'Why?'

'Because I can think of nothing I'd like more. It will be the incentive I need to trace this brother of yours. And then–' he looked at her '–when you've spent the evening with me, and know me a little better, perhaps you'll manage to call me Jack.'

'Does it matter?' Her voice was impatient.

'Yes, it does. I long to hear my name on your lips.'

'Why?' It was all she could think of to say, and even that one word was a struggle.

'Because I'm totally besotted with you, Mary Montrose.'

'Well – really!' Mary rose to her feet. 'I've taken up far too much of your time, Mr Keller. Thank you for the tea. It was very – er, nice.'

'My pleasure.' And he had the cheek to

laugh at her. 'I hope we'll meet again soon, Mary. Meanwhile, I'll do all I can to see if I can find out anything for you.'

'Thank you. Goodbye, Mr Keller...'

Afterwards, Mary wasn't quite sure how she had managed to walk out of his house. The man was incorrigible.

What was worse, much worse, was the way her mind kept dwelling on that evening out.

Dinner and dancing, he'd said. Every time she thought of it, her heart started to beat a little faster.

Once again she tried, with very little success, to put Jack Keller from her mind. There were far more important things to worry about.

This evening, she and her mother were going to write to Ishbel and break the news of Robbie's disappearance. One of those 'there's nothing to worry about, but...' type of letters, the very worst sort to receive.

They'd put it off, waiting until they had news, but no news had come.

They'd thought that, as the mail took so long to reach Shanghai, Robbie would be safely home before Ishbel even received the letter.

But Robbie could be anywhere, and they could put it off no longer...

Chapter Five

'It was kind of you to bring me home, Adam,' Ishbel said. 'After what I've just seen of Sun Chen's company, I feel ridiculous offering you tea, but–'

'I'll accept graciously,' he said with a laugh. 'Thank you, Ishbel.'

The mission was deserted when they went inside. Gordon would still be at his meeting, but Ishbel had expected Jane to be there. She had probably taken Teddy for a walk.

'I'm always complaining I get no peace,' Ishbel remarked with a rueful smile, 'and now there's no-one in sight.'

She took Adam into the sitting-room. The room was Ishbel's favourite, but compared to the Chens' sumptuous home, it was slightly shabby.

It was also a little untidy, she noticed, which was rare. Usually Jane was over-conscientious about tidying Teddy's toys away.

She wondered briefly what Adam's home was like. Did he favour elaborate surroundings or, like her, choose comfort in preference to style?

'Have a seat, Adam, and make yourself at home. I'll bring our tea.'

While she made the tea, Ishbel's mind was still reeling from their tour of Sun Chen and Company. She had enjoyed the day immensely.

It had crossed her mind that Liang, going round yet again, might be bored, but she gave no sign of it. In fact, Sun Chen's daughter appeared to enjoy it just as much as Ishbel.

Adam had shown them where the tea was made, and then they had returned to the offices on Nanking Road.

The tea-making process, despite Liang having already explained it, was a real eye-opener.

The offices came as an even bigger surprise. The building was huge, and so modern.

Sun Chen's own office was the most amazing Ishbel had even seen. She had been touched to see, in pride of place on his huge desk, a photograph of Helen and their two daughters...

Ishbel carried their tea into the sitting-room, and Adam rose to his feet to take the tray.

'Wasn't it wonderful to see Liang so light-hearted today?' Ishbel remarked. 'I really admire the way she's so proper and correct, but I love to see her smile.'

'I know.' Adam laughed fondly. 'She even giggled today! I've never known that happen before.'

'How could she help it, when you were

teasing me about my knowledge of the tea business?' Ishbel asked solemnly.

'And what knowledge would that be?' he enquired, deadpan.

Ishbel spluttered with laughter.

'I've never felt so ignorant in my life!'

'And now you know all there is to know.' He sat back and sipped his tea.

Ishbel wasn't so sure about that, but she'd certainly learned a lot, not only about the tea business, but also about the people who worked in it. Which reminded her—

'Edward Clements should be back in Shanghai soon, shouldn't he?'

'Yes.' Adam nodded. 'He's due back at work on the fourteenth.' He gave her a wry smile. 'I almost feel sorry for him... I'm sure you don't have good news for him.'

Ishbel simply didn't know. Good news or bad – that would depend on Mr Clements.

'I hope I can tell you all about it one day, Adam, but—'

He held up his hands.

'I appreciate that it has to be confidential.'

She nodded gratefully.

Obviously, she couldn't tell him – she had no right. But a part of her had longed to explain how they were hoping Edward Clements would accept Teddy as his son.

Perhaps it was because Adam actually knew Edward Clements, albeit not on a personal level – or perhaps it was because she suspected he wouldn't judge anyone.

Maybe she simply wanted someone to convince her the outcome would be a happy one.

Just then the air was rent by a baby's yells, and Jane herself came into the sitting-room. She held Teddy against her hip, and an assortment of envelopes in her free hand.

That was no easy task. Almost sixteen months old now, Teddy was very heavy.

Ishbel made introductions over the noise, but further conversation was impossible.

'He'll be over-tired,' Jane said apologetically. 'I'll take him upstairs and see if he'll sleep.

'I only came to bring you the mail, Ishbel... I've left Gordon's in the hall.'

'Thank you, Jane.'

Ishbel's heart always raced at the thought of mail. News from home brought her family closer.

She put the envelopes on the table, ready to open when Adam had left, but he leaned forward and flicked one with a local stamp.

'Don't think I'm being nosy, but the handwriting on that envelope belongs to Lizzie McKie, your fellow missionary.'

'Really?' Ishbel swooped on it and tore it open. 'Oh, what a lovely letter!'

'How do you know that?' Adam asked in amazement. 'You haven't read it!'

'Well, no, but four pages in small, neat

handwriting? How can it be anything but lovely?'

And it *was* wonderful, Ishbel discovered as she read it.

Lizzie McKie was six years older than herself. When she wrote of her missionary training back at St Colm's in Edinburgh, she mentioned a couple of people that Ishbel knew.

'She says we must have a chat and compare experiences,' Ishbel said, glancing up. 'She sounds lovely.'

'She is.'

Lizzie was working in one of the villages in the north of China. Her life there sounded very different.

'Listen to this, Adam. She's coming to Shanghai! She says, *I would love to meet you, Ishbel, and will call at the mission on the seventeenth of this month. I won't receive any reply in time so don't bother writing – if you're unavailable, don't worry.'* Ishbel beamed at Adam.

'Isn't that exciting?'

She laughed aloud as she reached the end of the letter.

'Lizzie sends her regards,' she told Adam. 'And she adds a PS. *Don't make the mistake of spending half your time cooking for him – as I did!*

'Oh, really, Adam.'

'She's a lovely woman,' Adam said, grinning, 'but she is prone to exaggeration.'

Laughing, Ishbel returned the letter to its envelope.

The handwriting on another envelope was familiar, too.

'That's from my sister,' she told Adam with a smile. 'Knowing Mary, it will be short, and full of horror-stories about the state of the country.' She grew serious.

'Mind you, she does have a point. In her last letter, she told me that because unemployment's so bad, ex-Servicemen have been reduced to selling matches on the street.'

'That's terrible.' He seemed as shocked as she was. 'I'll take my leave, Ishbel, and let you read your sister's letter in peace.'

'Oh, no – really. I'll read it later.'

She enjoyed his company immensely. Without her family around her, life seemed a little too serious at times.

It wasn't that she didn't take her work seriously, but she missed the banter of her family, and Adam never failed to make her laugh.

There was very little that he took seriously. His favourite phrase, she'd discovered, was 'Life's too short.'

She asked now about his life in America, and he regaled her with tales of his childhood in New York, where he'd grown up with five brothers.

'Someone said New Yorkers feel at home in Shanghai because the climate is the same.

Is that true, Adam?'

'Yes. The cities are very different, but the weather is the same – too hot in summer and too cold in winter!'

'Unlike Edinburgh,' she joked. 'That's too cold in winter and too cold in summer.'

Adam nodded at Mary's letter.

'You're longing to open it. I'll go–'

'No.' She reached for the envelope and opened it. 'I'll skim through it quickly, then read it later at my leisure. Mary's letters are always full of–'

But then her hand flew to her chest as if she could somehow calm the hammering of her heart.

'Ishbel?'

His voice seemed to come from miles away. All she could do was read Mary's words with a growing sense of horror and disbelief.

'My dear girl, whatever is it? Bad news?' He was on his feet, leaning over her. 'Can I get you something? A glass of water?'

She looked up at him.

'No. Thank you.' She took a deep breath. 'I'm so sorry, Adam. It's my young brother, you see. Robbie's run away from home.'

She saw her own shock mirrored in his eyes.

'He left a note saying he was coming here – coming to Shanghai. He said he wanted to find me!' She bit her lip hard.

'How old is he?'

'Fourteen – fifteen at the end of the month.' Again, she put her hand to her chest. 'They've had no word at home. They've no idea where he is.'

She couldn't bear to think about it, but she read Mary's letter again. This time she could hear her mother's voice in every word.

'Try not to worry, they say. How can I do anything *but* worry? How on earth does he expect to get here?'

'Try to keep calm, Ishbel,' Adam said gently. 'You know how irregular the mail service is. For all you know, Robbie could have given up on his plan and be back home by now. You know what fifteen-year-olds are like.'

Ishbel shook her head.

'They left it a while before they wrote, hoping for just that.' She looked into his face, hoping to find an answer there.

'What on earth can I do, Adam?'

He patted her hand gently, but he didn't answer. How could he? They both knew there was nothing she could do. Nothing at all.

'What do you mean?' Mary Montrose stopped with one arm in her coat. 'Your brother Gordon…?'

'Exactly what I said,' Flora Campbell replied impatiently. They'd finished work for the day and were getting ready to go home.

'But you told me Gordon wasn't inter-

110

ested in girls,' Mary reminded her.

'I didn't think he was.'

Mary shook her head in a bemused fashion. Flora had always worshipped her twin brother yet she didn't seem to know him too well.

'So what did he say about Ishbel?'

'Och, when he writes to me and Mum, he mentions Ishbel in every sentence!' Flora grinned. 'Mum reckons we ought to ask Ishbel how *Gordon* is, because all he does is tell us about her. I'm telling you, Mary, there's something going on there.' Flora buttoned up her coat and pulled up the collar.

'I told you ages ago,' Mary said, hunting in her pockets for her gloves, 'before they even left for Shanghai, that Ishbel was half in love with him.'

'Well, I reckon he's half in love with her, too. Our Gordon! Who'd have thought it?'

As they stepped into the front office, Mary was making a mental note to mention Gordon in her next letter to Ishbel.

When she saw who was standing in the office, though, all thoughts of her sister flew from her mind.

'Hello,' she managed to say.

'Good evening, Miss Montrose,' Jack Keller said. 'I'm rushing to an appointment, I'm afraid, but I'd like a quick word, if I may.'

'I'll see you in the morning, Mary.' Then Flora had gone, leaving a blast of welcome cold air on Mary's face.

'Of course,' she said to Jack, as her thoughts slowly gathered themselves and her heart skipped a beat. 'Is it about Rob?'

'It may be,' he answered cautiously. 'I've heard of a lad who hid on a ship bound for Newcastle-upon-Tyne.

'The skipper chased him off and threatened to fetch the police when they docked – more to frighten him than anything else, I gather.' He took a watch from his waistcoat pocket and glanced at it.

'May we walk? I don't want to be late for my appointment.'

'Of course.'

Unless Mary was mistaken, and she doubted it, the watch was gold, with a small object attached to the chain. She wondered what it was.

Outside, walking at a pace too quick for Mary, she fired question after question at him.

What made him think it was Robbie? What was the boy wearing? Where did he go when the boat docked?

'I wish I could be of more help,' Jack Keller said, 'but that's all I can tell you. And now I'm sorry, but I must leave you.'

'Yes,' Mary's mind was racing. 'Thank you, Mr Keller.'

'My pleasure, Miss Montrose.' He touched his hat. 'If I find out anything more, I'll let you know. Meanwhile, I'll bid you good-night.'

'Goodnight, Mr Keller. And thank you again.'

Moira stepped inside Donald's kirk and closed the heavy old door behind her. She'd been right – her daughter was there, sitting in a pew and staring into space.

She wasn't praying or her head would be bowed. No, Veronica was just worrying.

Moira sympathised. She'd lost several nights' sleep herself. She touched Veronica on the shoulder.

'Mum! You startled me.'

'Sorry, love. I thought you'd be busy cleaning.'

'No.' Veronica was about to rise from her pew, but then changed her mind. 'What are you doing here?'

'I was out for a walk, and thought I'd see if you were still here.'

Veronica nodded. It was obvious she didn't care if she had company or not.

She didn't care about anything. Ishbel's departure had been bad enough, but all this long time without news of Robbie – it was too much for her to bear.

Moira sat beside Veronica. Sympathetic though she was, the time had come for some stern words.

'None of this is easy for Mary, you know,'

she began. 'She misses Ishbel, and she's just as worried as you are about Rob—'

'I know that, Mum.'

'Yes, but on top of all that, she's got you to worry about, too. Robbie won't be home any quicker whether you starve yourself or not.' A bit of plain speaking was long overdue.

'You don't sleep, you refuse to eat,' Moira went on. 'All you're doing is worrying Donald and Mary – aye, and me, too. Well, lass, we've got enough to worry about without you adding to it!'

Her words were harsh, she knew that, but she didn't regret them.

'Robbie's all but fifteen,' she pointed out. 'He's no longer a bairn, Veronica. He's old enough to be working at sea, in the yards – anywhere.'

'What are you saying?' Veronica demanded hurt. 'That I should pretend I'd never brought him into the world?'

'Of course not,' Moira said gently. 'But I think you could be stronger – for Don's sake, and for Mary's. They need you, love. And when Rob comes home, he'll need you too.'

'If he comes home,' Veronica gulped back a sob.

Moira didn't know what to say to that.

'I'm going home now.' Veronica got to her feet.

'I'll walk with you,' her mother said at once.

Apart from comments from Moira about the weather, they walked in silence.

'I suppose Ishbel will know what's happened by now,' Veronica said. 'I dread to think how she'll be feeling. I wish we could have written a different letter, but—'

'Ishbel will feel as dreadful as the rest of us,' Moira said frankly, 'but she'll cope. She's a strong, sensible young woman.'

'And I'm not, I suppose! It's all right for you, Mum, you've—' Veronica stopped suddenly.

'Is this our Mary?'

Sure enough, Mary was racing along the street towards them, her coat flying behind her.

Only when she stopped in front of them did Mary realise she'd no breath left to speak.

'I thought you were at the kirk, Mum,' she said breathlessly. 'I was on my way there. I've got news of Rob!'

Her mother went completely white.

'What do you mean? What news?'

Mary wished she'd phrased it differently, but the faster she'd run, the more she'd managed to convince herself that it *had* been Robbie on that boat.

This was the first spark of life she'd seen in her mother's eyes since that brother of hers had taken off, and she couldn't bear to dash those hopes.

'Well – it *may* be news of Rob. I went and

asked Mr Keller if he could help. He knows everyone in Edinburgh.'

She didn't miss the way her grandmother's mouth tightened in disapproval at the mention of Jack Keller's name.

'He came to see me when I finished work today,' she went on. 'Apparently, a lad looking like our Rob hid on a boat that left Leith for Newcastle. Now, it might not have been Rob, but the date and time fits, and from the description Jack – Mr Keller – got, it sounds as if it could have been him.'

'Newcastle?' Veronica shook her head.

'It could be. He might have taken off to anywhere nearer to Southampton – nearer the boat for Shanghai.'

All light had gone from her mother's eyes again.

'It's good news, Mary,' Moira said firmly. 'At least we've got something to go on. At long last, we can actually *do* something.'

'Like what?' Veronica asked, voicing Mary's own doubts.

'Well, first of all, I'll visit Bridget – you know her, Veronica, at my bridge club. She has family in Newcastle. I'll ask her for any names and addresses she can give me – people, shops, factories – anything.'

'But even if it was Rob, we don't know that he stopped in Newcastle for more than five minutes,' Veronica said wretchedly.

'Of course we don't,' her mother agreed

impatiently. 'We don't know that the three of us will still be alive this time tomorrow, either!'

She took a breath and spoke more calmly.

'But at least we can do something.'

'I suppose you're right.' Veronica nodded. Then she rounded on Mary.

'But why you had to go to that Jack Keller, I don't know. Your father will have something to say about that, my girl. Broadcasting our problems to a man like that!'

Mary gave her mother an apologetic grimace, but she welcomed those sharp words. At least Mum had sounded like her old self for a moment.

Anything had to be better than sitting and waiting for news that didn't come.

Every time there was a knock on the manse door, and that was often – every time a letter was delivered – they all held their breath, hoping and praying. And every time, they'd been disappointed.

They walked on to the manse, each lost in their own thoughts.

Had it been Robbie? Mary wished she knew. Jack Keller hadn't sounded too confident.

At the time, it had been in the back of Mary's mind to tell him in no uncertain terms that as they didn't even know if this was Rob, she had no intention of fulfilling her part of the bargain – spending an evening in his company.

Yet he hadn't even mentioned it.

Perhaps he'd turned his attentions else-where, Mary thought suddenly. Who was he in such a rush to meet?

Well, if he had his eye on someone else, it could only be a good thing. The last thing Mary wanted was the likes of Jack Keller taking an interest in her.

So why was the prospect he'd cooled towards her such a depressing one?

For once, the Shanghai weather was kind, and Ishbel appreciated the gentle warmth on her face as she walked. She'd strolled along the Bund and turned into Nanking Road.

She liked walking, and the sights, sounds and smells of the city still had the power to amaze and fascinate her…

'Ishbel!'

She stopped and turned. She'd walked past the offices of Sun Chen and Company without even glancing at the buildings; she'd been too wrapped up in her thoughts.

But there was Liang, just leaving the building with a young servant girl.

After a brief word with the girl, who nodded in response, Liang walked along the street in her usual sedate manner towards Ishbel. The servant girl followed.

'I'm so pleased to see you, Ishbel! I've been wanting to call on you. I'm so sorry to hear about your brother. I hope you don't mind, but Mr Butler mentioned it to me. Have you had any news?'

'None at all,' Ishbel said softly, 'but thank you for your concern. Everyone's been so thoughtful. I'm glad Adam told you. He was there when I opened the letter, you know. It's always better to have someone with you when you receive bad news, isn't it?'

'I don't know.' Liang was thoughtful. 'I think I would prefer to be alone.' She paused.

'May I walk with you?'

'Can you? Oh, yes, please!'

Liang turned and spoke in Chinese to the servant girl, far too quickly for Ishbel to understand.

They walked on. Ishbel felt slightly strange to have the girl following them.

Liang, as always, looked very pretty in her traditional dress. There were several pairs of mandarin ducks embroidered on the sleeves of her jacket today, but Liang's beauty went far deeper than the clothes she wore.

'You must be very worried,' Liang said quietly. 'I know how close you are to your brother.'

'Very close.' Ishbel nodded. 'I'm worried to death. It's just the sort of thing Robbie would do, though. He's always got himself into mischief. He's a lovely, sensitive boy, but he's completely fearless. He will have got it into his head to come to China, and that will be that. He won't have stopped to consider the dangers involved.'

'My sister, Mei Li, is the same.' Liang nodded. 'If she wants something, she gets it. She never stops to consider the consequences.'

'Are you very close to your sister?'

Liang considered the question.

'Most of the time. We're very different, though.'

They side-stepped a couple who were trying to pacify two rickshaw men.

'Mei Li is stronger than me,' Liang said. 'More headstrong. Instead of talking through her problems, she'll shout them at anyone who will listen.'

'That doesn't make her stronger,' Ishbel protested.

'She's certainly braver than me,' Liang said with a small smile. 'She says things to our father that I wouldn't dare!'

'She sounds like my sister, Mary. She's very headstrong, too. She and my father are often at loggerheads over something or other.'

Her smile faded.

Were Dad and Mary at loggerheads now? She doubted it. They'd both be so worried over Robbie...

'I've often wished for a brother,' Liang confessed. 'A brother would have taken the pressure off me. Instead of worrying about finding a suitable husband for me, my father would be preparing his son to take over the business.'

'*Is* he worrying?' Ishbel asked. 'About finding a suitable husband, I mean?'

'More than I find comfortable,' Liang admitted. 'Your brother is young, isn't he? Younger than Mei Li?'

'Yes.'

'I'm so sorry, Ishbel. I know how you long for your home and family. It must be very difficult for you.'

'Thank you, Liang. Everyone has been very kind. It helps more than you'll know.'

It should have helped, but there had been times when Ishbel could have jumped on the first ship home.

She needed to know Robbie was safe. She needed to know what her family were doing. She needed to be there, worrying with them...

A week later, Ishbel and Gordon were sitting in Adam Butler's office, waiting. Ishbel's heart was thumping wildly – so much rested on this meeting.

Fortunately, Adam didn't keep them long. Within a few minutes, he entered the office. It was the tall man who followed him Ishbel was interested in.

She couldn't take her eyes from him. He looked nothing like the man she had imagined.

'Miss Monstrose, Mr Gordon Campbell – Mr Edward Clements,' Adam introduced them.

Ishbel shook hands with Edward Clements, her mind in a whirl.

'Pleased to meet you both. Mr Butler said you wished to see me. How may I be of assistance?'

'I'll leave you alone,' Adam said. 'I'll only be in the outer office.'

'Yes. Thank you, Adam,' Gordon murmured.

As soon as the door closed behind Adam, Ishbel gestured to a seat.

'Please, sit down, Mr Clements.'

Ishbel sat opposite, with Gordon by her side, and tried to gather her thoughts.

She was at a complete loss. Instead of the foolish youth she had been expecting to see, she was facing a mature, intelligent man, dressed immaculately in a dark suit. How old would he be? Thirty?

It seemed impossible this could be Jane's Mr Clements. But it was too much of a coincidence, surely – his name, the fact that he worked in the tea business, his trips to England…

Before they even arrived in Shanghai, Gordon had pointed out that Edward Clements might be married with a family of his own. Looking at the man opposite her Ishbel thought that more than likely.

He was well-educated, well-spoken, and had a good job on the European liaison side of Sun Chen and Company. She would be surprised if he wasn't married...

Edward Clements was waiting patiently for them to speak, and Ishbel didn't even know where to begin.

She had insisted on dealing with this matter herself. She was Jane's friend, and she'd felt that Gordon might be too intimidating, too disapproving – but now she was pleased he was with her.

'It's a very delicate matter, Mr Clements.' She decided to start at the beginning.

'When we were on our way out last year, we met a young girl on the ship. She had her baby with her – a wee boy called Teddy.'

He was listening patiently.

'An English girl,' Ishbel went on. 'She was coming to Shanghai in an attempt to find the father of her child.'

She ground to a halt and offered a silent prayer for help.

'I'm afraid I still don't see how I can help, Miss Montrose,' the suave voice said.

'Her name is Jane Terry, Mr Clements. She claims that you are her child's father...'

Chapter Six

The noise that was Shanghai, muted inside that modern office, but everpresent, seemed to cease for a moment. And little wonder.

Ishbel looked at the man sitting opposite her. Minutes ago, Edward Clements had been a confident, self-assured businessman. Now he was a changed man.

His face was frighteningly pale, dominated by eyes that held a mixture of shock, fear and disbelief.

'I realise what a shock this must be, Mr Clements,' Ishbel murmured.

'Do you?'

There was anger in his voice, but Ishbel didn't think it was because of her.

'I'm sorry, Miss Montrose – Mr Campbell. None of this is your fault.' Edward Clements rose to his feet, walked to the window and rested his forehead against the glass. 'You're right; it is a shock.'

How would a man feel on hearing such news? That a part of him, his own flesh and blood, could pass him in the street and he wouldn't even know him?

The tense silence stretched on until Ishbel could bear it no longer.

'Do you remember Jane Terry?' she asked.

He turned from the window, rubbed his eyes as if exhaustion had overtaken him, and sat back in his seat.

'Oh, I remember her. Vaguely. Young – about your age. Pretty. Huge blue eyes.'

Ishbel felt Gordon tense beside her. The young woman they knew was more than young and pretty with huge blue eyes. A lot more!

'So it is possible that–?' Ishbel's voice trailed away. She was hopeless at discussing such delicate matters.

'Is it possible that you're the child's father?' Gordon had none of her qualms.

'It's possible – yes,' Edward Clements stated flatly. 'It's also possible that a dozen other men could–'

'I refuse to accept that!' Ishbel retorted. 'I *know* Jane, and I won't believe that of her.'

'You have the advantage, Miss Montrose. I don't know her at all.'

'You clearly knew her well enough–' Again, she stumbled to a halt.

'No,' he said with a heavy sigh. 'I met Jane Terry when I was on leave. With hindsight, I can see what a fool I was, but I was flattered by her attention. We had a brief, very brief affair, and yes, it went too far.'

'That's not how Jane sees it.' Ishbel was shaking now, but tried to speak calmly. 'According to Jane, you told her that you weren't yet financially secure, but that you would keep in touch.'

That made him blush.

'That's correct, up to a point.' He paused. 'In the tea business – well, the salary is so poor for the first five or six years that a man can't entertain the idea of marrying. My circumstances have improved now, but – well, I've come to realise that Miss Terry and I had nothing in common.'

'You have something in common now,' Ishbel reminded him sharply. 'You have a son.'

'So she says.'

Ishbel held his eyes.

'And I believe her.'

It was Edward Clements' turn to remain silent.

'When I first met Jane, I thought her naïve, foolish and a little irresponsible,' Ishbel said. 'I imagine you did, too. My opinion soon changed – or, rather, *she* changed. She's a good mother to wee Teddy – she would die for that boy – but there's more to her than that. She helps us so much at the mission.'

He made a sound, swiftly suppressed, and she met his gaze.

'You look surprised, Mr Clements, but it's a fact. She's marvellous with the young children, and we would be lost without her. There's more to Jane than a pretty face, you know. She's very hard working, honest and reliable.'

He said nothing to that.

'What does she want from me?' He looked at Gordon. 'Money?'

'No!' Ishbel saw red at once. 'No,' she said more calmly. 'At first, I think she hoped that you would fall in love with her and Teddy, marry her and live happily ever after.'

He shook his head, bemused.

'You said "at first". She doesn't hope that now?'

'Now, her ideas are more realistic. She wants you to acknowledge Teddy as your son, and for Teddy to know his father. I think she still hopes you will marry her. She isn't expecting miracles, though. She knows life won't be easy. But she is prepared to work hard to make a marriage successful.'

Gordon, watching the other man's face, felt his heart sink.

'Are you married, Mr Clements?' he asked.

'I'm engaged to be married. My fiancée is living in England at present, but we plan to marry early next year.' He spread his hands. 'You'll appreciate, Mr Campbell, I could do without this – complication.'

'*You* could do without it?' Ishbel was on her feet, shaking with fury. 'You enjoy a holiday in England, you have your fun with Jane, you leave her without a second thought for a more suitable fiancée – and then you have the nerve to call your son a complication?'

He stared at her, startled.

'I didn't mean–'

'I know exactly what you meant, Mr Clements!'

Silence followed her outburst. Ishbel stood by the window, with her back to the two men, as she tried to regain her composure.

Maybe she should have let Gordon deal with this after all. Already worried sick about Robbie, she wasn't at her best. Losing her temper would get them nowhere.

When she turned round, Edward Clements was looking a little sheepish, and Gordon was looking at her as if he'd never seen her before.

She looked at Edward Clements.

'Will you at least see Jane and your – her son?'

'Yes.' He didn't hesitate – Ishbel supposed they should be grateful for that.

'But I can't promise nothing more, Miss Montrose. None of us know for sure that this child is mine...'

Once she'd talked things over with Gordon that evening, Ishbel felt slightly better – but only slightly.

'Have you spoken to Jane?' Gordon asked.

'Yes, but I think the only thing that registered was that he'll be calling here on the second of the month – and that's another two weeks away.'

'I wish it could have been sooner, too,' Gordon agreed. 'I'm sure he's very busy catching up with his workload, but I suspect what he really wants is time to think.'

'I expect so. But Jane – well, I think she's choosing to forget he's engaged. And she can't afford to do that. So much will hang on this meeting...'

She knelt on the floor beside Gordon's armchair.

Usually, this was her favourite time. Most evenings, they sat in this room, discussing their respective days, the successes and the failures.

This evening, however, Ishbel was too wrapped up in what she could only see as her failure.

'I'm sorry I lost my temper with him, Gordon. It was the way he described Jane that irked me – the huge blue eyes part.'

'Don't apologise – he deserved it. Although I must admit,' Gordon added with a gentle smile, 'it took me by surprise. I don't think I've ever seen you so angry in my life!'

'I was furious,' she admitted. 'But I suppose he's right – he doesn't really *know* that Teddy's his child.'

'He should have thought of that at the time,' Gordon said at once. 'He should have had the good sense to think of the consequences.'

Knowing he was right didn't help.

'It's too late for recriminations now,' she pointed out.

'I know.' He shook his head. 'It's a sorry state of affairs.'

Ishbel's heart ached for Jane, who so longed for Teddy to know his father.

'And there's another thing. How on earth will his fiancée feel when she hears about it?' she asked.

There was silence. It didn't bear thinking about.

'She may *not* hear about it,' Gordon pointed out. 'Would there be any point in his telling her?'

'What? You mean–?' Ishbel stared at him. In Edward Clements' shoes, she would *have* to tell the poor girl.

'But – surely he couldn't enter into marriage with such a thing lying between them? I know I couldn't!'

'Of course *you* couldn't.' Gordon placed a gentle hand on her shoulder. 'But you're not Edward Clements.'

Instinctively, Ishbel grasped the hand on her shoulder and lifted her face to his.

'Could you, Gordon?' she insisted. 'Could you marry someone with that secret lying between you?'

'Of course not,' he answered immediately. 'When I marry, there will be no secrets, no shame.' He leaned forward in his chair and cupped her face in his hands.

'And you'll be the same, Ishbel.'

'Yes.' Her gaze was fixed on his lips as they

came closer to hers. 'Oh, Gordon–'

The kiss was brief, but intense.

'You know how I feel about you, don't you, Ishbel?'

It was more statement than question. Still tingling from the feel of his lips on hers, Ishbel nodded.

'Do you – can you feel the same?'

'Yes, oh, yes. Gordon I've loved you for – oh, for ever, it seems.'

Ishbel wasn't quite sure how it happened. One minute, she was kneeling on the floor by the chair in which Gordon was sitting – the next, they were standing with their arms wrapped tightly around each other.

This time, Gordon's kiss went on and on – filled with passion, with love, and with desire…

Robbie Montrose lay on his back in the narrow bed, staring at the ceiling. It was too dark to see the crack that ran from the corner of the room to the centre, but he knew it was there.

There was a crack in his own ceiling at the manse, but much smaller. They were the same jagged shape, though.

In the bed beside him, Victor was snoring loudly. That was something he wouldn't miss, he thought with a smile. It was about the only thing, though…

As things had turned out, bumping into

Victor when he arrived in Newcastle-upon-Tyne had been the best thing that could have happened to Robbie. Thanks to Victor, and the generosity of his parents, he'd been given a welcome, a warm bed and hot food.

Victor's father, a big, loud man whose bark, thankfully, was a lot worse than his bite, had got Robbie his job in the yard, helping to build the huge ship that, one day perhaps, would visit Shanghai.

Robbie wouldn't see the ship finished, but at least he knew he'd done his bit. The hours were long, and the work hard enough to bring tears to his eyes on occasions, but he could pay Mam for his keep and put some aside...

Yes, he'd miss Victor and his parents.

He'd miss Victor's sister, too. Betty was four months older than Robbie, a fact she reminded him of most days. She was out-spoken to the point of rudeness, but she was pretty and she made him laugh.

Yes, he would miss her.

This time tomorrow, he would be on board the *Northern Light,* working his way to Southampton, and, once there, he was bound to get to Shanghai...

By the time he woke, Victor was dressed and ready for a day's work at the yard. For a brief moment, Robbie envied him. Victor's life seemed so simple compared to his own.

'You'll miss breakfast if you don't get a

move on,' Victor said, as he jumped out of bed and pulled on his shirt, trying to ignore the atmosphere.

He knew the reason for it, but he didn't know what to do about it.

'I'll walk to the yard with you, shall I, Vic?' Robbie ventured.

'If you like.'

In the kitchen, Victor's mother was already cooking breakfast and Betty was setting the table.

It was a strange meal, despite Mam's efforts to talk as if all was normal. In such a short time, Robbie had become almost a member of the family, and it was strange to know that he'd never see these people again. Strange, and very sad.

He was relieved when it was over, and he and Victor were walking to the yard.

'Betty was a bit funny with me,' Robbie remarked. 'Did you notice? She wouldn't speak to me at all. Do you think I've done something wrong?'

'Betty's sweet on you!' Victor grinned. 'I reckon she wants you to kiss her.'

'Kiss her?' Robbie stopped in his tracks, horrified.

'You know what girls are like,' Victor said with a shrug.

Robbie didn't, not really. He knew what his sisters were like, and he couldn't imagine either of them wanting anyone to kiss them.

But sisters were different. Betty was different...

They were almost at the yard.

'I'll write, shall I?' Robbie suggested uncertainly.

'Why not? Yes, that would be good.'

Robbie was pleased.

'You'd better not come any further,' Victor said with a grin, 'or you'll find yourself back at work.'

'Right.' He laughed, but it was a very shaky laugh. 'Well, then, Vic–'

'Yes – be seeing you, Rob.'

'Yes.'

Both boys moved at once. They hugged, and patted each other on the back.

'Write soon,' Victor said gruffly, and he was gone, soon lost in the crowd of men and boys ready to start the day's work.

As he walked slowly back to the house for the last time, Robbie's thoughts returned to what Victor had said about Betty. Could she really want him to kiss her?

Initially, the thought had appalled him. Now, though, it didn't sound quite so bad.

He'd never kissed a girl before, and he wasn't entirely sure how to go about it, but he reckoned that if he did have to, he'd quite like it to be Betty.

He'd kissed Aunt Matilda, after all, many times, and it couldn't be any worse than that...

At first, he thought the house was empty, but although Victor's mother was nowhere in sight, Betty was in the hall.

She strode past him without saying a word as he walked up the stairs to his room. Robbie couldn't understand it.

In his room, he forgot Betty and began the difficult task of writing to his parents. It was made all the worse because of the guilt he felt ... he knew he should have written sooner. He'd just felt too ashamed.

He picked up his pen.

He wanted to let them know he was safe but, other than that, there was little he could say.

He would have liked to tell them about Victor and his family, and how he'd worked in the shipyard, but if they knew about that, they'd soon have him home.

Much as he missed them, he refused to give up. It might take a while, but he was determined to get to Shanghai and find Ishbel...

With the letter finally written, he went downstairs. It was almost time to leave.

Betty was sweeping the kitchen floor. She was a hard worker, which was just as well, because next week she was going into service.

'Would you like me to write to you, Betty?' His face was tinged with red.

'You can write,' she replied airily, 'but that doesn't mean I'll read your letters.'

'True. Tell you what then, I'll write, and you can decide later if you want to read them or not.'

'As you like.' She shrugged.

Robbie took a deep breath, crossed his fingers, uncrossed them, and walked over to her.

Nothing went quite as he'd planned. He'd meant to kiss her on the lips, but she was so startled that she jumped, and he ended up kissing the tip of her nose.

It was a kiss, though, and he hoped she'd be pleased.

'Ouch!' Unlike his kiss, the flat of her hand had connected with the side of his face with perfect accuracy.

'That hurt, Betty!'

'Good! I hate you, Robert Montrose!'

As she fled from the room, Robbie rubbed his sore cheek. That was the first and last time he'd kiss a girl!'

Donald Montrose sat at the desk in his study, staring at the letter in his hand with a mixture of anger and despair.

He wondered briefly how long it had taken to write. The ink was a little smudged in places, but the handwriting was neat and precise.

My dearest father and mother,

This is just to let you know that I am safe and well. I'm sorry to have caused you distress, but I could see no other choice. I hope you can find it in your hearts to understand and forgive me.

I'm hoping to reach Shanghai soon and I shall write more then. Meanwhile, please don't worry about me.

My thoughts and my love are with you, and with Gran and Mary.

Your ever loving son,

Robert.

His Sunday name. No matter that the women in his family always called him Robbie. But Donald wasn't feeling affectionate towards the young writer of this letter.

He had read it several times, looking for some clue as to his son's whereabouts, but there was nothing. The postmark was so badly smudged that it could have been posted anywhere.

What would his wife say when she read it? She'd be relieved that Robert was safe.

Donald knew Veronica well, though, and the relief would last only as long as it took her to realise anything might have happened since the letter had been posted!

How he wished Ishbel was still at home. Until now, he hadn't realised just how much the family relied on her steadying influence.

Ishbel, with her calm serenity, might have been able to talk to her mother – something Donald seemed incapable of. Whenever he tried, nothing seemed to register, and they usually ended up having sharp words.

137

Mary, too, would benefit from Ishbel's influence. She became more headstrong every day. Donald still couldn't understand what had possessed her to run to Jack Keller with their problems.

Donald didn't know the man personally, but there were more than enough rumours flying around Edinburgh about how he and his father had obtained their wealth.

As a rule, Donald paid no heed to rumours, but he suspected that in this case there was no smoke without fire.

Yes, they needed Ishbel at the moment, and she was so far away ... albeit on the Lord's work.

Of course, if Ishbel were here, Robert would never have dreamed up such a ridiculous scheme...

The sound of the front door interrupted his thoughts. Veronica was back.

For the first time in twenty-four years of marriage, Donald didn't want to face his wife.

Their discussions always seemed to end with Veronica in floods of tears, and Donald quite incapable of consoling her. It saddened him more than she would know.

However, face her he must. He got slowly to his feet.

In the kitchen, his mother-in-law greeted him.

'We just missed the downpour, Donald.'

He was pleased to see Moira. Her frankness could be just what they needed. Like Ishbel, Moira had a steadying influence.

He was aware of the rain lashing the window as Vernoica gave him a brief peck on the cheek.

'I'll get lunch on, Don,' she said. 'Sorry it's late, but–'

'It doesn't matter, my dear. We've had a letter,' Donald announced abruptly. 'From Robert.'

'A letter? Oh, my!' Veronica's hand flew to her mouth for a brief instant. 'Is Robbie safe? What does he say?'

Donald handed it to her.

She must have read it half a dozen times. She said nothing – she didn't have to. The pain was in her eyes for all to see.

'May I?' Moira asked at last, and Veronica handed the brief letter to her mother without a word.

Moira read it through. As she handed it back, Donald saw understanding in her eyes.

'This calls for a celebration,' she said briskly. 'I'll put the kettle on.'

'Celebration?' Veronica echoed in amazement. 'But he's told us nothing!'

'Nonsense!' Moira scoffed. 'Robbie's told us he's safe, and he's told us not to worry. What more is there?'

'Plenty! Where is he? How is he living? Is he eating? Is he happy? When is he coming home?' Veronica's voice broke.

'It doesn't matter where he is, or how he's living,' Moira said in her practical way. 'He's clearly eating, and happy – if he wasn't, he'd have scurried home before now! And he can't tell us when he's coming home because he doesn't know. Now then, Donald, a cup of tea?'

Donald was staring at her in admiration.

'Yes, that would be grand, Moira. Thank you.'

Veronica, he saw, was still mulling over her mother's words, but she was at least sitting at the table now. He sat down beside her, his anger gone.

'It was good of Robbie to let us know he's safe and well,' he told Veronica, and she smiled at him through her tears.

'Yes,' she murmured.

Oh, Donald would still have a few words to say to their errant son when he got the chance, but … no, perhaps he wouldn't.

Robbie was the first thought that came to mind when Donald woke, and the last thought before he drifted off to sleep – if he was lucky enough to sleep…

Veronica put his feelings into words.

'I just wish he'd come home!'

Even if she hadn't been counting the minutes until her visit, Ishbel would have recognised the woman at her door as her fellow-missionary, Lizzie McKie. She had the young, laughing face Ishbel had pictured from her letters.

Because Lizzie had had to delay her visit to the mission, Ishbel had had to wait an extra two weeks.

'Ishbel?'

'Yes. Oh, I'm so thrilled to meet you at last, Lizzie!'

They hugged on the doorstep as if they had known each other for years, and Ishbel felt the tears flowing. This was almost as good as going home!

Lizzie was about Ishbel's height, and slim, with dark, neatly cut hair, and that lovely smiling face.

'Come in, Lizzie. How long can you stay? Gordon – I told you about him, didn't I? Well, he has an appointment, but he'll be back about five. Can you stay that long?'

'Yes.' Lizzie laughed. 'This is wonderful, Ishbel.'

It was. Wonderful to meet a friend, and wonderful to hear that lovely accent of home.

'I've so missed another Scottish voice, Lizzie! Gordon and I are sick of listening to each other... Oh, here's Jane.'

Jane made them tea, and the three of them chatted about Edinburgh, Scotland, England, the long voyage out, St Colm's College, where Ishbel and Lizzie trained, and a hundred other things. All the while they fussed over Teddy who, as always, enjoyed being the centre of attention.

'What an adorable little chap,' Lizzie said, once Jane had taken him out for his walk.

'Isn't he? Everyone loves him.'

Ishbel only hoped that Edward Clements would learn to love him, too, when he came to visit his son. She refused to think of Teddy as anything other than that.

Then they had a caller – Adam Butler.

He and Lizzie were old friends. He strode into the sitting-room and gave Lizzie a huge hug, which she happily returned.

'Adam, I thought you must be ill,' she teased. 'I've written two letters and neither have been answered!'

'Patience is a virtue, Lizzie. I've been busy educating your fellow countrywoman in the basics of tea making. Ishbel, I'm afraid, knew as much about the process as you did.'

'Ah, but what do you known about whisky making, Adam Butler?'

'As much as you, Lizzie McKie!'

Lizzie looked at Ishbel and laughed.

Adam kept them amused for almost half an hour.

'I assume you've had no news of your brother, Ishbel?' he said as he was leaving.

'None.' Ishbel was trying to put a brave face on it. There was little else she could do. 'The mail takes so long, though. Perhaps tomorrow…'

'I do hope so.'

When he'd gone, Ishbel explained about her brother's escapade, and Lizzie sympathised.

'He sounds a very determined lad. I wouldn't be at all surprised if he didn't end up in Shanghai, after all.'

Ishbel shuddered at the thought.

'I hope not. It's hardly the sort of city for Robbie.' But she didn't want to spoil Lizzie's visit with her own worries.

'Adam's lovely, isn't he?' she said, changing the subject.

'He is, but don't be taken in by that American charm. Everyone falls in love with him. From what I gather, it's a dangerous occupation.'

'I wouldn't do that!' Ishbel laughed at the idea. 'Adam's great fun, and I enjoy his company immensely, but—'

At that point, the man she was thinking of walked into the room.

Ishbel felt self conscious as she introduced Gordon to Lizzie. She knew Lizzie would realise immediately why there was no danger of her falling in love with Adam Butler. Ishbel wore her love for all the world to see.

Gordon was everything she had ever dreamed of, everything any girl could dream of. She swelled with pride as she listened to him discussing their work with Lizzie...

Stupidly, she found herself in tears as she

said goodbye to Lizzie.

'None of that,' Lizzie said gently. 'There'll be other visits, and we'll write – oh, we'll write!'

That thought was an enormous comfort. Ishbel had been more homesick than she would have believed, and a friend who had walked the much-missed streets of Edinburgh lessened the ache...

Lizzie had been gone less than five minutes when Liang arrived. It was the first time she had visited the mission, and at first, Ishbel was thrilled to see her.

The young servant girl, her almost constant chaperone, was with her and Ishbel ushered them both inside. Liang was looking as close to upset as Ishbel had ever seen her.

'Something's wrong,' Ishbel said. 'Come into the sitting-room and talk, Liang. Tell me what's happened.'

Liang said something in Chinese. To Ishbel's surprise and dismay, the servant sat on the upright chair in the hall and prepared to wait.

Ishbel could tell that Liang wanted to talk in private, but her conscience wouldn't allow the poor girl to sit in the hall like that.

Jane had returned from her walk, so Ishbel dashed upstairs to ask if she would mind making the girl tea and keeping her company.

'I think Liang needs to talk to me.'

'It will give me the chance to practice my

Chinese!' Jane followed her downstairs at once.

Liang said how nice the sitting-room was, how sorry she was to call without an appointment, and how well Ishbel was looking.

'But what's happened, Liang?' Ishbel asked impatiently. 'You look dreadful. You look as if you've been crying.'

'So do you, Ishbel,' Liang countered softly. 'Have you had news of Robbie?'

'Nothing.' Ishbel bit her lip. 'My only consolation is that the mail takes such a long time to get here. I try to convince myself that he's home – safe and well – and that I'll hear tomorrow.'

Yet, only yesterday, she'd spent too long gazing at a ship bound for home. Part of her had longed to board it. Instead, she'd watched it leave Shanghai, then sat and wept at the quayside...

'I'm so sorry, Ishbel,' said Liang's gentle voice. 'I feel awful now, coming here to burden you with my own problems.'

'Please don't, Liang. That's what friends are for. Besides, I'm grateful for anything that stops me worrying about Rob – even for a second.'

Liang nodded.

'I don't know what to do, Ishbel,' she confessed shakily. 'My father spoke with me yesterday. He told me about his friend's cousin, a man I'd never heard mentioned, but apparently Mr Butler knows him.'

'But what exactly is the problem, Liang?'

'This man, Mr Han Hsien, comes from Shanghai, but he's been living and working in America for five years. He's older than – than us. He's thirty. Anyway, he will be returning to Shanghai at the end of this year, to work at Sun Chen and Company.'

Realisation was beginning to dawn. Liang was worried that this man, this Mr Han Hsien, would steal the place she longed to hold at her father's side.

But surely Liang had accepted that her father wouldn't allow her to work for the company?

'So he'll be doing the work you wanted to do?' Ishbel asked Liang.

'Oh, no. Well, yes, he will, but it's not that.'

'Then what is it?'

As always, the traditional coat Liang wore was beautifully embroidered. She absently fingered the mandarin ducks on her sleeve, and a tear dropped on to her exquisite work.

'My father has decided that I am to marry Mr Han Hsien,' she said.

Chapter Seven

Ishbel needed a full minute to take in what Liang had said.

She knew all about arranged marriages, of course. It was the custom in China. She and Liang had even discussed the probability of a marriage being arranged for Liang, but the cold reality came as a shock.

'Do you like him?' she asked.

But she could see from her friend's red-rimmed, fear-filled eyes that the whole idea was abhorrent to her.

'I don't *know* him,' Liang replied shakily. 'I've been told that the two of us met when I was seven, but I have no recollection. I know he's an astute businessman, I know he's thirty-six, and I know he wishes to marry me – for business reasons, I suspect.'

'Oh, Liang!' No wonder the poor girl was so distraught. 'And he's fifteen years older? That's quite an age gap.'

'The same as that between my grandmother and my grandfather.' Liang nodded.

'Another arranged marriage? Was it a happy one?'

'Not on my grandmother's side, at least. To my grandfather, it was satisfactory, a marriage of convenience. These marriages always are. He was happy enough with it. He had a suitable marriage, and his wife gave him a son – my father.'

In the cosy, slightly shabby sitting-room at the mission, this kind of talk seemed out of place.

There were many aspects of the Chinese way of life that Ishbel struggled with – which was why she and Gordon were here, why Lizzie McKie was here. And they *would* make a difference.

Liang was still absently fingering the embroidered mandarin ducks on her sleeve.

'Grandmother fell in love with a local boy,' she remarked. 'When she was forced to marry my grandfather, she had two choices – die of a broken heart, like the mandarins, or stand and be strong. Fortunately, she chose to be strong. She never forgot her young love, though, through all the long years of her marriage, and she always embroidered mandarin ducks on her tiny shoes.'

Ishbel's heart ached for the unknown woman who had spent a lifetime embroidering symbols of fidelity – and had herself kept faith with her husband.

She wondered how her own grandmother, back in Edinburgh, would have coped with an arranged marriage. It was impossible to say.

'Do you know the legend of the Crystal

River?' Liang asked, and Ishbel shook her head.

'Many centuries ago, the Emperor tried to make peace with the Huns by offering their king a bride.

'The Emperor chose the ugliest woman he could find from the portraits of three thousand. However, when it was time for her to leave, he discovered that the girl wasn't ugly at all. She was very beautiful; she just hadn't bribed the artist, as all the others had.

'The Emperor was so angry that he had the artist executed. It didn't help the lady, though. She was so upset at having to live with barbarians that she wept by the river.

'It's said that the wind carried off her hairpin and dropped it in the river, so that a part of her would remain in China. The water turned crystal clear where her hairpin landed, which is why it's called the Crystal River.'

Ishbel found this story so moving. The Crystal River had been nothing more to her than a Yangtse tributary, but from now on she would always remember the story of the beautiful lady losing her hairpin.

'Perhaps she was happy with the Huns,' she murmured.

Liang shook her head sadly.

'She found the thought unbearable. She killed herself.'

An icy shiver ran down Ishbel's spine,

caused less by the legend than by Liang's matter-of-fact voice.

'What do you intend to do, Liang?' Ishbel asked, dragging her mind back from the Crystal River. 'About your father's plans, I mean?'

'What can I do?' Liang, usually so composed, threw up her hands in despair.

'My mother and I will try to talk to my father, but his mind is made up. He sees it as the best thing for me.'

'But surely – he married your mother because he loved her, and she's English! I know his family was against the marriage, and I can imagine what they both went through, but surely, he wouldn't have wanted it any other way? He wouldn't have wanted to marry a stranger. And let's face it, that's what you will be doing. That's what Mr Han Hsien will be doing, too.'

'It's the way, Ishbel.' Liang's voice was cold.

'Then it's high time the way was changed,' Ishbel said firmly. 'Good grief, this is 1921!'

Liang smiled fondly at her, but they both knew that Ishbel's frustration wouldn't – couldn't – change 'the way' just like that.

'May I discuss this with Gordon?' Ishbel asked. 'He may be able to talk to your father.'

'Of course, but–'

'I know – it's "the way".' Ishbel's smile took any sting from her words.

'You're very lucky, Ishbel – you can choose your husband. You can even choose whether to take a husband or not!' Liang smiled knowingly. 'And I expect you'll choose Mr Campbell.'

'If he asks me,' Ishbel said with a laugh.

But she hoped that one day, one day soon, Gordon *would* ask. And she knew what her answer would be. The thought of it brought a warm glow to her heart.

'He is a good man,' Liang said. 'A handsome one, too.'

Ishbel was surprised Liang had noticed. It was also 'the way' for Chinese girls not to look directly at a foreigner…

'Yes, he is. And I'm sure he'll think of something,' she said briskly. 'Don't despair, Liang. It's only March, and this man isn't coming to Shanghai until the end of the year. At least time is on our side.'

'Ishbel, please. I came today because you're my friend and I had to tell you, nothing more.

'There is nothing you can do. Nothing I would ask of you. But I do feel so much better for having talked to you.'

'But all isn't lost, Liang,' Ishbel said urgently. 'Please don't think that it is.'

Liang simply nodded.

Ishbel wished she had something more constructive to offer her friend. She couldn't bear the thought of seeing Liang waste her days in a loveless marriage, a marriage 'for business purposes'.

This could not be allowed to happen!

Saturday, April 2, 1921. Ishbel wrote the date in her diary, and stopped.

She'd been a bundle of nerves thinking about Edward Clements' visit, but now that the day had finally arrived, she felt strangely calm.

Whatever happened today, God would be with them, and He would ensure that everything worked out for the best.

They might not like the outcome, but none of them knew what was best.

Jane thought she did, of course, but to marry a man who was to all intents and purposes a stranger was not necessarily for the best. In Ishbel's eyes, it was almost as bad as Liang's predicament.

Not that Edward Clements was considering marriage. Ishbel had formed her opinion of the man, and she couldn't imagine him offering to marry Jane.

Ishbel closed her diary again. She would make her entry this evening, when Mr Clements had been and gone...

That afternoon, Jane was wearing her best dress and looked prettier than Ishbel had ever seen her.

Her fair hair positively shone, her eyes were bright with excitement and she looked

152

a picture of health and vitality.

Teddy, dressed in his Sunday best, looked adorable. It would take a very hard man to deny him.

'I only hope I can keep Teddy looking clean until he arrives,' Jane said.

'He should be here in another half hour,' Ishbel soothed. 'Try not to worry too much, Jane. Whether Teddy looks spotless or not won't matter to him.'

'It will to me, though!'

Jane was justifiably proud of the way she was bringing up her son, and she always liked him to look presentable. Teddy was a lively, active boy, so it was no easy task.

When Edward Clements arrived, Jane's face drained completely of colour, reminding Ishbel of their seasickness on the long journey to Shanghai.

'Don't worry,' Ishbel repeated. 'I'll go and bring him in here – I've made sure we won't be disturbed.'

Once again, Ishbel was surprised by Edward Clements' self-assurance. He, too, was looking immaculate. If ever they were to pose for a family portrait, she thought grimly, now was the time to do it...

'Good afternoon, Mr Clements,' she greeted him, her voice cool. 'Thank you for coming.'

'My pleasure, Miss Montrose.'

Despite the self-assurance, he looked as if

he wished himself a million miles away.

'Miss Terry and her son are in the sitting-room. Please follow me.'

'Thank you.'

He was so stiff and formal that Ishbel couldn't imagine how Jane would react. But then, Ishbel realised she was being equally stiff and formal. The walk from the hall to the sitting-room had never seemed longer...

She pushed open the door of the sitting-room.

Jane was standing, rooted to the spot, and her complexion was still that sickly shade.

Teddy was leaning against his mother. Usually, he was happy enough to meet strangers, but it seemed her nerves had rubbed off on him.

'Miss Terry.' Edward Clements walked forward and shook her hand. 'It's a pleasure to see you again.'

Met with such formality, poor Jane could only nod.

'Let's sit down, shall we?' Ishbel suggested.

With Teddy still clinging to her, Jane struggled to move, but eventually they were sitting down. Ishbel sat next to Jane; Edward Clements sat as far away from them as possible.

'I'm sorry I couldn't visit you sooner.' He spoke directly to Jane. 'I've been in England–'

'Visiting your fianceé?' she said calmly.

'On business.' Her frank question took him by surprise. 'But yes, while I was there, I visited Claire.' He cleared his throat.

'Once I returned to Shanghai, I had a heavy workload to catch up with.'

'Of course.'

Silence stretched between them. Ishbel was grateful when Edward Clements finally broke it.

'He's a fine boy.'

To Ishbel's surprise, he managed a smile as Teddy finally released his grip on his mother and eyed Edward with interest.

'Yes, he is.'

That awful silence again.

'Are you feeling unwell, Mr Clements?'

Jane's voice showed genuine concern. Ishbel had to admit he did look ill.

'A little shaky. And I think, in view of the circumstances, we can dispense with the Mr Clements, don't you, Jane?'

'I'm sorry about this,' Jane blurted out. 'Not about Teddy,' she added quickly, 'but about the rest. I realise you're engaged to be married, and I realise you can't have proof that Teddy is your son – but he is, you know. You have my word on that.'

'I know he is.'

Ishbel looked up in surprise.

'Actually, I'm not feeling too well.' He rose to his feet. 'I need to walk in the fresh air. I wonder if I might call again – say, on Tuesday evening? About seven? We'll talk then, Jane. When the shock has worn off. Would you mind?'

'Er – yes. I mean, no.' Jane got to her feet. 'Tuesday evening will be fine. Are you sure you'll be all right?'

'Can I get you something, Mr Clements?' Ishbel asked. 'A glass of water? Tea?'

'Nothing, but thank you for your kindness.' He gave them a smile. Just for a moment, Ishbel thought he was going to reach down to Teddy, but abruptly he moved away.

'Until Tuesday, then,' he said.

The fresh air was welcome, even the cloying air of Shanghai. Edward Clements breathed deeply as he walked away from the mission.

He'd have to apologise on Tuesday for his abrupt departure, but looking at that small boy, he'd thought he was going to faint...

He'd had all of this worked out. He'd planned to visit Jane Terry, tell her there was no reason why he should accept responsibility for her child.

Then he'd planned to walk out of her life again – for ever. At worst, he'd provide for the child financially – not because he felt obliged to, but as a token of their brief relationship...

As he talked, he could see Claire, sitting at her piano, his engagement ring sparkling on her hand. He could see her eyes shining with happiness as he'd put that ring on her finger...

That room at the mission had seemed totally devoid of air. It seemed a lifetime ago that he and Jane had laughed together, taken that crazy, fun-filled river trip together...

It was shock, he knew that. He'd felt the same sense of shock when Ishbel Montrose had broken the news to him, but that had been short-lived.

Then, he'd been able to dismiss any likelihood of his having a son. He couldn't do that now.

The child was his; there could be no doubt. As soon as he'd seen the boy, he'd known.

Teddy looked nothing like him, but Edward favoured his father's side of the family. It was his younger brother, David, who took after their mother's side.

And when he looked at young Teddy, he was looking into David's face.

'Oh, Dave!' he muttered aloud. 'Dear Dave...'

Edward had longed for a brother and, as soon as David was born, he rarely left his side. They played together, talked together, laughed together, planned together...

Inevitably, they'd gone their separate ways, with Edward coming to Shanghai, but they remained close until the bond had been broken four years ago.

David had been killed at Passchendaele.

He'd been just eighteen.

As Edward had been leaving, overcome by the concern shown to him by Jane, he'd longed to reach down and ruffle Teddy's hair.

He wished now that he had at least touched his son.

His son!

That was Jack Keller standing at the staff door of the printing works! Mary could have sworn her heart had stopped beating.

Was he waiting for her?

The last time she'd seen him had been almost a month ago, in church, listening to her father's sermon. She'd glanced sideways and spotted him in the congregation – the very last person she'd expected to see there!

'Good morning, Miss Montrose.' He greeted her easily.

'Mr Keller,' she acknowledged breathlessly. There were two minutes before she was due to start work.

'I don't want to raise your hopes, but I'm fairly sure that I've found your brother.'

Mary had to lean against the door jamb for support.

'You've found Robbie?' She hardly dared to believe it. 'Where is he? Is he safe and well?'

'I'm fairly sure he's in Southampton.'

'Southampton! But how? I mean, those letters we've had – two of the postmarks were definitely Birmingham.'

'I know, but I think he must have asked someone to post them for him. Perhaps he knows someone who travels between the two places.' He was having to squint against the bright June sunlight.

'When you told me that your grandmother's friend had found out he'd been working in the shipyard in Newcastle – well, I sent someone to ask around. He found a young boy, around your brother's age, called Victor, who clammed up as soon as Robbie's name was mentioned. My friend found this lad's father, and it turned out that your brother had lodged with the family while in Newcastle. Apparently, Robbie then worked his passage on a boat to Southampton.'

Mary was shaking. She couldn't quite believe it. Despite the three letters Robbie had written, she had despaired of ever seeing her brother again.

'This friend of mine–'

'Who exactly is he?' Mary asked, curious.

'Oh, you don't need to know that.'

Mary suspected she was better off not knowing. She could imagine that Jack Keller had friends on both sides of the law, and probably more on the wrong side than on the right...

'He's due back in Leith on Monday. Hopefully, he'll bring with him all the information we need.'

'Oh, I hope so!' Mary's eyes were shining

now as it all began to sink in.

'So do I,' Jack said quietly. 'When I saw your mother in church that day, I was shocked. I think you can afford to raise her hopes now. I would have saved this news until Monday, but–' He shifted his weight from one foot to the other. 'I was wondering if you remembered your part of our bargain, Miss Montrose?'

Mary's face reddened. She hadn't forgotten. In return for news of Robbie, she'd promised to spend an evening in Jack Keller's company.

'I haven't forgotten, Mr Keller.'

'The thing is, I have to attend a dinner and dance this evening, and I would very much like you to accompany me.'

'This evening?' She stared at him. 'But I can't – I mean, it's very short notice.'

'It is, and I apologise for that.' But he was still waiting.

'Well, I suppose – yes,' she said, with the recklessness born of knowing she was now well and truly late for work. 'Yes, I'll go with you.'

'Marvellous! Thank you.' His smile was devastating. 'Shall I call for you at–?'

'No.' Mary cut him off. 'I'll meet you at your house. What time?'

'Seven?'

'Fine. I must dash. I'm late for work, Mr Keller.'

'Of course. Good morning, Miss Montrose.'

Mary watched him stride away, and then dashed inside the building.

What on earth had she agreed to? And how was she going to manage it?

But what did it matter? Robbie was safe! That was the important thing. She was dying to tell her parents, but how could she keep Jack Keller out of it? If she even hinted that she was going dancing with that man, her father would forbid it, she well knew.

Her thoughts chased themselves in circles all afternoon, but then she had an idea. After work, she dashed to Ruth McKinlay's house.

Ruth had changed so much since the day, a year ago now, that Mary had found her on the manse doorstep, clinging to her hungry, frightened children.

She was still renting her home from Jack Keller, but the rent was no longer a problem. Ruth's skill with a needle had become common knowledge in Edinburgh, and work was pouring in from all sides. She had two girls helping her now.

'Where are the bairns?' Mary asked.

'Playing with next door's lot. And what brings you here looking as if the devil himself is after you?'

It was no laughing matter, but Mary had to smile.

'I think he probably is!'

She quickly explained.

'Mary!' Ruth hugged her tight. 'Oh, I'm so pleased, and so relieved. I do hope Mr Keller's right – your mother can't take much more of this.'

'I know. And those letters Robbie writes – if he'd just tell us where he is!'

'What did your parents say?' Ruth asked.

'That's just it, I haven't told them yet.'

'Why on earth not? Ah – because of Jack Keller?'

'Yes.' Mary took a deep breath, and told Ruth the rest.

'A dinner followed by dancing?' Ruth said in amazement. 'But your father will never allow it.'

'I know he won't. Which is why I need your help, Ruth.'

'What can I do?'

Mary knew then that Ruth would do all she could without judging her actions. Somehow, that made it easier.

'I want to tell my parents I'm spending the night with you,' Mary explained. 'And I shall, actually, if that's all right?'

'You know it is. There's always a bed for you here, Mary.'

'Thank you. I really appreciate it.'

'So you're actually going out with him?'

'Well, I promised I would if he'd help us find Robbie. Anyway, I thought I could tell my parents I was helping you with some work, or something. You said yourself that you're rushed off your feet.'

'Aye.' Ruth laughed. 'But I can do without your help, Mary! No offence, but I'd soon lose customers if I let you loose with a needle. So you're not going to mention Mr Keller to the minister?'

'Not until tomorrow,' Mary said firmly. 'I'll say Mr Keller called here, on his way to the manse to tell us all about Robbie. I'll tell them how lucky and coincidental it was that I was here.'

'Right,' Ruth's voice was flat.

'Yes, I know, and I feel awful about it, too,' Mary rushed on, 'but I don't see what other choice I have. I'll tell them that he'll call at the manse when this friend of his gets into Leith on Monday. That way, they'll be more prepared for him. And hopefully, they'll be concentrating on Robbie, not me.'

'Mm.' Ruth looked doubtful. 'And meanwhile, you're going to enjoy an evening in Mr Keller's company?'

'Enjoy? Not at all!'

'I would.' Ruth laughed at Mary's shocked expression. 'He's got looks, charm, money–'

'Ruth! He's the biggest rogue walking the streets of Edinburgh.'

'That's as maybe. But still...'

'I'm going out with him simply because I agreed – from what I gather, it must have cost him money to send this friend of his to Newcastle. There's no more to it than that.'

But as she spoke, Mary knew there was a *lot* more to it than that.

'What do you plan to wear?' Ruth was ever practical.

'I haven't the faintest notion. I thought perhaps my blue dress, the pale blue one. It's not exactly–'

'It's not,' Ruth cut her off. 'Mary, I'm sure we're talking really posh here. Tell you what, your green dress is still here, the one you left with me to have the hem altered. Why don't I have a look at that? I can have it ready for you – you'll need to call here on your way, if you plan to spend the night here.'

'Would you? Ruth, you're an angel...'

By the time Mary arrived at Jack Keller's house that evening, she was breathless, exhausted and almost overcome with guilt.

It wasn't so much the lies she'd told her parents, it was more the way they had tripped so effortlessly from her tongue.

'You look stunning, Mary!' Jack greeted her warmly.

'Thank you.' She felt overdressed, but she accepted the compliment. He was the one who looked stunning. Ruth was right; few girls would refuse an evening in his company.

By dinner followed by dancing, Mary soon discovered that Jack Keller meant spending the evening with the best-known faces in

Edinburgh. And at the North British Hotel, no less!

Everyone who was anyone was there. Far from feeling overdressed, Mary felt dowdy and plain.

Dinner was a banquet. How could these posh folk sit down to such mountains of food when people were starving on the streets of their own city? Mary could barely swallow.

It wasn't only that her principles wouldn't allow it, it was the sure knowledge that her parents would inevitably find out she'd been here.

'Are you all right, Miss Montrose?' Jack enquired.

'Not really.' She nodded towards the assembled guests. 'I didn't realise it would be quite so–' Words failed her.

'Stuffy?' Jack spared her the embarrassment of having to answer.

'If you're not enjoying yourself, we can leave as soon as you like. I need to show my face, that's all. We've endured the dinner, so I'm sure we can sneak away now.'

Mary was incredibly grateful to him.

'It's not that I'm not enjoying myself,' she tried to explain. 'Although, to be honest, it sickens me to see so much food and drink going to waste on these people. It's just that–'

He waited, eyebrows raised.

'My parents don't know I'm here,' she confessed, feeling all of twelve years old. 'I told them I was spending the night with a friend – with Mrs McKinlay.'

'I see.'

'Well, I am spending the night at her home,' she put in quickly. 'It's just that I didn't mention–'

'My name?' he guessed, and she nodded.

'They wouldn't approve,' she explained apologetically.

'*You* don't approve,' he reminded her, but she ignored that.

'An event like this – with so many of Father's acquaintance here – he's sure to find out I've been here with you.'

'Let's get away,' was all he said.

'We'll go back to my house for a night-cap,' he said as he drove away from the hotel. 'Then I'll take you back to Mrs McKinlay's.'

'Thank you.'

Mary wasn't sure what else to say. She felt guilty about not fulfilling her part of the bargain, and she was extremely grateful to have escaped all those people.

At his house, he poured Mary some brandy.

'That will make you feel better,' he said.

'Thank you. Where's your housekeeper?'

'She doesn't live in, but I'm sure she'll have left something to eat. I'll go and see. You must be hungry; you hardly ate a thing.'

Mary was starving.

When he returned, he was carrying a plate.

166

'Mabel's let me down,' he confessed. 'She must have thought I'd have eaten well this evening. However, I've made us ham sandwiches.'

He set a small table between their chairs, and put the plate on that.

'Help yourself,' he said.

Mary soon began to relax. Tucking into ham sandwiches personally made by Jack, drinking brandy which had made her cough at first, but was now warming her nicely, it was difficult not to.

She still felt guilty, though.

'I'm sorry about this evening,' she murmured.

'There's nothing to be sorry about,' he assured her immediately. 'I was promised dinner and dancing with you. I had dinner in your company, and soon I shall have dancing. We can dance jut as well here.'

'Dancing? Here?' Mary struggled to get the words out. 'But there's no music!'

'I have music,' he said softly. 'Although I'm sure we don't need it. You do dance, don't you?'

'Well, yes.' But not with the likes of Jack Keller in his own home!

'Excellent!'

Before Mary knew what was happening, he was on his feet, reaching for her hand. She didn't seem to have any choice.

Dancing with Jack was like nothing Mary

had ever experienced. He held her close as they moved slowly. There was no music, no sound except for the pounding of her heart.

He didn't say a word. Or if he did, Mary couldn't hear it over the sound of her heartbeat.

For some reason that she couldn't understand, she had to rest her head against his shoulder...

'Mary – I'd like to see you again. May I?' His voice was soft.

'I can't, Jack.' She managed to pull back from him.

'Because your parents wouldn't approve?'

Mary was silent.

'Is that the only reason?' he persisted.

'Yes,' she admitted.

If the choice had been her own, she would have seen him tomorrow, the next day, whenever he could fit her in. The knowledge shocked her – frightened her, too...

'You can't live your life like that,' Jack told her. 'You make your own choices in this world. There are times when we have to go against our parents' wishes.'

If she wanted to see Jack again, and Mary did, very much, then Father would simply have to accept it. She refused to lie to him again, and she refused to be ashamed of her actions. But...

'Give me time,' she whispered. 'Wait until the fuss has died down. I'll tell my parents that you called at Ruth's house this evening, with news of Robbie. If you come to the manse on Monday, once your friend gets back to Leith – well, that will be enough for my father. He'll be relieved about Robbie, but he'll still be furious that I've involved you in all this. And if he finds out where I was this evening–' She couldn't begin to imagine how her father would react to that one!

'Will you give me time, Jack?'

'All the time in the world, Mary.'

His soft reply had her trembling in his arms…

She tried to imagine her father's wrath, to feel ashamed of where she was and what she was doing, but her mind refused to co-operate. It was too full of Jack.

The days ahead were going to be difficult, in more ways than one, but her parents would have to accept that she was seeing Jack. They would have to…

Chapter Eight

'I hope Mary will be all right,' Veronica Montrose said anxiously.

'Mary will be fine,' Donald said patiently, patting his wife's hand. 'Your mother's there if anything crops up.'

This was going to be an awfully long journey unless Veronica could relax a little. They'd only just pulled out of Waverley Station, and they weren't due to arrive at King's Cross until half-past six that evening. At this rate, she'd be fit for nothing.

'What time do we leave London?' she fretted.

'Seven-thirty from Waterloo.' He gave her a smile. 'This Underground sounds a bit complicated to me, so we'll cross London by taxi.'

She continued to clasp and unclasp her hands in her lap, and Donald fervently wished he was making this journey alone.

They had no idea what they would find when they reached Southampton, and he would rather deal with whatever came up on his own.

That had been out of the question, though. If Donald was taking leave from the kirk, and there was a chance of seeing Robbie and bringing him home, nothing would keep Veronica at the manse.

Absently fingering the slip of paper in his pocket, Donald felt his jaw tighten. On it was the address of the boarding-house in Southampton where Robbie was supposedly staying.

It was the man who had given him the address that set Donald's teeth on edge – Jack Keller.

'What use will my mother be,' Veronica asked, 'when it comes to Mary?'

'Sorry?' Donald hadn't a clue what she was talking about.

'Mary has a will of her own. There's something – different about her these days.' She turned worried eyes on him.

'I don't like the way she is with that Jack Keller, Don. There's something not right about it.'

Mary's father knew exactly what she meant. The mere thought of being indebted to a man like Jack Keller was abhorrent to him.

And just what was Mary's part in it all?

'We know she asked for his help,' he said carefully. 'I had some firm words with her about that, and she knows it was wrong to involve him.'

But had it been so very wrong? After all, if it hadn't been for Jack Keller, they wouldn't be sitting on this train in the hope of seeing their son.

'She was wrong and she knows it,' Donald said firmly. 'It's past now, Veronica.'

'But did we get through to her, Don? I'm sure she's seen him since we spoke to her, you see.'

That thought had crossed Donald's mind, too.

'Well, he's Ruth's landlord – I suppose it's only natural he should call on his tenants from time to time. It was pure coincidence that Mary happened to be there on Friday evening, and as she said, he was on his way to see us anyway...'

'I suppose you're right. I keep getting the feeling that Mary's a little too – oh, I don't know – at ease with him, somehow. There's nothing I can put my finger on...'

Before Donald could respond Veronica went on.

'He's not really her type, is he? Mary's far too level-headed and sensible to be impressed with the likes of Jack Keller.'

'Of course she is,' Donald agreed. 'She was worried about Robbie, that's all, and if she thought Jack Keller could use his position to help, she wouldn't hesitate to ask him.'

'Yes. That'll be it.'

Veronica was right, there was a strong familiarity between Jack Keller and their daughter. Or perhaps it was simply the way the youth of today behaved.

Mary was strong-willed, too much so at times, eager to grasp life with both hands and solve all the world's problems single-handed...

How different she was from her sister!

How was Ishbel faring? That was something else Donald couldn't discuss with Veronica.

As soon as she'd heard civil war had broken out over Sun Yat-sen's election as president, she'd been all for insisting that Ishbel came home immediately.

Ishbel's letters told them very little, but peraps there was little to tell. Shanghai, according to their daughter, was like a separate world from the rest of China. The civil war, so far, was having little effect on the city.

'Even the Chinese see Shanghai as a foreign country when they visit,' she'd told them.

Donald was more proud of his elder girl than he could say but, like her mother, there were times when he wished with all his heart that she could be working safely in Edinburgh...

'We ought to eat something,' Veronica suggested eventually. She delved in her bag for sandwiches, and Donald tried to look enthusiastic. They'd only just left Newcastle-upon-Tyne, so they still had a long journey ahead of them.

They needed something to do, even if it was only eating. With two poor appetites, however, it didn't take long and they both fell silent again.

Veronica's hand was resting in his. They'd left Grantham before she finally broke the silence.

'Do you think we'll see Robbie tonight?'

'No.' Donald was firm. 'It will be almost ten o'clock by the time we reach Southampton. We'll both be exhausted, and likely to say things that won't help. No. We'll get a good night's sleep and then visit his boarding-house first thing in the morning.'

'*You* might get a good night's sleep.'

Donald didn't comment, but at least she didn't argue with him this time.

He sat back, still holding his wife's hand, and closed his eyes to concentrate on the rhythmic sound of the train speeding along the track...

When she arrived at Ruth's house, Mary was already feeling guilty. She felt even worse when she saw her friend.

'Ruth! What in the world's happened?' she asked in amazement. Ruth's eyes were red and swollen.

'Oh, it's nothing. But what brings you here on a Wednesday? You've not lost your job?'

'Not yet,' Mary said. 'Never mind that now. Let me put the kettle on, and you can tell me what's happened. It's not one of the bairns, is it?'

'No, no. I told you, it's nothing.'

Mary wasn't convinced. Ruth, she knew, was a proud woman – it took a lot to make her admit to worries and fears.

'You're making me nervous, Ruth.' She thrust a cup of tea into her friend's hand. 'What's wrong?'

'Oh–' Ruth took a long breath, then sat down at the kitchen table, cradling her cup in her hands.

'It's two years today since my Angus was taken, and when I went to bed last night, it all caught up with me. Not a day passes when it doesn't hurt, but last night – I relived it all.'

'Oh, no. I am so very sorry, Ruth. I had no idea.'

Mary felt humble. What were her own problems, compared to Ruth's? Ruth rarely mentioned her late husband. When she did, it was only in passing and always with a smile on her face.

It was all too easy to forget the pain that she had been through. Typical of Ruth … the last person in the world to want sympathy.

'What was he like?' Mary asked quietly. 'You've never really spoken of Angus.'

'I talk about him to the children a lot, John especially. I want them to know what he was like, and how much he loved them. But with other people – no, I rarely mention him. It only embarrasses folk.'

'So what was he like?'

'Oh!' Ruth smiled then. 'I thought he was the best man who ever walked this earth.

'Good and kind. He was for ever teasing me and making me laugh. And handsome. Gosh, he was handsome!' The smile broadened.

'He never knew it, though, never believed it. He used to think himself so lucky to have found someone like me!'

She shook her head, bemused.

'He loved me and the bairns to distraction,' she added. 'He couldn't do enough for us. Wanted the perfect life for us.'

'He sounds lovely,' Mary said softly.

'He was. I was very lucky,' Ruth said firmly, taking a sip of her tea. 'But that doesn't tell me what you're doing here on a Wednesday. What are you up to, Mary Montrose?'

Thinking of Ruth's loss, a loss she had to live with every day of her life, Mary's problems didn't seem quite so important.

'I asked for a day's holiday,' she said. 'Mum and Dad caught the train for Southampton this morning, and I couldn't face spending all day at work wondering what was happening.'

Ruth nodded and then frowned.

'And why are you dressed up? You're not wearing your best skirt and blouse for my benefit.'

'I'm on my way to visit Jack,' Mary admitted.

'Ah!'

'Don't say it like that, Ruth,' Mary pleaded. 'I know my father would have a fit, but I thought that while they're away, I could spend a little time with him without anyone knowing.'

'So that's why you asked for a day's holiday?'

'Partly ... but I honestly wouldn't be able to concentrate with Mum and Father on their way. Will they bring Robbie home?

And if he doesn't come home, how will Mum cope? Oh, it's dreadful.'

'I know, lass,' Ruth sympathised.

'But yes, I want to see Jack,' Mary went on. 'I know it's wrong, but–'

'I'm not sure it is,' Ruth said vaguely. 'Even before we were wed, I'd have done all I could to spend five minutes with my Angus. And now that he's gone– Well, you have to take what you can get, Mary. Life's too short to worry about what other people think.' She pulled a face. 'But don't tell your father I said that!'

'I won't!' Mary chuckled. 'And thank you, Ruth. Thank you for understanding.'

They drank their tea in silence. Their cups had been empty for some minutes before Mary spoke again.

'I need to spend time with Jack, so that I can really get to know him. Half of me thinks he's the most wonderful man, and the other half believes him to be the biggest rogue in the city. I can't concentrate on anything for thinking about him, and I'm so confused!'

Ruth thought for a moment.

'You have to bear in mind he's a wealthy man,' she said at last. 'Anyone like that is going to have enemies. People will be jealous of his good fortune, and that jealousy will start rumours. Forget the rumours, Mary. Forget everything you've ever heard about the man.'

'I do try,' Mary said, 'but it's difficult to forget how he put you, John and Bella out of the house when you were too ill to meet the rent. I'll never be able to forgive him for that.'

'What else could he do, Mary? If people brought sewing to me when they had no hope of paying me, you'd think I was mad to keep doing it.'

'That's completely different,' Mary scoffed.

'It's not so different. He's a businessman, not a charity. If Jack Keller let folk off with the rent all the time, he'd be out of business before you could click your fingers.'

'Yes, but...'

Mary knew that. She also knew there were times when business had to be forgotten. And the day Ruth had been unable to pay her rent was one of those times.

'Give him a chance,' Ruth said softly. 'Everyone deserves that.'

Mary *was* giving him a chance. She simply didn't want to allow her heart to rule her head, yet she had the feeling she was doing exactly that.

'Does Jack know you've taken a day off work?' Ruth asked suddenly.

'Yes. I dropped a note through his letter-box last night.'

'So what are you waiting for?' Ruth asked with amusement. 'Get yourself along to his house, lass.'

The walk to Jack's didn't take long. Mary's

178

mind was so full that the distance soon passed. Her thoughts would flit from Jack, to her parents in Southampton, and back to Jack again.

No sooner had she reached the top step than the front door swung open and she was face to face with him.

'You got my note?' she asked.

'I did, thank you.' He smiled.

'I was afraid you might have prior engagements.'

'I did. I cancelled them.' He stepped back. 'Come inside, Mary.'

As soon as he'd closed the door behind them, he cut short Mary's garbled chattering by pulling her into his arms.

'Jack!'

'I was beginning to think you were a dream,' he murmured.

He traced a finger slowly along her bottom lip until Mary's whole body was quivering. She'd relived every moment of Friday evening. When she'd closed her eyes, she'd been able to feel, once again, his lips on hers—

'Jack, don't!' she said shakily, trying to get free.

'I've given Mabel the day off,' he explained, his hands still firmly on Mary's waist. 'It's such a lovely day that I thought we might share a picnic lunch in Princes Street Gardens. How does that sound?'

It sounded wonderful, but—

'I shouldn't be here, you know.' She couldn't bring herself to meet his gaze, in case he saw the longing in her eyes, so she focused on his lapel.

'My parents would – well, I don't know what they'd do! And if anyone from McIntyre's should see me–'

'Your parents are miles away,' he reminded her, 'and if anyone from work sees you, they will simply think you're enjoying the sun. You've taken a day's holiday, Mary. You're entitled to do exactly what you choose.'

'You have such a simple view of life!'

'I don't believe in making life more complicated than it already is.' He finally let her go, clasped her hand in his, and led her into the kitchen. 'See what Mabel's prepared for us.'

Predictably, his housekeeper had made enough food for the whole of Edinburgh. There was a selection of cold meats, pies, plenty of salad, an apple pie–

'I realise that there are people far more deserving than us, but they're not getting it,' Jack said with a grin. 'Not today. Today is for us, Mary.'

She had to smile...

They travelled in Jack's car, and joined a surprisingly large number of folk enjoying the sunshine and the gardens.

They spread the rug not far from the Scott Monument.

'Well?' Jack said as they sat down.

'Well what?'

'How did your parents react to my visit on Monday evening?'

'It was all quite strange, actually,' Mary answered thoughtfully. 'And chaotic. Once it had sunk in that Robbie could be in Southampton, my father was busy making plans to rush off on the next available train, and my mother was berating him for daring to think of going alone. And in the midst of all that, both of them were saying at regular intervals, "How could a daughter of ours approach a man like Jack Keller?" It was very strange.'

'And what sort of man is Jack Keller?' he mused.

'You tell me.'

He pulled a blade of grass and twisted it round his finger.

'Oh, he's a fairly ordinary sort of chap,' he said at last. 'And I believe that most – not all, admittedly – of his bad reputation is due to his father.'

'In what way?' Mary asked, curious.

'My mother died when I was born.' There was no emotion in his voice at all. 'My father had loved her to distraction, by all accounts, and when she died, he became very bitter.'

'I'm sorry,' Mary murmured. 'I didn't know that.'

'There's no reason why you should. He wasn't wealthy then and, consequently, was of no interest to anyone. I think he blamed me for my mother's death, so our relationship was never good. He was a great believer in blood being thicker than water, but we were never – close.'

Mary listened, both fascinated and horrified.

'He had his first property left to him by my mother's uncle,' Jack went on. 'He didn't need to live in it, so he rented it out. I was about five at the time, I suppose. Anyway, he soon saw this as an easy way to make money. In money, he found something else to love.'

'Jack, don't say such things!' She tried to imagine the life he described, but couldn't. 'Didn't you have any other family – aunts, uncles or cousins?'

'Several aunts.' He nodded. 'The trouble was that none of them could bear to be in the same place as my father. And who could blame them? He could have remarried and found happiness but, instead, he chose to believe that life had treated him unfairly. In turn, he treated everyone else unfairly. He wasn't a good man.' He thought for a moment. 'On the other hand, I've been given a very comfortable life. I've never wanted for anything.'

'And are you like him?' Mary asked.

Jack carefully cut a tomato into thin slices.

'No. At least, I hope not.' He looked at her. 'What about you, Mary? Are you like

182

your father?'

'Probably. We argue constantly, and his attitude frustrates me – but, yes, we're very alike. Don't misunderstand,' she put in quickly. 'I think the world of him, but our temperaments are too alike at times.'

'And your mother?'

'I love Mum, and we're very close, but I'm nothing like her.' Mary thought for a moment. 'I'm far more selfish than she is. Everything she does is for us. She never seems to want for herself, just wants the best for us.'

'She sounds lovely.'

'She is.' Mary smiled fondly. 'They're good people, both of them. But they don't approve of you, Jack, and I hate deceiving them.'

'I know you do.'

Mary tried to forget her parents and concentrate on enjoying the moment. She did hate deceiving them, but she felt sure that if they got to know Jack, they would like him.

Or – would they? She still hardly knew the man herself, though he seemed to occupy her every waking thought these days.

For all she knew, he might make a habit of having picnic lunches with young girls. This clearly wasn't the first picnic Mabel had ever prepared.

And judging by his expertise, Mary wasn't the first girl he'd ever kissed...

'Stop looking so serious,' Jack admonished

her, 'and try some of Mabel's apple pie. It's the finest in Edinburgh.'

'Ha!' Laughing, she took the plate from him. 'You wouldn't dare say that to my grandmother...'

Moira Kerr was listening to her friends, chattering over the teacups in Jenner's restaurant, as usual, but she was taking little part in the conversation.

Her mind was miles away, with her daughter and son-in-law, on that train to Southampton.

Moira didn't envy Donald. Her daughter would be a bag of nerves by the time they arrived, and who could blame her? They simply didn't know what to expect...

She dragged her mind back to the here and now.

Every other Wednesday for the last three years or so, she and her friends, Dorothy, Margaret and Bridget, had set the world to rights over tea in Jenner's.

Today, Moira had thought of cancelling, but where was the point in that? All she would have done was sit at home and worry about Robbie.

In any case, Bridget was keen to tell them the latest news of her daughter's wedding preparations.

'Oh, and yellow roses,' she was saying as Moira returned to the present.

Moira smiled and nodded approvingly, but her mind insisted on wandering. Perhaps she'd meet Mary out of her work.

Yes, that was a good idea. It would do them both good, because Mary was sure to be worrying, too...

The waitress, immaculate in black and white, brought them fresh tea. Moira helped herself to a scone and gazed idly out of the window, smiling to herself at two children chasing a dog in Princes Street Gardens.

Then something else caught her attention.

Directly below the window, a very striking young couple were clearing away the remains of their picnic. The man, tall and dark, was folding a rug. He dropped it on top of the hamper and reached for the girl's hands...

At first, Moira thought her eyes must be deceiving her.

The image seemed to freeze in her mind. She knew it would remain there for the rest of her days.

The girl lifted her arms, draped them around the man's neck, and there – in full view of everyone, like a common shop girl – kissed him.

Moira felt the colour drain from her face. It was her granddaughter, Mary.

Mr Sun Chen was a charming, courteous man, but Ishbel was relieved when he left Helen and herself alone.

Ishbel had always found the Chens' home a place in which to relax; now, it felt anything but. The atmosphere between Helen Chen and her husband was distinctly chilly.

Ishbel didn't intend to mention the bone of contention here, but she had to ask after her friend.

'How's Liang? I was hoping to see her while I was here.'

'And you will. She'll be back shortly.' Helen raised her eyebrows. 'As to how she is, well, you'll see for yourself. She feels as we would all feel in her situation. I imagine she's discussed it with you? You're so close...'

'Yes.' Ishbel chose her words with care. 'She's terribly unhappy about her father's decision.'

'I know.' Helen gestured to the doors. 'Come – let's sit outside in the shade. I always feel better in the fresh air.'

They sat in two comfortable chairs in the courtyard. It was an idyllic setting, but neither paid it any heed.

'I know I can trust you, Ishbel. This is a matter of–' Helen hesitated.

'I understand perfectly, Helen. Believe me, nothing you say will be repeated. But I have to say that I feel deeply for poor Liang.'

'So do I, my dear.' Helen's eyes were suddenly bright with tears. 'Unfortunately, my hands are tied. I've known for many years now that my husband wishes Liang to marry

186

Mr Hsien. It's the custom in China, and no matter how much I hate it, I must accept it. A wife cannot go against her husband.'

Ishbel still found the custom impossible to accept.

'I thought, or hoped, that your husband would–' It was very difficult to find the right words.

'Your husband *chose* you for his wife, Helen, and it's obvious that he loves you very much. I just hoped he might remember – that he might allow Liang to choose her husband, too.'

'Mr Chen truly believes that Liang will be happier this way,' Helen said softly. 'He doesn't want her to choose an unsuitable husband. He doesn't want her to go through everything he had to face when he married me. There's the business to consider, too. He wants to make sure that Liang, and her sister, of course, are well provided for. Mr Hsien, he believes, is the perfect man to run the business.'

'I see,' Ishbel said blankly.

'I've told Liang the same thing; I've even tried to believe it myself. But it's very difficult, Ishbel. It's so hard to witness your daughter's unhappiness and feel so helpless. I've talked to my husband, even argued with him. It's done no good, though.'

She gazed up at the cloudless blue sky.

'This is the price I pay for falling in love

with a man like Mr Chen.'

Shanghai was having another stifling hot day, but Ishbel's skin was suddenly covered in goosebumps. She shivered.

In other circumstances, Mr Chen might have been right. But he was wrong about his elder daughter.

Liang wasn't the type to settle happily into an arranged marriage. She was too bright, too clever, too independent, too spirited.

Thinking of her friend, spending the rest of her life embroidering mandarin ducks and caring for babies, her eyes stung with painful tears. It was so very, very wrong…

'Ishbel! What a lovely surprise!'

The unexpected sound of Liang's voice, as gentle and composed as ever, made Ishbel jump. With tears still in her eyes, she rose to her feet and gave her friend a fierce hug.

'I was hoping to see you.' It was all she could say.

Fortunately, Mei Li was close on her sister's heels, and she immediately began chattering about her school work.

Liang, it seemed, was able to distract herself with her sister's talk. Ishbel tried to do the same, but it was impossible.

Something had to be done to stop this marriage. But what? Could no-one make an intelligent, caring man like Mr Chen see that he was wrong?

Robbie's stomach churned with a mixture of nervousness and anticipation, excitement and dread as he gazed up at the huge ship. He wished he could climb aboard now and have done with it, but he had to wait a whole three hours yet.

It had been a strange morning altogether.

His landlady, Mrs Jeffrey, had given him a guinea.

'For the journey,' she'd said.

For the whole time Robbie had spent with her, he'd been convinced he would never meet a more disagreeable woman, and the generous gesture had taken him completely by surprise.

When she'd added, 'Good luck, lad,' it had left him close to tears.

Less than half an hour later, walking down to the docks, he'd had the second shock of the day.

There was a man striding along, in the opposite direction to Robbie and on the other side of the road, who was the image of his father.

The man had quickly rounded the corner, but the likeness had been so striking that Robbie hadn't been able to get it out of his mind.

The word 'omen' popped into his mind, though Robbie had no time for such non-sense.

Was he making the right decision? Would

he be able to find Ishbel when he finally reached Shanghai?

Now that civil war had broken out over there, he was even less sure of what he might find. If the city was dangerous, perhaps Ishbel would be sent home!

It was too late to worry now, though. Robbie had fought hard to earn himself a place as crew member on this ship. In another few hours, he would be on his way...

He wasted money he could ill afford on a cup of tea, then returned to the docks to wait until they'd allow the crew to board—

There he was again. That man. Walking straight towards him!

Robbie stopped in his tracks, his heart hammering.

'Robert!'

The voice was strained, but oh, so blessedly familiar. Robbie dropped his few belongings to the ground, and before he could draw breath, he was clasped tightly in his father's arms.

'Oh, Father!' he gasped. 'I thought I saw you – this morning– I thought–'

'We arrived last night. Your mother's here–' Donald gestured behind him, but Robbie couldn't see his mother.

'But what – how?'

'It's a long story.' His father hugged him again. 'It's so good to see you again.'

He held Robbie at arms' length, and there

was an expression in his eyes his son had never seen before.

'I'm so proud of you, son.'

Proud? Had he heard right? Robbie was shaking so much that it was difficult to tell.

'You've led a sheltered life at the manse compared to most boys,' his father said, seemingly oblivious to the increasing number of people gathering, 'and I know you've never found it easy. But you've proved yourself a fine and capable young man. I had no idea you would cope with–' He looked around him, and then back at Robbie, his eyes brimming with admiration.

'All this! Getting to Newcastle, working in a shipyard, working your way to Southampton, and then–' His expression changed.

'I spoke to Mrs Jeffrey. She told me you've been given work on this ship?'

'Er – yes.'

His father was shaking, too, Robbie saw.

'It's unbelievable. Another twenty-four hours, and–'

'Robbie!'

They both swung round as they heard his mother's shout. She was running, pushing her way past people, until she almost crushed the breath from Robbie's body.

He couldn't look at his mother, and even if had he wouldn't have seen her through his tears.

'Oh, Rob!'

Robbie was struggling to breathe, not because she was holding him so tightly, which she was, but because every feeling from his months away from home had welled up inside him.

His shoulders were shaking. Tears were pouring freely down his face.

'Come home with us!' Mum was in tears, too. 'We all want you back home, son. We need you there. It's where you belong, Robbie!'

Chapter Nine

Ishbel took her mother's letter from the envelope, and smiled as three more and a couple of newspaper cuttings dropped out. As always, Robbie, Mary and Father had included short notes.

She read her brother's first. Ever since he'd returned home, almost six months ago now, Ishbel had noticed a new maturity in Robbie.

The note had more news about what his friends were doing than anything else, but he seemed more grown up, more settled, happier with life.

Robbie had never found it easy being a son of the manse, but he seemed more able to accept it these days.

Her sister's note was shorter still – little more than a rushed promise to write soon.

Father's letter hoped she was safe, and referred to one of the newspaper cuttings – an article about another missionary in China.

Mum's letters were full of cheer and optimism these days, and Ishbel thanked the Lord for that.

Reading between the lines of letters she'd had during the long months of Robbie's absence, Ishbel realised her mother had found it hard to deal with.

But then, none of them had coped well. Ishbel would never forget the day the good news had finally come and she'd been able, once again, to sleep soundly...

I'll look forward to Lizzie McKie calling if she has time, her mother had written. *It will be lovely to meet your friend, and hear all about the mission, but I do so wish it was you, Ishbel. I'll soon have forgotten what you look like...*

Ishbel smiled wistfully. She didn't begrudge Lizzie her leave, far from it – Lizzie would be able to give her all the home news when she got back – but Ishbel dearly wished she could be going home, too.

I do feel for your friend Liang, my dear, but I suppose we have to accept that different cultures have their own way of doing things. Not that it helps, of course. The poor girl must be almost out of her mind...

The strange thing was that Liang seemed calmer than anyone. Now that the day she'd meet Han Hsien was approaching, she seemed to have resigned herself to her fate.

Or had she? *Was* Liang accepting it, or was she refusing to think about it? Ishbel had the awful feeling that, one of these days, Liang was going to crack under the strain.

How would Ishbel feel in that situation? The idea was too awful to contemplate.

Without Gordon, without the knowledge that he was hers, and the future was theirs to share, Ishbel didn't know what she would do.

She was so deep in thought that it took a few moments for her to realise she had a caller. She dashed to the door, wondering how long she'd ignored the knocking.

'Edward! We weren't expecting you.' She stood back to let Edward Clements in. 'I'm afraid there's no-one here but me, but come in anyway.'

'Thank you, Ishbel.'

It was so unlike Edward to call unexpectedly that she was alarmed, though she said nothing. Ishbel wished they could be something other than polite towards each other, but nothing seemed able to break down that barrier.

'I've no idea where Jane and Teddy are, but if you'd like to wait–'

'If I may. I'm sorry to turn up unannounced, but we, or rather Sun Chen and

Company, have something of a crisis on our hands. I'm leaving for France in the morning.'

'The company?' Ishbel met his eyes. 'Is it serious?'

'I hope not.' He gave her a reassuring smile. 'Unfortunately, it's the last thing Mr Chen needs with his daughter's wedding looming.'

'Indeed.'

Ishbel knew just how strained things were between Sun Chen and his wife at the moment.

'Please – sit down, Edward. How long will you be gone?'

'I'm not sure. Apart from business problems, Mr Chen has given me permission to visit England to see Claire – my fiancée – while I'm away.'

'Oh?' Ishbel's heart began to race. What exactly did he plan to say to his fiancée? More importantly, what was he going to say to Jane?

'It's very difficult.' His eyes clouded. 'I've written to Claire, but I don't feel able to break off our engagement in a letter. She deserves more than that. A lot more.'

'Are you ending your engagement?' Ishbel could barely breathe.

'Yes.'

He said no more, and Ishbel knew it wasn't her place to pry, but suddenly there was hope in her heart for Jane.

They carried on a stilted conversation until the door burst open and Teddy raced inside.

'Dada!' he cried, his face shining with joy.

Edward was on his feet in an instant, ready to catch him mid-stride and swing him in the air.

'Edward!' Jane was not far behind. 'What are you doing here? Is something wrong?'

'No, I was just explaining to Ishbel that something's cropped up – business – and I need to go to France. I'm leaving in the morning.'

Jane's disappointment was clear.

'I'll soon be back.' The gentle smile on his face as Edward spoke touched something deep inside Ishbel.

'I'll leave you alone,' she said. 'I've already wasted far too much time this morning. If I don't see you again, Edward, I hope you have a good journey.'

'Thank you, Ishbel.'

Ishbel was still puzzling over that smile. It wasn't simply that Edward was pleased to know Jane would miss him. There had been something protective there … a wish to look after Jane for the rest of her days…

Or was Ishbel just being fanciful?

Gordon Campbell, too, was thinking about Edward as he walked back to the mission a week later. He was remembering how he, with a bright-eyed Jane and a tearful Teddy, had watched his ship leave Shanghai.

Gordon hoped that Jane and Teddy's future was bright. Edward had acted foolishly, true, but Gordon was beginning to like the man.

He was almost home when he saw Liang Chen walking towards him.

'I've been to the mission. Ishbel's not there!'

Liang was normally so composed, but there was a wildness to her, and she seemed to be struggling to breathe properly.

'She and Jane have taken the school-children out for the day, Miss Chen. She'll be sorry–'

'Oh, no!' Liang swallowed several times, but seemed unable to say more.

'Come in to the mission with me,' Gordon said. She seemed past caring, and followed him in silence.

Inside the mission, Gordon wondered what on earth he was going to do with the poor girl. Given who her father was, it seemed ridiculous to offer her tea. She clearly needed something, though…

Then realisation dawned.

'Of course! I believe you're meeting Mr Hsien today?'

'Yes. And I don't think I can bear it.' Her voice shook alarmingly.

'It will be difficult, I'm sure, but–'

'No, it will be more than difficult.' Her

voice broke. 'It will be impossible. This evening I have to meet the man I must marry, and in a few days' time, I shall marry him. My life is as good as over, Mr Campbell, and I can't bear it.'

Her eyes, gazing into his, seemed to believe he had the power to change everything. If only he did!

'You can, Liang.'

It was the first time he had ever used her name, and he'd done it without thinking.

'I can't!' To Gordon's horror, she covered her face with her hands and burst into tears.

Gordon put his arms around her and pulled her close. What else was he to do?

Her small hands, curled into fists, were digging into his back as Liang clung to him. She wept in his arms like a child, and his heart melted...

'You look beautiful,' Helen Chen told her daughter. 'Truly beautiful.'

'You do,' her sister agreed.

'Don't sound so surprised.' Liang teased Mei Li, smiling in spite of herself. But the atmosphere in the room was soon as tense as ever.

'Leave us alone for a few minutes, Mei Li,' their mother suggested. 'Go to your room. I'll join you there.'

Mei Li didn't argue. She gave Liang a hug, and a look that said more than words ever could. It sympathised, but it also said, 'I won't allow myself to be in your situation.'

'You're very brave, Liang,' her mother said, when they were alone.

'No. Believe me, I'm not brave!' Liang's eyes were dry, her mouth a thin line.

'Your father promises me that Mr Hsien's family are good, kind people,' her mother said earnestly. 'We'll still see you, Liang. It's not like it was years ago, when brides didn't see their families again. Times have changed.'

'I know.'

'There's nothing more I can say.' Helen's eyes were bright with tears. 'I love you so much, Liang, and so does your father. Never forget that. We'll always be here for you.'

Helen held her close, then took a deep breath.

'We'll see you downstairs in a few minutes...'

Totally alone, Liang went to her window and gazed down at the courtyard below. If she felt like this now, how would she feel on her wedding day?

Mr Campbell had said this afternoon that God never gave people a burden too great for them to bear. Could she bear this?

She remembered how he'd gathered her close and tried to soothe her, and her face flamed with colour at the memory.

She had embarrassed him; she had humiliated herself. Yet, he hadn't seemed embarrassed, and she hadn't felt humiliated.

She'd felt as if, just for a few minutes, she'd found a safe haven. She wished she could be there now, held close in those strong arms.

He'd called her Liang...

She needed all the strength his words could give her now, meeting the Hsien family. When she was summoned to join their guests, she wasn't sure her legs would carry her into the room.

But they did. Her heart pounding furiously, her gaze immediately sought out Han Hsien.

He stood and bowed slightly, which pleased her.

He wasn't tall, she noticed, but he didn't look as old as she'd imagined, and he seemed open and friendly. He also looked nervous.

Did he think her father might not accept the betrothal? Or was it because this was just as much of an ordeal for him as it was for her?

True, he had to take her as his wife, just as she had to accept him as her husband, but then, he was the one who would step straight into her father's business...

She took little notice of the other guests; she was too busy watching Han. Later, she gained the distinct impression that his mother wasn't overjoyed by the betrothal. Perhaps she'd had someone else in mind for her son?

Liang hoped not. Mrs Hsien would be welcoming her into her home; it would be impossible if they didn't get on…

The Hsien family presented gifts, including the Dragon and Phoenix bridal cakes. It was the cakes, more than anything else, that made the whole thing seem frighteningly real to Liang.

The bridal cakes, a symbol of their pairing, would be distributed to friends and family as an invitation to the wedding feast.

And that would be that. Liang was being given to this man's family. There was no escape…

At last they were free to talk to each other.

'I have lived in America for some years,' Han said, 'and you, of course, have grown up with your lovely English mother. We shall have the best of both worlds.'

He must have seen her confusion, because he tried to explain.

'We have our more modern Western ways, yet we also have our culture and traditions behind us. We'll have a good marriage, Liang, if that's what you want.'

What Liang wanted was to ask Mr Campbell what he'd meant, about God never giving a person a burden heavier than they could carry… But no.

'Yes,' she answered simply.

'Your father tells me you've always shown

an interest in his business. I gather he doesn't approve – well, of course he wouldn't.'

There was a simple shyness in him that Liang found appealing.

'I don't have such beliefs, Liang. I don't hold with the view that ignorant women make better wives.'

A small spark of hope leapt in her heart.

'I'm glad,' she said, not sure what else he expected.

The spark of hope soon died, though. She still had to marry this man. No matter how kind, how friendly he was, he was still a stranger to her. She had to marry him, bear his children–

Glancing across the room, she caught her mother's eyes. The love she saw there helped more than anyone could ever know...

Ever since Lizzie McKie's note had arrived at the manse, Veronica Montrose had been rushing round cleaning up.

Now, though, as the family hung on every word Ishbel's colleague uttered, she realised the rushing around had been pointless.

Lizzie was the type to slide effortlessly into any surroundings. It was easy to see why she and Ishbel were such good friends.

'What's this American like?' Mary asked curiously. 'The one Ishbel mentions so often. Adam, is it?'

'Adam Butler. He's the Chens' accountant.' Smiling, Lizzie nodded.

'Oh, how would you describe him? He's very – American. He's a lot of fun, and I think he keeps us all sane. I don't see much of him now that I've moved from Shanghai, but I know he's still a regular visitor to the mission. We try to show him the error of his ways,' she added with a twinkle in her eyes, 'but he's incorrigible.'

Veronica saw her husband's face alight with laughter.

'We need people like Adam to stop us taking ourselves too seriously,' Lizzie added soberly. 'Our work *is* serious, but if we didn't keep a sense of humour, we wouldn't cope.'

Donald nodded thoughtfully at that. He, naturally enough, was interested in the mission work, whereas Veronica and Mary were more interested in Ishbel's life and her friends.

For once, Veronica's mother was struggling to get a word in. She wanted to hear all about life in Shanghai.

'But how *is* Ishbel?' Veronica asked again. 'You say she's well, Lizzie, and enjoying the work, but–'

Lizzie smiled, understanding Veronica perfectly.

'She's fine, I promise. As you know, she makes friends easily. At first, she was very homesick – I think we all go through that. But now, although I know she'd love nothing more than to be taking my place, sitting here with you all, I'm sure she's happy – not just in her work, but in herself.'

Lizzie smiled at Robbie.

'As for you, young man, you worried the life out of her!'

Robbie had the grace to blush.

'The young rascal worried the life out of all of us.' Veronica glanced sternly at her son.

But he was home now, and that was all that mattered. Veronica even thought that his adventure had done him good.

Perhaps it was the realisation that life's not so easy when you have to fend for yourself; perhaps it was pride that he *had* fended for himself.

Or perhaps it was simply mixing with so many people from different walks of life.

Whatever it was, it had given Robbie a maturity that hadn't been there before...

'And what's Teddy's father like?' Moira put in. 'This Edward Clements?'

'I've only met him once,' Lizzie answered. 'He seems a good man, and I know wee Teddy adores him. He's very good with children.'

'Jane is, too,' Veronica said. 'Ishbel says she's a marvel with the wee ones at the mission.'

'She is. Endless patience.'

Veronica sat back in her chair, happy just

to hear Lizzie bring the characters from Ishbel's letters to life. She'd found it all difficult to visualise – the strange people, the strange city, the strange customs – but Lizzie made it real, made it sound almost normal...

'Ishbel and Gordon make a wonderful team,' Lizzie was saying. 'Gordon keeps Ishbel's feet on the ground, and Ishbel stops him being so–' she paused suddenly.

'I was going to say – stuffy, but–'

Her words were met with a roar of laughter.

'He's not stuffy, of course,' Lizzie said, sharing their amusement. 'I just think he could be seen that way, without Ishbel's influence. But stuffy, no. Heavens, one evening, just before I left for Scotland, he showed me a few things about Highland dancing! And he almost danced poor Ishbel off her feet...'

Veronica wondered just how good a team they made. For some time now Ishbel's letters had been full of 'Gordon says...' or 'Gordon thinks...'

She wasn't worried, though. Once there was anything to know, Ishbel would tell them. There was nothing secretive about Ishbel.

Unlike Mary. Veronica frowned. Mary had just turned to look at the clock for the third time in as many minutes. Why? She wasn't going anywhere.

Something had happened when she and

Donald had been in Southampton, she was sure of it. And Mary's grandmother was in on the secret. At the time, Veronica had been too relieved to have Robbie back home to push the issue.

Nevertheless, there had always been a secretive side to Mary. Veronica couldn't get close to her as she was to Ishbel.

'Mum, look!' Robbie nudged her. 'It's Ishbel with her friend, Liang! Look at what she's wearing...'

She pushed her worries aside and concentrated on Lizzie's photographs.

On Liang's wedding day, Ishbel awoke with a knot of tension inside her. It was a bitterly cold day, but at least it was bright.

How was poor Liang feeling? How could she go through with it?

How could she not...

There were so many customs involved, too – like the installing of the bridal bed. Ishbel wasn't sure she'd grasped half of it, but she knew she'd never heard anything so ridiculous.

The bed was moved into position by a carefully selected 'good luck man' – someone wealthy and successful.

A good luck woman, who'd borne lots of sons, then made the bed, and covered it with red dates, oranges, lotus seeds and pomegranates.

The children were then invited on to the bed and left to scramble for the fruit.

It hurt to think of her bright, intelligent friend going along with such nonsense... But then, there were customs in Scotland that Liang would no doubt find just as silly.

Ishbel dressed carefully and went through to the sitting-room.

'Until today,' Gordon declared moodily, striding in, 'I had a great deal of respect for Mr and Mrs Chen.'

Ishbel looked at him in surprise. Usually, he had endless patience with the local customs, but not today, it seemed.

'I don't think Helen can be blamed,' she said quickly. 'This is breaking the poor woman's heart.'

'Breaking *hers?*' Gordon muttered.

'And I suppose we can't blame Mr Chen, either. For centuries, this is the way it's been done. The young have always been considered too foolish to choose wisely.'

'I know all that,' he said testily, 'but when a girl's been raised by an English mother–'

'I know.'

'Are you ready?' Gordon asked, sighing heavily. 'Let's go.'

Ishbel had expected Gordon to compliment her on the outfit she'd had made especially for the wedding, but he didn't appear to have noticed.

She'd even hoped that Liang's marriage,

different and unwelcome though it was, might spur Gordon to think of his marriage – *their* marriage...

Helen Chen woke to the worst day of her life, feeling resentment for everything Chinese. It was a resentment she couldn't shake off.

She'd been only a couple of years older than Liang was now when she married. She remembered believing she would grow to love China, with all its strange customs, as much as her husband did.

She remembered how nervous she had been, and how much she had looked forward to meeting Sun's family and friends...

Instead of the welcome she'd hoped for, there had been pure hostility. Even Sun's mother – but, no, after the initial disappointment and disapproval, over the years, the dear woman had become Helen's closest friend.

It would have been so easy during those first difficult months for Helen to have left her husband and returned to her beloved Devon.

Instead, she'd done all she could to make Sun proud. She'd raised their children in the proper manner.

The only time she had gone against custom was when she had refused to have their daughters' feet bound. Other than that, she had been a loyal and obedient wife.

And all it had done was bring her to this day – the worst day of her life.

In all those years of marriage, she had visited England only six times. Now, she felt a fierce longing for 'home'. She wished she could go there, this minute, taking both her girls with her...

But the ceremony had to happen. During the intricate ritual, pride in her daughter had Helen close to tears, and the longing for home increased. This was so unfair!

Holding the teacup in both hands, Liang served her parents the traditional tea, with lotus seeds and red dates added to ensure the couple would have children soon.

The sweetness of the tea was supposed to be a wish for sweet relations between the bride and her new family, and Helen hoped desperately for that. Her daughter would be living with Han Hsien's family for a year, and Helen couldn't see it being easy.

Helen watched her husband, smiling at Liang, proud and happy.

The pride she could understand – their lovely daughter was serving tea as a sign of respect, and to thank them – but how could he look happy?

All too soon, it was time for Liang to leave for the groom's house. Then Helen did break down.

The house was already decorated in so

much red that Helen had thought she would scream at the sight of more, but Liang, resplendent in her bright red wedding gown, with her face hidden by a red veil, couldn't have looked more beautiful...

The procession, with Liang carried in the red sedan chair, was the usual noisy affair. Everyone was high-spirited. Everyone looked happy.

It never failed to amaze Helen that, compared to the many rituals leading up to it, the actual ceremony itself was so short.

Now it was over. Her lovely Liang was married...

At the wedding feast, she felt a little better.

For one thing, Liang's veil had been removed, and it was a huge relief to see her daughter smiling. For another, she could distract herself by talking to the guests.

'How are you feeling, Helen?' Ishbel's friendly voice came as a relief. This was probably the only guest who *could* understand how Helen was feeling.

But she refused to put Ishbel in an awkward position. It wasn't fair.

'What did you think of your first Chinese wedding?'

'I'm overwhelmed.' Ishbel smiled. 'All this red! But it does give a sense of joy to the occasion. And a twelve-course banquet – really, Helen, I had no idea.'

'It's tradition.'

They both fell silent as they watched Liang and her new husband chatting to guests.

'Mr Hsien is a lovely man,' Ishbel said with feeling.

'He is.'

Helen was grateful for that. She knew that her husband had made his best choice for their daughter, but a 'lovely man' wasn't necessarily the right man for Liang.

'Liang's been laughing at things he's said on several occasions,' Ishbel added.

Helen had noticed that, too. It had warmed her frozen heart a little.

'Pray God he makes her happy, Helen.' Ishbel patted her arm.

Biting her lip, Liang's mother nodded.

Even Gordon Campbell's calm sense of reason seemed to have deserted him today.

In a way, Helen found it touching that these dear people from Scotland should understand just how hopeless and painful Liang's situation was. In another way, it only increased her outrage.

'I saw you having a long chat with Han, Gordon. What are your impressions of my new son-in-law?'

He thought for a while before answering.

'What can you learn about a man on his wedding day?' he said at last. 'I only hope he realises how very lucky he is.'

'So do I!' Helen linked arms with them both.

'We mustn't be so gloomy,' she said briskly, her eyes moist. 'Come along. We must toast the – toast their future…'

That night, sitting in front of her mirror, brushing her hair with a ferocity that was painful, Helen relived the day in her mind.

In the mirror, she could see Sun, waiting for her to join him in bed. All she could think of was her lovely Liang, having to share a bed with a man she hardly knew…

For the first time in her life, she couldn't bring herself to speak to Sun. She wasn't sure she would ever forgive him for this.

'Come to bed, my dear,' he said at last.

She continued to turn her back to him.

'Helen, my love–' he sighed. 'It's for the best, you'll see. You wouldn't want Liang to go through what we did?'

'What?' Helen was on her feet, spinning round to face the bed. 'We fell in love! So deeply that no family, no stupid tradition, no business, nothing could ever harm that love. You don't want our daughter to know that neither great wealth nor abject poverty would ever matter a jot?'

'Helen, listen–'

'No, Sun, you listen, for a change!' Her hairbrush slapping against her hand as she spoke was the only outward sign of her anger.

'In a month's time, I'm going to England. I'm taking Mei Li and Liang with me.'

'Helen, you know you can't do that. Liang

belongs to—'

'Liang belongs to no-one!' Helen yelled at him. 'She's my daughter, and nothing will ever change that. If she doesn't want to come with me, fine. But if she does, I'll take her. And nothing, or no-one, will stop me. Not even you, Sun!'

Chapter Ten

For the first time in her life, Mary Montrose envied her sister. How she wished she was in Shanghai, far away from Edinburgh and the manse!

This evening, Ishbel would be attending the party for Helen and Mei Li Chen before they sailed to Britain. It would be a grand, colourful affair, and Ishbel wouldn't have a care in the world.

What would her sister say if she could see Mary now, curled up in the armchair in Jack Keller's sitting-room, waiting for him to come home, her teeth chattering with fear? Mary would have given all she had to be able to talk to her at this moment. Perhaps Ishbel would have been able to calm her.

This was real fear, that had her stomach churning, and made her feel faint.

If she didn't know what Ishbel would say,

she certainly had no idea how Jack would react when she broke the news to him. But tell him she must.

Here, in this very room, he'd shattered all her dreams.

At the time, of course, she hadn't thought them dreams. She had truly believed that one day she would become Mrs Jack Keller. One day, her parents would grow to love Jack as much as she did.

She had even pictured herself walking down the aisle of her father's church, wearing a long, floating creation of white satin and lace, and carrying yellow roses...

She knew now, of course, that could never be.

'Why have you never married, Jack?'

She would never forget asking him that simple question. At least, it had seemed simple at the time.

They'd been sitting here together. As soon as she'd asked the question, he'd risen to stand with his back to her.

It was shortly after Christmas, and the room had been warm and bright.

'Jack?'

He'd turned around then, and she'd seen it in his eyes. She'd known the truth before he even spoke.

'I was eighteen,' he said with a sigh. 'Gilly was the same age. We were young, and my father and her parents were against the relationship from the start. But Gilly and I had big ideas, we wanted to change to world–'

Mary had stopped breathing then, it seemed. Even if she'd been capable of speech, she would only have begged him not to tell her any more.

'We were married against everyone's wishes. I often wonder if we hadn't faced such opposition – but we did, so it's no use wondering. We were happy for a few months – only a few months.' He shook his head.

'We divorced, Mary. Gilly's living in London now, or she was the last time I heard. I haven't seen her for five years.'

Silence settled on the room. Outside, a blackbird, perched on the window-sill, fixed a pair of bright eyes on them.

'Divorced?' Mary said at last, getting the word out with difficulty. 'Oh, Jack, why didn't you tell me before?'

'Because I knew what your reaction would be,' he answered simply. 'You would have wanted nothing to do with me.'

'It's not that,' Mary murmured. A divorced man...

Her legs felt shaky, but she stood and paced the length of the room, her arms wrapped tightly around herself. A divorced man!

All her dreams, all her hopes for the future – crushed to dust.

'I love you, Mary.'

'Jack, don't! Please!'

She was shaking with shock and misery – and yes, anger. How could he keep such a thing from her?

'Do you have children?' she asked.

'No.'

'Really? You're not saving that little shock for another time?'

'Mary, listen–' He moved towards her.

'But there won't be another time, Jack. There can't be. You've known that all along, haven't you? You know perfectly well that, in my position, bearing in mind who my father is–'

'Mary!' He reached for her, but she flinched and stepped back.

'No, Jack.' She picked up her jacket. 'As I said, there won't – can't be another time. Goodbye!'

'Mary!' he'd called after her. 'I'm ten years older than you and, consequently, I have a past. It's not one that I'm proud of, but–'

Mary had refused to listen. She'd walked out, her head held high and her heart smashed to pieces...

In the weeks that followed, jealousy had been added to the shock and hurt.

The unknown Gilly – and what sort of name was that, for heaven's sake? – had soon become the most beautiful, intelligent, glamorous, witty female Mary had ever imagined.

Why hadn't she known? The locals loved to gossip about Jack. How had he managed

216

to keep this secret?

It had been easy to walk out of Jack's house compared to the task of stopping loving him. She hadn't been able to master that.

So she'd gone back to him. Working on the principle that half a loaf was better than no bread at all, she'd gone back, craving anything he could give her.

She'd known, of course, they had no future, but she needed any crumb she could have...

The front door opened and closed, and she jumped. Instead of dwelling on the past and reliving all that misery, she should have thought about how to tell him...

She heard Mabel, the housekeeper, speaking in hushed tones, but she didn't hear his reply. A moment later, the sitting-room door was thrown open.

'Mary, what are you doing here?'

She was on her feet, facing him. She opened her mouth to speak, but no words came.

'Mary? Sweetheart, what is it?' He wrapped his arms around her, and that was Mary's undoing. She gave a choked sob, covered her face with her hands and broke down completely.

She cried and she cried, not knowing, or even caring, if she would ever stop.

'Nothing's this bad,' Jack said, worried. 'Whatever it is, we'll sort it out. *I'll* sort it out, darling. I'm here now. There's nothing to worry about, nothing to upset yourself about.'

'Oh, Jack.' She took huge breaths, and used her hands to rub the tears from her face. 'Do you really believe you can solve every problem?'

'I can do my best. What is it, sweetheart?'

'You can't solve this one, Jack. I'm pregnant!'

Sun Chen gazed out of his office window, for the first time in his life gaining no satisfaction from the view.

His six-storey building on Nanking Road, at the nerve centre of the International Concession, was less than a mile from the Bund.

He'd had lifts installed, and modern plumbing with hot and cold running water. Some of his staff lived in comfortable dormitories on the upper floor.

The building had the most prestigious business address in China and it was a symbol of his success.

Today, however, it all meant nothing.

He was a man used to looking forward; it was rare for him to look back. This afternoon, though, his mind kept taking him back to the thirteen-year-old boy he'd been when he'd left Shanghai for Europe; taking him back to the very different twenty-year-old he'd been when he'd brought his lovely English wife home to Shanghai.

The young Sun Chen had been a changed man in many ways.

Like all his fellow students, he'd been instructed to stay away from Western women, and although those dire warnings in themselves aroused his, and his friends' curiosity, he'd never dreamed he would meet a woman who touched his heart so deeply.

It had taken him a month to fall in love with Helen, many more months trying to kill that love, and almost as long to accept he couldn't face life without her.

They'd had their problems, perhaps more than most couples.

Helen was strong-willed and stubborn, and Sun's background hadn't prepared him for anything other than a compliant Chinese wife. But their love had remained strong and true.

Apart from his dear mother, none of his family had been able to understand just how much he loved his new bride. Their prejudices had torn at his heart, for Helen's sake.

He had vowed then that, one day, he would give her everything. He had worked like a man possessed – he had *been* a man possessed, possessed with ambition.

Now, of course, he could provide Helen with anything she could want. That seemed so hollow to his ears.

Did Helen still love him? A year ago, he

would never have dreamed of asking himself such a question. But now...

There was a light tap on his door. He turned away from the window and smiled at his elder daughter.

'Liang – I was beginning to think you were lost.'

As soon as he'd spoken, he regretted it. She was only a few minutes late – he didn't want her to think he was chastising her.

She gave him a brief hug, which touched him. At least Liang didn't blame him as her mother did.

Embroidered on the sleeves of her gown were two pairs of mandarin ducks. Normally Sun wouldn't have noticed them, but a sudden memory of his mother came to him.

She, too, loved to stitch those ducks, the symbol of fidelity. Everyone believed it was because she'd been unhappy in her marriage...

Of course, his mother had already fallen in love with someone she'd had to give up, to marry the man her parents had chosen for her.

For Liang, it was different...

'I'm sorry to be late.' Her gentle voice recalled him to the present. 'I stopped to talk to Mr Butler. You wanted to speak to me, Father?'

'Yes.' He wasn't quite sure what to say. The last thing he wanted was Liang worrying about the state of her parents' marriage.

'It's about your mother's visit to England. I know she was very keen to take you with her. She wanted to take you both – you and Mei Li.'

'I know.' Liang was frowning. 'She spoke to me about it.'

All Helen had told him about their discussion was that Liang wouldn't be accompanying them.

Liang's fingers absently traced the outline of one of those ducks on her sleeve, but she looked straight at him.

'My marriage to Han has upset her a great deal,' she remarked. 'Perhaps, like me, she never believed it would really happen.'

That 'like me' made Sun shiver, but he said nothing.

'I think a holiday in England will do her good,' Liang went on. 'Mei Li will enjoy it. It's a long time since we went.' She smiled suddenly. 'I think I was ten years old last time, so Mei Li would only have been five.'

'Do you wish you were going with them?'

Although he had to ask, he knew in his heart what her answer would be.

'I should love to be leaving with them tomorrow, I really would. But my place is with Han.'

'It is,' Sun agreed urgently. 'Han is a good man, Liang.'

'I know that.'

'Was your mother very disappointed?'

'In a way.' She was thoughtful. 'Although, in another way, I think she was quite relieved – I really don't know. When I told her about the party tonight, she seemed happy about that...'

Sun watched her closely as she spoke of the arrangements both she and Han – and Han's family, of course – had made for this evening's party at the Hsiens'. Never in his life had he been so unutterably proud of her.

'Does Han make you happy, Liang?'

'He's a very good, kind man.' She didn't hesitate. 'He treats me almost as an equal, which I like. He allows me to see my family and friends whenever I choose. He's very kind, and I consider myself lucky.'

Sun was pleased with that, but his pleasure was short-lived. When Liang had left his office, he realised that she hadn't answered his question at all...

'Isn't this lovely, Adam?' Ishbel's gesture took in everything – the beautifully furnished room, the well-dressed, smiling guests, the sumptuous food.

'This house wouldn't look out of place in England, would it?' she added, smiling at the Chens' American contrast. 'Somewhere in rural England?'

'It is nice,' he agreed. 'It's cosier than Sun and Helen's home.'

Ishbel knew exactly what he meant.

The house Liang shared with her husband and his family was in the French Concession, sandwiched between the Japanese in the north, the British in the south and the Russians across the river.

It was the way the area was laid out that impressed Ishbel most, though. The tree-lined avenues and green parks were a delight to walk through, especially in this warm May sunshine.

'But I have to confess to preferring the Old Town,' Adam admitted.

He meant the old walled Chinese city, immediately south of the French Concession.

'I love the low buildings of Nantao,' he went on. 'The small markets, and all those alleyways with the colourful shop signs hanging overhead. And the mobile stoves on bamboo poles, and those one-room cafés... I love being there.'

'You would.' Ishbel smiled. 'I have to say I prefer the French Concession. I feel more at home.'

'Yes, but I think it's so wrong that all subjects in the foreign concessions, whether they be foreign or Chinese, are governed by the laws of the foreigner.' Then he smiled. 'Don't let me get on my soapbox today. We're supposed to be enjoying ourselves.'

'I *am* enjoying myself,' Ishbel said happily. 'It's wonderful to see Liang looking so settled. It doesn't seem so long since we were all dreading her marriage, but it's been – what? – almost six months now.

'She looks – content, doesn't she?'

'She does.'

Ishbel had seen Liang many times since her marriage, and although they chatted happily for hours, Liang hadn't spoken much about her husband. Picking up on what Liang didn't say, rather than what she did, Ishbel gained the distinct impression Liang didn't share a good relationship with her mother-in-law.

Ishbel hoped she was wrong. On the few occasions she had met Mrs Hsien, she'd found her polite, but cool.

As for Liang's relationship with Han – well, that seemed better than either she or Liang had dared to hope. He was courteous, charming and friendly. Compared to her Chinese friends, Liang had a good life.

'It's a pity the same can't be said for Helen.' Adam's voice broke into her thoughts.

Ishbel followed his gaze to Helen, standing by her husband's side. She and Sun were together – yet not together. Helen seemed to be angry and Sun bewildered.

'Liang's marriage hit her hard,' Ishbel said softly.

'Yes, but it's done now.' Adam rubbed his chin thoughtfully. 'Do you think she's really looking forward to visiting England?'

Ishbel had asked herself that several times. It was completely out of character for Helen – almost as if the sole reason behind this trip to England was to hurt Sun.

'She must be,' Ishbel answered positively. 'So is Mei Li – it will do them both good. When Helen comes back, she'll be in a far better frame of mind – you'll see.'

'I hope you're right.' Adam couldn't say more because Mei Li joined them.

At seventeen, Mei Li was almost as tall as her sister now, but whereas Liang was quiet and composed, Mei Li was filled with restless energy.

'Mother says we'll be able to visit your family during our holiday, Ishbel,' she greeted them. 'Won't that be wonderful?'

'Won't it just!' Ishbel had to smile to herself. Heaven alone knew what her parents would make of this fiery young girl.

'I only wish I could go with you,' she added, 'but it won't be too long before I get my leave. And, Mei Li, don't forget to take the photographs of Liang's wedding.'

'They're already packed.' Mei Li looked around the room. 'This is lovely, isn't it? But I wish tomorrow would hurry up and come. I can't wait to board the ship. I'm so excited!'

'We'd never have guessed,' Adam said, and Mei Li spluttered with laughter.

'I want to see some life,' she told him earnestly.

'Life? My dear girl, you live in one of the most exciting cities in the world!'

'Oh, nonsense!' Mei Li looked to Ishbel for support, but Ishbel could only agree with Adam.

'You may find Devon very quiet compared to Shanghai,' she warned.

'Surely not!' And Mei Li flounced off to find someone else to share her excitement with.

'We could both be wrong.' Adam smiled as they watched her. 'I imagine Mei Li could find excitement anywhere. Sun and Helen will find her a handful in a few years!'

'In a few years?' Ishbel echoed on a splutter of laughter. 'She's been a handful, as you put it, from the moment she was born!'

Adam fetched them some tea and they sat down to chat.

'Aren't you off to your up-country station soon, Ishbel?'

No dates had been agreed yet, but Ishbel knew she was going to a village in the north, fairly close to where her friend, Lizzie McKie was working.

'Are you looking forward to it?' Adam asked.

'In a way. I'll miss everyone here, of course, but it should be an interesting experience. I'll enjoy seeing how the villagers live – it must be so different from the city.'

'You'll need to be careful, Ishbel. There's

been some trouble up there with bandits.'

'Yes. I heard about it.' Heard about it, and tried not to think about it.

'A friend of mine, Warren Dean, is heading that way soon. I've spoken to you about him, haven't I?'

'The American journalist?'

'That's him.' Adam was thoughtful. 'He might be useful to have around on your journey.'

'The journey doesn't worry me—' Ishbel began.

'Then it should. Anyway, I'd feel happier if he was about. He's used to talking his way out of trouble.' He smiled at her.

'I hope you don't stay away too long, Ishbel. I'll miss you.'

Before Ishbel could comment on that, Liang joined them.

Ishbel always felt dowdy in her friend's company and today was no exception. Liang's gown was of pale blue silk and, as always, exquisitely embroidered.

'I thought I'd never get a chance to talk to you both.' She smiled that gentle smile of hers. 'I'm so grateful to you for coming. This should remind my mother she has many friends to come back to.'

'The break will do her good.' Ishbel tried to cheer her up. 'After six months away, she'll be pleased to get home. Try not to worry about her too much, Liang.'

'Ishbel's right,' Adam put in. 'She'll miss her family and friends more than she perhaps realises.'

'I hope so. And talking of missing people, where's Mr Campbell today? I'm beginning to think he's avoiding us. We haven't seen him since our wedding day.'

Liang spoke lightly, but Ishbel thought Gordon's absence hurt.

'He would have loved to be here.' She leapt to Gordon's defence. 'But he's so terribly busy at the moment.'

Had it really been six months since Liang had seen him? True, Gordon *was* busy. He was also very – preoccupied.

There was nothing Ishbel could put her finger on, but there was no escaping the fact that Gordon wasn't his normal self...

'Of course he is,' Liang said. 'He's doing very important work, like you, Ishbel. Tell me – have you heard when you'll be leaving Shanghai? I hope you won't be away for too long...'

All the time they spoke, Ishbel's mind was on Gordon.

He wasn't his usual self. These days, his kisses seemed to stem from habit more than passion.

He seemed to have no enthusiasm for the future – for their future ... and Ishbel had no idea why.

It seemed to Mary that half Edinburgh was enjoying the sunshine in Princes Street Gardens. She only wished she could enjoy it, too.

Instead of coming here, she should have gone to see Ruth. Ruth and bairns might help take her mind off things. Here, all she was doing was dwelling on her problems.

She was meeting Jack in an hour – though not here, where her grandmother had seen her kissing him.

'Like a common shop girl!' Moira Kerr had said furiously. 'What about your parents, Mary Montrose? What about respect? Ashamed?' she'd thundered, her face red with anger. 'I've never been so ashamed in my life!'

The familiar knot of pain tightened in Mary's chest. What on earth would Gran say if she knew what had happened?

At least Gran hadn't told her parents about that kiss, for which Mary was grateful. Not that Gran had kept it a secret for her benefit.

'It would kill your father,' she'd said, and that had been the end of it.

Things had never been the same between them since, and it saddened Mary.

Her thoughts returned to Jack. She'd been terrified of his reaction to the news, but he'd behaved in typical Jack fashion.

'Pregnant?' His eyes had lit up. 'My darling girl!' And he'd hugged her so tightly that she'd struggled to breathe.

Despite the fear in her heart, the guilt and the shame, the memory still brought a small smile to her face.

'That's the most wonderful thing I've ever heard,' he'd declared. 'Oh, I know you're frightened, and I know we wouldn't have planned things this way, my love, but just think—' He held her close.

'Our child, Mary, who'll grow tall and strong ... a boy or a girl with his or her own future ... just because you and I fell in love.'

At the time, Mary had been incapable of doing anything but cry. At first she'd cried out of pure fear, but then she'd cried from relief – the relief of no longer feeling so alone.

'But what will we do, Jack? My parents – my father—' And she'd started to tremble.

'We'll get married, of course.'

'But it will be no marriage! You're divorced, Jack. I can't marry at the registrar's! My father would never be able to show his face—'

'We'll elope.' Jack cut her off. 'In the eyes of the law we'll be married, my love...'

Moments later, he had their future mapped out.

'We'll go to America.'

Mary had sat there gasping. Jack's simplistic view of life never failed to amaze her.

It wasn't due only to his wealth, Mary decided, although that had a lot to do with it. She didn't have a clue how much money he had, only that it was more than enough to take them both to America in comfort.

Jack's attitude to life came from his personality. If he'd been a pauper, he would still have refused to be beaten.

'America's the place to be these days,' he went on. 'We'll make a new life for ourselves, a good life for our child. A wonderful life, Mary. Just me, you and our child – with the rest of our lives stretching before us.'

He'd spoken as if it was Stirling or Glasgow he was discussing.

'We'd come back for holidays, sweetheart. I know, or I can imagine, how your family will react to this news, but they'll come round–'

'But they won't, Jack. That's what you don't understand. They'll never get over this. Never!' Mary knew that was true – especially of her father.

'People always do, my love. As soon as the baby's born–'

'No, Jack!'

'I love you, Mary.' Jack held her gaze. 'I love you more than I believed it possible to love anyone or anything. I have since the moment I first saw you. I want you with me until the day I die. I want to love you, cherish you, protect you – you and our child, my love. Do you love me?'

'Yes.' He was her whole world. 'Yes, of course I love you.' Her voice faltered. 'But I love my family, too, Jack, and they don't deserve this.'

'I know that.'

She'd felt instantly bereft when he let her go.

'Mary, I wish I could be everything you want. I wish I was the respectable, God-fearing bachelor your parents would approve of. But I'm not. I can't be what I'm not!'

Mary had wanted to feel his arms around her again, but he'd been standing by the window, sounding almost angry. Then, suddenly, he'd spun round to face her.

'All I can say is that I love you, and our unborn child. I want the best – for both of you. Think things over, Mary, and let me know your decision...'

How could a man sound so angry when he told a woman he loved her?

She shivered in the June sunshine.

It hadn't been anger, of course. It had been frustration – and hurt. He'd wanted her to be as pleased about the child as he was, and her reaction had hurt.

If they'd been married in the eyes of God, with her family's blessing, Mary would have been the happiest girl in the world.

But she couldn't alter the circumstances...

It was time she left the Gardens, and went to see Jack, to give him her answer.

As she walked, she found herself longing for Ishbel. Her head was full of memories –

the happy childhood days they'd shared.

By the time she reached Jack's house, tears were falling freely down her cheeks. He opened the door and took her in his arms.

'I hope this is the last time I ever see you cry, my love.' He kissed the tears away.

'So do I.' She gave him a wobbly smile.

'Well?' he asked uncertainly. 'Have you thought about – everything?'

'Yes.' She nodded, and once again, her heart yearned for Ishbel.

'Yes, Jack, I've decided. I'll marry you. I'll go to America with you…'

Chapter Eleven

'Happy, Mrs Keller?' Mary spun round, startled by the sound of her husband's voice.

'Of course! I've spent the evening being wined and dined in the most luxurious style imaginable. Who wouldn't be happy?'

'Someone who missed their home.' Jack slipped his arms round her waist. 'Someone who missed their family.'

'Yes, well–' Mary turned in his arms and gazed out across the twinkling lights of Chicago. She gripped his arms so that he wouldn't let her go.

'This view fascinates me,' she murmured.

But it alarmed her, too. Chicago was a huge city; around two million people lived there. It was so modern, too.

Not surprising, she supposed, given that only a couple of buildings had survived the fire of 1871.

'The lights are pretty, aren't they?' she added.

'They are, but stop changing the subject. What's wrong, Mary?'

'Nothing.' But she couldn't fool Jack; he knew her too well.

'It's just that it's all happened so quickly, Jack. One minute I was panicking in Edinburgh, the next–'

'The next you were married to me,' he finished for her.

'Yes.' She smiled, and touched his face. 'Marrying you was the easy part.'

Had her entire family disowned her?

The thought brought tears to her eyes, and she had to blink them back rapidly. Jack was so kind, she didn't want to hurt him by appearing sad.

She still had her friends, even if they were an ocean away. Or perhaps her friend, in the singular.

Ruth McKinlay had proved to be the best friend a girl could have. She'd hugged Mary tight, wished her well, and promised to take Jack up on his offer of a holiday in America.

Ruth was busy with her dressmaking business, and with the children, but one day, Mary hoped, she would visit them. Meanwhile, they could exchange long letters.

Her workmate Flora Campbell – well, Mary knew not to expect a letter from that quarter. Flora had made her feelings known in no uncertain terms. She was Gordon's sister, and shared his strict moral views.

The day before Mary had left, she'd seen Flora in Edinburgh, walking along the street towards her.

Mary had hoped they might have a friendly word, but Flora had made a point of crossing over. That had hurt.

No doubt Flora had written to her brother and he would have shown the letter to Ishbel...

'Who were those men you were talking to this evening?' She dragged her mind back to the here and now.

'Oh, it was just a business matter,' Jack said. 'Nothing for you to worry about. But that reminds me – we'll have to get you a car.'

'A car? Jack, no! I can't drive!'

'You'll soon learn.' He laughed and ruffled her hair.

'But what would I want with a car?' she protested. 'I can walk everywhere. Chicago's so flat, and–'

'I want only the best for you, Mary. You and Junior.' He ran a gentle hand over her thickening waistline.

'The best, as you call it, can't be bought, Jack. The best is two happy, loving parents. The best is a loving family.'

The best would be grandparents, aunts, uncles and cousins, family christenings and family Christmases...

How could she and Jack give their child the best when they couldn't provide any of those things? Between them, they had no family at all.

'I'm tired, Jack.' She tried to smile, despite the tears swimming in her eyes. 'We've had too many late nights recently.'

'Let's go to bed, then.' He turned her away from the window.

'Will you hold me close all night?'

'Of course, my love...'

With difficulty, Mary managed to hold back her tears until Jack slept.

It all seemed so unfair. Jack was a kind, caring, generous, sensitive man, and she'd fallen in love with him almost the first moment she saw him. She would have given all she had to be his wife, to bear his children–

A lump wedged in her throat. But she *had* given it all – family, home, friends.

Even so, she should have been the happiest girl in the world. If it weren't for the guilt and the shame, she would have been.

'You have to forgive yourself, Mary,' Jack murmured sleepily, startling her. 'You've done what's right for you, and for our child…'

She held him tighter. He was right, they'd had no other choice. She was truly sorry for the pain she'd caused her family, but it was their child who mattered now.

As she drifted off to sleep, she was smiling. What did the future hold for their child? Happiness, she hoped. Good health and happiness.

It would be a November baby. Together, she and the baby would discover Chicago in November. It had been hot and humid for the last couple of weeks, but from what she'd heard, few folk ventured outdoors in the winter, when the temperature was well below zero and the wind almost knocked a person off their feet.

Oh, but it would be a magical Christmas…

'Mary!'

Mary woke with a start at the sound of Jack's voice, high with excitement.

When he burst into the bedroom, she wasn't sure which surprised her most – the fact that it was already morning when she felt as if she'd only been asleep for a few minutes, or the huge smile on Jack's face.

'What's happened?' she asked, sitting up.

'A letter from China!'

'What?' Mary grabbed the envelope from his hand. 'It's from Ishbel!'

Tears blurred the wonderfully familiar

sight of her sister's handwriting.

'Oh, Jack! She hasn't abandoned me after all!'

'This is the first time I've been out of Shanghai since we arrived,' Ishbel remarked. 'I can't tell you how grateful I am for your company, Adam.'

'I'm just as grateful for yours.' The Chens' American accountant smiled at her. 'I have to inspect the tea plantation so it was only a matter of choosing the right date.

'Besides,' he added, 'I knew Gordon would feel much happier if you had company.'

Ishbel smiled back. She stared out of the window at rows of houses, and tried to think of something that had showed her Gordon was concerned for her safety.

'Take care,' he'd said. 'There are all sorts of problems out in the country.'

And that had been it.

Ishbel knew that bandits lurked in remote places. When you lived in a country caught up in civil war, there were bound to be problems.

It would have been nice, she decided grimly, if he'd remembered that today was her birthday...

Perhaps when she returned to Shanghai, he would be more – what? Interested in her? Was it that he took her for granted?

'You're frowning.' Adam's voice broke into her thoughts.

'Sorry.' She smiled at him. 'I was miles away.'

'Thinking of your family?' he asked curiously.

'No.' Her smiled faded.

'I gather there are problems,' Adam said quietly. 'Gordon said as much.'

Did he indeed! What right did he have to broadcast her problems to the world?

'Did he tell you about Mary?' Ishbel asked sharply.

'No – he simply hinted that there were problems.'

Ishbel had confided in Jane, who'd been sympathetic and understanding, and in Gordon, who hadn't. Perhaps it would be good to talk to Adam...

'My sister became friendly with a man called Jack Keller,' she began. 'I don't know him, but he's a bit of a character by all accounts. Probably a crook.' Her self-conscious smile belied her worries. 'She fell in love, and then discovered he was divorced.'

'Oh, dear.' Adam nodded his understanding. 'That won't be popular with your parents. So what's happening? Is she refusing to give him up, or what?'

'It's worse than that. Much worse.' Ishbel realised her hands were shaking, and made a play of straightening her skirt. 'She's having his child.'

Adam winced.

'She's taken off to America with him – they're living in Chicago. She's married him.'

'Good heavens!' Adam took a few moments to digest this. 'What do your parents think about it?'

'I'm sure you can imagine,' she replied with a sigh. 'My father is furious – deeply hurt and upset, but furious all the same. I mean, for a man in his position–'

'And your mother?'

'Distraught,' Ishbel said simply.

'What did Mary do? Leave a note and sail to America?'

'No. She and Jack told them their plans.'

'That took courage.'

'Yes.' She was surprised that, like her, he'd thought of that. 'The result was the same, though. My father has disowned her, forbidden my mother to contact her. It's all very–' she paused to think '–sad.'

Ishbel hadn't been able to believe such things of her young sister, but when the shock had worn off the whole situation had saddened her.

'I had a letter from my mother telling me what had happened,' she told Adam, 'and then one from Mary. My mother sounded sick with worry, and Mary was trying to convince me, or herself, that everything was fine. They both sounded desperately un-

240

happy, though.'

And no wonder. The family was disintegrating before their eyes, and poor Mary was living in a strange city with no family, no friends...

Ishbel hadn't known what to say to Mary, but nothing would be gained by lecturing. What was done was done, and nothing Ishbel could say or do could alter it.

In the end, she'd tried to reassure her sister that time would help, and faith would help. She'd made sure Mary knew that her thoughts and her love were with her...

'It is sad.' Adam reached for her hand and gave it a quick squeeze. 'I'm so sorry, Ishbel.'

'Thank you.'

For some reason, his quiet concern brought foolish tears to her eyes. How different his reaction had been from Gordon's. Gordon had been almost as angry as her father must be, and she'd never forget what he'd called Mary...

'When I get some leave,' Adam said suddenly, 'I must make a point of visiting your sister and her husband.'

'Oh, Adam, that would be wonderful!'

'Don't get too excited,' he warned her with a smile. 'I'm not due leave for another six months.'

'But even so, Mary would love to see you if you could manage it. She must be feeling very lost and lonely... She and her husband, of course, and in November, she'll have a child, but–' She shook her head. 'Mary with a child! Heaven help us. It doesn't seem possible.'

'How old is she? Nineteen?'

'Yes.' Ishbel smiled suddenly. 'But she'll always be about twelve in my eyes.'

She felt better for having talked to Adam. Suddenly it all seemed more acceptable.

Her heart ached for her sister but, with God's help, it would all come right in the end.

And the best of it was that Father hadn't forbidden her to mention her sister, so she could easily pop news of Mary into the letters she sent to her parents.

Yes, she felt much better.

The train jerked to a stop, and she looked questioningly at Adam.

'Don't worry,' he said. 'It always stops here, and I've never yet understood why.'

A couple of minutes later, they were on their way again.

'Are you being met?' he asked.

'Yes.' She nodded. 'Actually, I'm quite excited about it. I'll only be there for twelve weeks, as a stand-in, but a new school is being set up and they want someone with experience to help. There's already a hospital not far away, but this is more in my field. I'm looking forward to seeing how the villagers live.'

'Very differently,' Adam said. 'Give me Shanghai any day!'

Ishbel laughed as he gazed with disdain at the Chinese countryside.

'I'm so glad you're with me, Adam,' she said again. 'I would have hated making this journey alone.'

'So am I.' He gave her hand another squeeze and, this time, he didn't release it.

All afternoon, Jane Terry had been convinced that Edward had things on his mind, and now she was really beginning to worry.

They were strolling along the Bund, Shanghai's grand seven-mile curl of waterfront. Teddy was walking between them, his hand in his father's as he listened intently to his stories.

'The Bund was originally a towpath. Can you imagine all the coolies pulling the Emperor's rice tribute along it?'

It amazed Jane that their son was almost three now, but she often felt Edward treated him as if he were older.

Perhaps that was a good thing. Teddy adored his father and was, as usual, hanging on Edward's every word.

'Shall we go back?' Edward asked her.

'Yes, of course.'

It was still early. Jane was disappointed – she would have preferred to carry on walking.

Edward wasn't his usual self today, quiet and preoccupied. Jane only hoped he had business matters on his mind.

They'd been getting along so well lately, too. In unguarded moments, she had almost been able to believe that Edward's feelings for her were the same as hers for him.

She'd imagined herself in love when they first met in England. Their time together had been so brief, though – she'd managed to put it down to spring madness.

As soon as she'd seen him again, it had all come flooding back – the strength of her feelings for him, the love she felt for his son...

He hadn't mentioned Claire for months, and Jane didn't want to ask in case she heard something she didn't like.

She felt for the woman Edward had been engaged to, but she couldn't bear the thought of anything or anyone coming between herself and Edward...

Back at the mission, Edward looked even more agitated. Finally, Jane had to ask.

'Is something wrong?'

'No, but I would like to talk to you, Jane.'

'Oh?' Her heart sank as she led the way into the sitting-room.

For a few minutes, Edward seemed happy enough to play with Teddy. His love for the boy and his pride were there to see.

Could he contemplate a life that didn't

include Teddy? Even if his feelings for her weren't as strong as she hoped, surely he wouldn't abandon his son?

An even worse fear gripped her. What if he wanted to take Teddy away from her – to marry Claire, and let her bring up their son?

'You wanted to talk, Edward?' Her voice was shrill with panic, but he didn't seem to notice.

'Yes.' He put Teddy down and faced her. 'As you know, Jane, when I visited England, I saw Claire.'

She nodded, but couldn't speak.

'I explained the situation here–' He broke off. 'I ended the engagement. When I returned,' he went on, leaving her no time to digest this, 'I planned to suggest that we marry – mainly for Teddy's sake.'

'I see.' Her mouth was painfully dry. 'Why didn't you?'

'Because my feelings were changing,' he said frankly. 'Even if Teddy wasn't here, I would still want to marry you. I've fallen in love with you, Jane.'

'Oh!' Jane's head flew up, and she hurled her arms around him in a most undignified manner. 'Edward – yes! If that was a proposal, I accept!'

She was thrilled to see the relief in his eyes as he held her close.

'I know we've had a bad start,' he said softly, 'but I can make you happy, darling –

I know I can.'

'I know it, too, Edward. I'll be a good wife to you, I promise you that.'

Teddy was tugging at his father's leg, demanding to know what was happening.

'Your mother and I are going to be married very soon,' Edward told him.

Jane liked that 'very soon'.

'You'll both come and live with me.' Edward picked him up and held him high. 'Won't that be wonderful? We'll see each other every day...'

Jane hadn't thought of leaving the mission, the only home she knew. Edward, she felt sure, would want her to carry on her work here.

She'd have a husband, a child and a home to care for, but she would still be able to find time for the mission.

'Mummy and Daddy are getting married!' Teddy announced as Gordon came into the sitting-room.

Gordon's face lit up, and he was soon shaking Edward's hand and showering them with congratulations and best wishes.

'Could you conduct the ceremony, Gordon?' Edward asked.

'I'd consider it an honour. I imagine you want to marry as soon as possible? Shall we say three weeks on Saturday? That's enough time for the banns.'

'Perfect!' Edward declared. 'Jane?'

'Yes – perfect!' She smiled at them both.

When Edward had long gone and Teddy was tucked up in bed, Jane realised why a shadow had fallen over her happiness.

She wanted nothing more than to marry Edward; it was a dream come true. But what about Ishbel?

Ishbel was the best friend she'd ever had. In fact, if it hadn't been for the way Ishbel had befriended her on the journey to Shanghai, she might never have found Edward.

It simply wouldn't feel right to get married when Ishbel was miles away in the north of the country. And how would Ishbel feel about it?

Moira Kerr felt every one of her seventy-seven years as she climbed out of bed. She pulled back the curtains and saw that already it looked set to be another scorching summer day.

As she gazed at the familiar view from her window, she ran a hand over her chest. All her life, she'd been blessed with good health, but this morning, she felt ill.

She hadn't slept well, though, so perhaps that was all it was. In truth, she hadn't slept well for the last few nights.

The heat didn't help. Her south-facing bedroom was usually a delight, but last night, she had felt as if she was being stifled.

Every time she'd closed her eyes, that

scene in Princes Street Gardens had come back to her. She would never forget the day she had seen her granddaughter kissing Jack Keller, in full view of anyone who cared to look.

At the time, Moira thought she had acted wisely. She'd had very stern words with Mary, and had been satisfied that her granddaughter was contrite.

Moira hadn't thought it necessary to trouble the girl's parents with it. They'd had far too much on their minds, and she'd wanted nothing to mar Veronica's joy at having Robbie home again.

It had been a fatal mistake. She should have done something to put an end to the nonsense between Mary and that awful Jack Keller.

'Oh, John. What would you have done?' she whispered. Her husband was still so much a part of her life.

John couldn't have loved his grandchildren more, and he would have been quick to put Mary's behaviour down to youthful high spirits – just as Moira had.

Mary had always been a self-willed child, and she was for ever clashing with her father, but Moira still couldn't believe how her granddaughter had behaved.

That she could form a friendship with Jack Keller, conceive his child, and then take off to America with him!

It took a lot to reduce Moira Kerr to tears, but this had, several times.

She went downstairs, walking more slowly than usual, and stopping once until a sudden dizzy spell cleared, to put the kettle on. A hot drink was sure to make her feel better.

She was sitting drinking it when her gaze fell on Mary's letter from America. There was no need to read it; she'd read it more than enough times since it had arrived to know it by heart.

The letter had been full of facts – details of the sailing to America, stark details of the wedding ceremony, a plan of their apartment in Chicago. There had been no remorse, no hint of shame.

It had ended with four simple words.

Please forgive me, Gran.

What was she to do? Moira had asked herself that question at least fifty times a day since the letter had arrived.

There was no question of discussing the matter with Donald. Nor with Veronica, either – her daughter had no choice but to obey her husband.

If Moira replied to Mary's letter, she would feel as if she had betrayed her daughter and son-in-law. If she didn't reply, she would feel as if she had betrayed her granddaughter.

More importantly, she would feel as if she had betrayed her faith. Forgiveness …

wasn't that what it was all about?

Mary had let them all down, and herself too, but–

Moira ran a hand across her chest again.

'John, I'm feeling like an old, done woman today. Help me get to grips with this,' she murmured.

As Veronica blinked at the sizzle of bacon in the pan, she thanked the Lord it was Ivy's day off. At least she'd have the maid's work to do to pass the hours.

There was plenty to do. Helen Chen and her daughter would be arriving any day, so there were preparations to be made.

She's a lovely woman, Ishbel had written, *and I know the two of you will get on well.*

Veronica hoped so, and she should have been longing to meet Mrs Chen, and hear news of her daughter. But now, she found it a struggle to face anyone.

'That smells good,' Donald announced in his usual falsely hearty manner.

He wrinkled his nose appreciatively at the smell of bacon, but Veronica knew neither of them would eat more than a couple of mouthfuls.

He was trying to make life as normal as possible. The problem was, it couldn't be normal. How could it, when Veronica daren't mention Mary, and Donald refused to?

She busied herself with breakfast. Sometimes it didn't pay to think, and certainly not now, when she wasn't sure of anything, except that her heart was breaking.

For instance, she thought, looking at Donald, sitting opposite, breaking into his egg, did she still love her husband?

The thought had come from nowhere and it shocked her.

She watched him as he made a show of eating, and wondered what had happened to them. Why did she feel no rush of love as she looked at him?

If she felt anything it was pity.

A couple of days after Mary left, Donald had broken down completely. It was the first time she had ever seen him cry, and the sight had torn at her heart.

She thanked God Mary wasn't there to witness it.

'Where did we go wrong?' he'd asked that night, over and over again.

She'd had no answer to the question she'd asked herself countless times, but she'd sympathised.

The shame for a man in his position was immeasurable. Veronica admired the way Donald could still stand in his pulpit, despite the gossip and unkind talk that was rife among his congregation.

It was all show, she knew that, but at least he was facing up to it all.

There was a world of difference between

pity and love, just as there was a world of difference between admiration and love.

She turned her thoughts to Helen Chen. Veronica couldn't imagine having to watch her daughter marry a man chosen by her husband.

What if she'd had to watch Ishbel or Mary vow to spend her life with a man Donald had forced them to marry?

In Mary's case, Donald couldn't have chosen anyone less suitable ... but still.

Helen Chen, faced with having to go on living with Sun, had taken their younger daughter and sailed for England. Of course, in Helen's case money was no object.

Veronica hadn't the remotest idea how much it cost to sail to America – a fortune, she imagined. But even if she had the means, would she – could she – defy Donald and book a place on that ship?

Helen Chen had sailed with her husband's blessing – something Veronica would never be able to do...

'You're very quiet,' Donald remarked. 'What are you thinking about?'

'I was thinking about Mary,' she admitted.

'Hmm.' He continued to eat.

Was that how it was going to be for the rest of their lives? If anyone so much as mentioned Mary's name, they would be ignored?

'I was thinking about Mary,' she repeated, 'and wondering whether, if I could afford it,

I would sail to America to see her.'

Donald stopped eating and stared at her in amazement. Even Veronica was shocked at her boldness. But hadn't they always valued honesty in their relationship?

'You would not!' Donald retorted. 'I would forbid it!'

'I'm going to write to her.' Her voice shook, but her resolve didn't. 'I remember what it's like to be expecting a first child – it's frightening. And for a slip of a girl like–'

'You will not write to her.' Donald's voice was frighteningly low.

'I'm sorry, Donald, but I'm going to. I'm her mother! I can't turn my back on her, no matter what she's done. I just can't do it. I couldn't live with myself if I did that.'

Donald rose to his feet.

'No!'

'I'm sorry,' Veronica said again.

She was sorry – sorry for Donald, and for the mess they were in – but she had to write to Mary.

'I won't allow it, Veronica.' His face was red with anger. 'Mary knew what she was doing. She's made her bed and now she must lie in it, no matter how uncomfortable it becomes.'

'But if–'

'No, Veronica!' Donald banged his fist down on the kitchen table. 'I will listen to no more on the subject. As far as I'm concerned, she's no daughter of mine.'

'Don't you ever say that to me again, Donald Montrose!' Veronica shouted. 'I've gone along with your views all my life, and where has it got me?

'I've one daughter in China, another in America, and a son who's desperate to sail off to heaven knows where with the Merchant Navy. I've had enough, Donald–'

She broke off as she heard someone knocking on the door. Whoever it was must have heard them shouting at the top of their voices, but Veronica was past caring.

With an icy look in Donald's direction, she went to answer it.

'Betty?' She was surprised, and slightly anxious, to see her mother's friend and neighbour standing on the step. 'Come away in.'

Betty didn't move.

'Veronica – it's your mother. I'm terribly sorry, but – when I called on her early this morning, I found her collapsed on the floor. She's at the Infirmary.'

Chapter Twelve

August 18, 1923. Land is in sight, Ishbel wrote in her diary. It was no use; her thoughts and emotions were too mixed. She'd just celebrated her birthday, and she was on her first furlough. It was so long since she'd seen Britain – it was bound to be an emotional time.

She blotted the ink and closed the book. There would be plenty of time to record her feelings later...

A crowd was beginning to gather on deck, impatient for the first glimpse of Southampton. Ishbel spotted Adam and made her way across to him.

'That sight must warm your heart,' he said, smiling.

'It does. But seeing Scotland will be even better!'

'It's been a long time.'

'Three years.' She nodded.

It was difficult to take in all that had happened during those years. One thing was certain, the family she'd left behind had been very different from the one she was going home to.

Robbie had run away from home and had all sorts of adventures, including being hours away from boarding a ship bound for Shanghai.

Mary, now married to Jack Keller, was living what sounded a luxurious life in Chicago.

And Gran – Ishbel bit her lip.

Gran had managed to survive two heart attacks, but Ishbel had no idea what news awaited her in Edinburgh.

One thing was certain, Moira Kerr was no longer the woman she'd once been.

'It sounds ridiculous,' she confided to Adam, 'but I'm almost frightened to go home. I so wish I was going home to the family I left!

'I can't wait to see Robbie again, but Mary's no longer there, my grandmother's in poor health, and my parents...'

Her voice trailed away. She had no idea how she would find her parents. Reading between the lines, relations between the two these days were very, very strained.

'I always feel a little strange as I'm going home.' Adam didn't press her to finish the sentence. 'I dwell on all that's changed since I've been away, and long for things to be as they were.'

'That's exactly how I feel,' Ishbel said eagerly.

'I suppose none of us welcomes change. But when I get home, it's always wonderful!' He smiled. 'It's just as I remember it – as if I'd never been away.'

Ishbel couldn't imagine feeling as if she'd never been away.

'It's a pity Gordon isn't sharing it with you,' Adam murmured.

'Yes.' Ishbel gave him her brightest smile. 'But he'll be joining us in a month or so.'

That still hurt. Ishbel hadn't been able to believe it when Gordon had said he wouldn't be travelling with her after all. She appreciated the amount of work that needed doing, but long after she and Gordon had left China, there would still be work to be done.

That was how it seemed to be with Gordon, though. Just as she thought their relationship was finally on an even keel, he did something that, to Ishbel at any rate, was completely out of character.

She'd been hurt beyond words when she heard Gordon had conducted Jane Terry's wedding to Edward Clements while she was still away, working in the village.

But that was childish, too. It had upset Jane, Ishbel knew, but for the sake of wee Teddy, the wedding couldn't have taken place too soon.

Edward and Jane were blissfully happy together, and that was the main thing. At least Jane's story had the traditional happy ending.

Ishbel missed Gordon terribly, though. She had so wanted them to travel home together, to catch sight of Scotland at the same time…

'Never mind.' Adam was grinning at her. 'Gordon's loss is my gain.'

'It's kind of you to say so.' Ishbel was used to his flattery, and took little notice of it.

'It's a pity your sister won't be there to meet you though,' he said softly. 'She must miss you terribly.'

'I miss her, too.' Again, Ishbel forced her brightest smile on her face. 'Tell me how she was when you saw her, when you were on leave.'

'Again?' He laughed. 'I've given you every detail time and time again!'

'Again, please.'

'She's very happy,' he said easily. 'And I still haven't got over the wonderful welcome she and Jack gave me. I'd booked into a hotel for one night, but they would have none of it. I ended up staying with them for almost a week. Oh, and did I tell you that I'm in love with your niece?'

'Only a couple of dozen times.' Ishbel chuckled. 'But tell me again. What does she look like, Adam?'

'Alice looks beautiful. There's a little of you in her – the eyes, I think – and yet she's the image of her father. You have the photographs, Ishbel.'

'I know, and I'm truly grateful for those, but it's not the same.' Ishbel's voice was wistful. 'It's not the same as being able to hold her, and watched her face.'

'True. Take my word for it – she's amazing. Jack is totally besotted with her! He can't do enough for either of the women in his life.'

'I still find that hard to believe.' Smiling, Ishbel shook her head. 'My little sister married, and to a man like Jack Keller, at that! Mind you, he must have his work cut out,' she finished with a laugh. 'Mary is very strong-minded.'

'She's also very much in love with her husband.'

Ishbel was pleased to hear him say that.

'I'm glad I've had your company on this trip, Adam,' she said, gazing up at him. 'It would have been awful to come over alone.'

'I've been glad of your company, too, but then I always am.'

'Thank you.'

'You'll have a wonderful time at home. You'll see.' He frowned for a moment. 'I only hope my own trip is successful.'

'So do I, Adam.'

Adam was making a business trip to Britain on behalf of Sun Chen and Company, but he'd also been given the task of escorting Sun's wife and daughter back to Shanghai.

That Helen could stay away from her husband and elder daughter for over a year was something else that Ishbel found difficult to understand.

Liang missed her mother, especially now that she was expecting a child, and it was clear to all who knew him that Sun missed his wife. He hadn't said much on the subject, but Ishbel recognised the pain and loneliness in his eyes.

Three times Helen had said she was returning to Shanghai, and three times she had changed her mind.

'I do wish Mr Chen had come himself,' Ishbel said. 'It would have meant so much to Helen if he'd come to take her and Mei Li home.'

Adam leaned on the rails and gazed down at the water below them.

'I think it's a matter of pride,' he said at last.

'I'm sure you're right, but that only makes it worse. And how has Helen managed to stay away for so long?' Ishbel asked. 'You'd think Liang's pregnancy would have sent her back to Shanghai in record time.'

'You would. I only hope she doesn't change her mind about going home again.' He shrugged.

'Not that there's anything I can do about it. I'll have to cross that bridge if and when I come to it...'

As Ishbel handed her grandmother yet another photograph of Alice Moira Keller, she felt that painful lump wedge itself in her throat again.

Adam had been wrong. Instead of feeling as if she'd never been away, she felt as if she'd been gone a lifetime.

Her grandmother, propped up in her chair, was a pale echo of her former self. It was sad to see her here at the manse, as Moira had fought so hard to stay in her own home.

She'd had no choice, though. The days when Gran could take care of herself were gone.

'You're honoured, Gran,' Ishbel said, smiling gently. 'Alice Moira, no less.'

'Aye.' Moira wasn't impressed. 'That'll be Mary's way of trying to get back into my good books!'

Ishbel had to smile. Gran might look old and frail, but her mind was as sharp as ever.

'It's a lovely name, though,' Ishbel remarked. 'Although I still can't imagine our Mary with a baby of her own.'

She held her grandmother's hand in her own.

'I'm glad you keep in touch with her, Gran. I know it means a lot to her.'

'What else was I to do, Ishbel? I can't turn my back on my granddaughter – no matter how she's behaved.'

'I know.' Ishbel sighed. 'I just wish Father would–'

'It's very difficult for him, love,' her grandmother said gently. 'Apart from the hurt we all felt, your father has had to carry a great burden of shame with him. People can be cruel, Ishbel, and his congregation expect better. Aye, and his colleagues, too.'

'I know.'

'It's worst for your mother, though,' Moira said quietly. 'You bairns have been her whole life. It breaks her heart to have you girls on the other side of the world.'

'But it could be so much better, Gran! Mary's husband is a rich man. Mary could easily come over to visit you all...'

'Your father will never allow it.'

Ishbel knew that, too.

'I'll go and make that cup of tea we promised ourselves an hour ago,' she said with a false brightness.

'Your mum won't write, you know,' Moira said suddenly, stopping her in her tracks. 'She was going to – I gather she and your father had words about it the day I had my first heart attack. She was going to defy your father. Then she decided that it was God's way of telling her–' She broke off. 'She won't write.'

Ishbel returned to her chair by her grandmother's side.

'Nothing's ever said,' Moira went on. 'I write to Mary, and Mary writes back. I leave the letters lying around for your mum to read. Oh, Ishbel, love, what a mess!' There was a mute appeal in her eyes. 'Will you talk to them?'

'And what can I say, Gran? What notice will Father take of me?'

'If you don't speak, you'll never know.' Moira patted her granddaughter's hand. 'Now – about that cup of tea?'

If a lot had changed at the manse, a lot had stayed the same. Ishbel could have found her way around the kitchen blindfolded.

Her parents were out, and it was Ivy's day off, but Ishbel would have no trouble making lunch for herself and her grandmother.

She could find her way around this kitchen more easily than she could at the mission.

When she carried the tea and biscuits into her Gran's bedroom, she found her looking brighter.

'So tell me all about life in Shanghai.' Gran's eagerness belied her frailty. 'And that village – is the school running well now?'

'It is.' Ishbel smiled as she poured out. 'It's early days, of course, but the signs are very promising. Gosh, the conditions are primitive, though. We've been spoiled in Shanghai. I told you about the rats?'

She shuddered at the memory of finding the rat in her bed, then laughed at herself.

'I didn't get another decent night's sleep until I was back in the city!'

Ishbel talked easily about her life and work in China for almost half an hour.

'I'll be wearing you out with all my chatter, Gran.'

'Nonsense! I've been as excited as a child at Christmas, waiting to hear all about it.' Moira's eyes misted. 'I can't tell you how good it is to see you, love.'

'And you, Gran. I've missed you so much. I knew I would, but it's been harder than I imagined.'

The two of them had never needed words, and they needed no more now.

Ishbel knew, though, that she had to make

the most of this visit. She knew – they both did – that it was unlikely she would see her grandmother again. She thanked God that at least she'd been given this time...

'And what about young Robbie?' Moira asked suddenly, chuckling to herself. 'He and Mei Li Chen are as thick as thieves.'

'Are they?' Ishbel had to smile, but when she thought about it, she wasn't too surprised. Robbie and Mei Li were around the same age and they were very alike.

'Oh, yes,' Moira went on. 'When Robbie heard that Mei Li and her mother were spending another week with us before returning to Shanghai, he blushed bright red. Ivy's been teasing the poor lad about it ever since!'

'Then he'll probably be pleased Mei Li's going home.' Ishbel laughed.

'Tell me about Liang.' Moira settled back in her chair. 'When's this baby due? Is she happy, do you think, Ishbel? Really happy?'

And Ishbel settled back to talk away the rest of the morning...

Robbie had never known a week pass so fast. One minute he'd been counting the seconds until Mei Li and her mother arrived in Edinburgh, and the next it was almost over.

Tomorrow, Mei Li and her mother would be leaving for Southampton, to board the ship that would carry them home. How

Robbie wished he were going too!

He and Mei Li were walking back from Waverley Station. Why they'd gone there, when they must have known that the sights of trains and of people saying fond farewells would depress them even more, he had no idea. He just wished they'd gone somewhere else.

They had little to say to each other; they simply walked, lost in their thoughts.

He'd been holding Mei Li's hand but now, as they walked side by side along the main street, he'd had to let it go. Occasionally, her shoulder would brush against his.

'I can't bear this.' Mei Li stopped, tugged on his sleeve and looked into his face. 'I really can't bear it.'

'Me neither. But it won't be for ever,' he reminded her. 'As soon as I'm able, I'll get to Shanghai. Meanwhile—'

'Meanwhile, my father will have married me off to some hateful man,' Mei Li said urgently. 'And I know that, just like Liang, I'll have no choice.'

'He can't,' Robbie said blankly.

'He will, Rob! He will!' She grasped his hands.

'I'm eighteen. Believe me, he'll already be looking for a suitable husband for me. Within the next twelve months, I'll be married.'

'You're far too young—'

'But that's just it, I'm not!' She looked as

if she was going to go into one of her sulks. 'Are you? Too young, I mean?'

Robbie knew he was. Much too young to think about marriage. He was training for the Merchant Navy – the last thing he needed was the responsibility of a wife and family...

'We both are,' he said quietly and, he hoped, firmly.

'You know I'd marry you tomorrow if it were possible.'

People would say he was mad, he knew, but he had been instantly and totally captivated by those beautiful Oriental eyes and that defiant smile.

He could remember every detail of that first meeting. The family had all been listening to Helen Chen talking about Shanghai, her husband, and her married daughter.

Mei Li had looked more bored by the minute. He'd thought her rude and spoilt, but part of him had also found her attitude vaguely amusing.

Since that meeting, he'd fallen in love with her spirit, her wildness, her passion for life, her sense of fun, her intelligence – everything that was Mei Li.

'Robbie, listen–' Her eyes were alight with excitement. 'Why don't we run away? By the time anyone notices, that ship will have long gone!'

'No!' He'd spoken too sharply, but he didn't want her planting the tiniest seed in his mind.

'No,' he said again. 'I won't even consider that, Mei Li. I've seen what it did to my parents. I've seen what Mary has done to them.'

'But this is different,' she argued.

'It's not. It's exactly the same.' He pulled her towards him, not caring who might spot them in the street.

'I promise I'll come to Shanghai for you – you have my word on that. But this time, I'm going to do things right.'

'Fine!' With a toss of her head, she began marching away from him.

'What's that supposed to mean?' he demanded when he caught her up.

'You say you love me, but it means nothing, does it? The prospect of not seeing each other for months – years – doesn't worry you at all!'

'Not true – but I could say the same for you,' he retorted. 'You say you love me and yet you can't even wait for me!'

They walked back towards the manse at a breakneck pace. Eventually, Robbie reached for her hand to slow her down, and saw the tears in her eyes.

'Mei Li, don't,' he said gently. 'Let's not fight. I love you. You mean everything to me, you know you do. But, for your sake, for my sake and for our families' sakes, we're going to do it right.'

Her tears spilled over and Robbie wiped

them away with his fingers.

'One day, we'll be together. I promise you that...'

Gordon Campbell felt chilled. The weather in Shanghai wasn't particularly cold, but it had rained all day. Three times, he'd been soaked to the skin. He wasn't entirely sure the weather was responsible for the chill in his bones, though.

'I had a letter from Ishbel yesterday.' Jane smiled at him across her dinner table. 'I'll show it to you when we've eaten.'

'Thank you. Is she still keeping busy? But I'm sure she is. It must be very rewarding for her to be able to help her father. In fact,' he added lightly, 'she seems busier than ever.'

'Will you–?' Jane hesitated. 'Will you manage to get home before she leaves, Gordon?'

'I hope so.' Unable to think of anything else to say, Gordon changed the subject.

'This is so kind of you, Jane. All these invitations to dinner, I mean.'

'It's nothing.' She coloured slightly. 'You know how much Edward enjoys your company – as I do, of course. And I enjoy cooking.'

It was difficult to equate this happy, confident young woman who ran her home so efficiently with the awkward girl that he and Ishbel had met on that long journey to Shanghai.

Under Edward's love and care, Jane had blossomed. They were such a happy, devoted couple; it was always a joy to be their guests.

Jane was still helping at the mission, of course, yet without Ishbel, it was—

Gordon had been thinking that it was a lonely place, but that was absurd. He was rarely alone – in the spiritual sense, never alone.

And yet, without Ishbel, he often felt—

He missed Ishbel desperately. He wished he was in Edinburgh with her. But what kept him in Shanghai was the knowledge that if he went home, Ishbel would expect him to make his intentions clear.

Most of the time, Gordon had no doubts about the future. If Ishbel accepted his proposal of marriage, he would be the happiest man alive.

So what was keeping him in Shanghai when he could so easily be by her side? If he could only answer that...

Gordon was relieved when dinner was served. Edward and Jane were easy companions. Conversation flowed effortlessly, pushing the unanswered questions to the back of his mind for a while.

Jane seemed tireless. Her day was devoted to Edward and Teddy, and their home, but the hours she put in at the mission were invaluable.

Perhaps because she had a child of her

own, she seemed to win the little ones' confidence more easily than either Ishbel or himself. Gordon often wondered how they would cope without her.

Jane had a gift for languages, as well. Gordon had never learned languages easily, but Jane seemed to hear a word once, and it was firmly in her mind.

Jane's house was always spotless, but the furnishings, the small touches, made it such a welcoming home.

Normally, Gordon wouldn't notice such things, but it was a pleasure to relax in such comfortable surroundings.

Just as Jane thrived under Edward's devotion, so did Teddy. A sturdy four-year-old now, he was a delight to his parents.

Gordon had imagine young Teddy would have had a brother or sister by now. He suspected Jane had hoped for it, too. There was plenty of time, though.

'Let me show you Ishbel's letter,' Jane said, as soon as she'd cleared away.

Gordon had to smile as he took it from her; from the slightly tattered corners and creases, he knew it had been read and reread, just as his own had.

He found it almost painful to see the familiar handwriting, but it was reassuring to read that Ishbel was in good spirits.

I'm sure Gordon has told you that my grandmother died.

Again, Gordon's heart ached for her. He knew just how much the old lady's passing would sadden her.

It wasn't unexpected, and in many ways it was a happy release. She was far too lively a woman to be confined to her bed. The family misses her dreadfully, of course, but I'm so grateful that God granted me those precious days with her...

Gordon handed the letter back to Jane.

'Good to hear she's keeping busy,' he murmured.

The evening was over all too soon, and Gordon walked slowly, thoughtfully, back to the mission. It had stopped raining, but he still felt chilled.

There was plenty of work to do, but all he did was wander around, picking up a book only to put it down again. Part of him kept expecting Ishbel to walk into the room.

It was late, almost eleven o'clock, when the visitor arrived. At first, he didn't recognise the young Chinese man, but as he eventually managed to catch and translate the man's words, he realised this was one of Han Hsien's employees.

'Mrs Hsien – she is asking for you. She wants you to pray for her child.'

Liang!

'I'll get my coat,' Gordon said at once. Even as he reached for it, he was already praying.

Liang's son, born a month early and less

than a week old, wasn't expected to live. It was several weeks since Gordon had seen her, but Helen Chen had kept him up to date on the news.

'Three doctors are in attendance,' Helen had told him yesterday, 'but the outlook isn't good, Gordon. If anything happens to this baby, I don't know what Liang will do. The poor girl is almost out of her mind...'

Now Liang had asked for him. What did Han Hsien think of that?

Gordon doubted if Liang's husband approved, but the mere fact she wanted him meant so much to Gordon. If medicine couldn't help her son, Liang was prepared to ask for God's help.

His heart was full as they made the journey to Liang's home. Full of prayer, full of concern for Liang and her child, full of memories...

As long as Gordon lived, he would never forget those few brief minutes when Liang, frightened at the prospect of her marriage, had broken down in his arms.

She'd aroused feelings that Gordon hadn't experienced before or since. Feelings that he couldn't explain...

Ishbel held the two letters in a hand that had started to tremble. Even if she hadn't recognised the handwriting on the envelopes, the Chicago postmark would have told

272

her that they were from her sister.

One was addressed to her parents, the other to herself.

Standing in the hall, she quickly opened her own letter. It was brief and quickly read.

I hope this reaches you before you return to Shanghai. Thank you for letting me know about Gran.

I wish that, like you, I'd been able to be with her before she died. I would have liked to have known if she really forgave me.

I know how much you'll miss her, but as you say, at least you were able to spend a little time with her. I know you'll take comfort from that.

I've written to our parents, but I'm not sure they'll even read the letter. Without Gran, I have no link with home, Ishbel.

The truth behind those words saddened Ishbel.

The rest of the letter was about Jack and baby Alice. Ishbel returned it to the envelope and put it in her skirt pocket. She would read it properly later.

Taking a deep breath, she walked into the dining-room, where her parents were finishing breakfast.

'There's a letter for you.' Her voice shook. 'It's from Mary.'

Seeing her mother's face light up, Ishbel handed it over. But it never reached Veronica's hand.

'No!' Her father snatched it from her,

stood up, tore the letter into four squares and marched across the room to drop the pieces into the wastepaper basket.

'Father, please. You can't do that!'

'Ishbel, do you dare to question my actions?' He rounded on her. 'I shall be in my study!'

The door closed behind him, leaving Ishbel and her mother to stare in horror at the wastepaper basket.

The silence was broken by a sudden choked cry from Ishbel's mother. Then she burst into tears.

Ishbel was by her side in an instant. She put her arm around her mother's shaking shoulders, and wished there was some comfort she could offer. But she was still too shocked by her father's actions.

'Oh, Ishbel–' Her mother wiped the tears from her cheeks. 'Just look at me! And just look at–' she nodded in the direction of her husband's study '–at him!'

She stood up, and took a steadying breath.

'I'll not take this, Ishbel,' she said, her voice even and calm. 'Not now. Not now my mother's in her grave.'

Ishbel hardly dared to breathe as she watched her cross the room to the waste-paper basket, and bend to pick up the four pieces of Mary's letter.

Alert to any sound that might indicate her father was returning to the dining-room,

Ishbel was torn between admiration for her mother, and fear that Father would burst in at any moment.

'Mum, you're upset–'

'Yes.' Veronica nodded. 'Yes, Ishbel, I am.'

She returned to the table and sat down, putting the two pages of Mary's letter on the table like a jigsaw puzzle.

Dry-eyed, and without comment, she read the letter over and over...

Ishbel wondered what Gran would have done, facing an outburst like Father's. One thing was certain, Gran wouldn't have stood there quivering!

'Mum, you have to speak to him.' She tried to keep the frustration from her voice. 'The two of you can't carry on like this.'

'I'll not speak to him!' Her mother was still gazing at Mary's letter.

Ishbel knew what she had to do. If you don't speak, you'll never know, Gran had said...

Quietly, she left the room and walked along the hall to her father's study. She knocked on the door.

'Yes, Ishbel?' Her father's face wore its usual welcoming smile, and that helped enormously.

'Father, I need to talk to you.'

'If it's about–'

'It's about Mary, yes,' she replied firmly.

'Before she died–' Ishbel stopped. She

didn't see any point in bringing Gran's name into this.

'Well, I feel I have to say something, Father. I can't sit back and watch this continue.'

'Sit down, Ishbel.' He gestured to the chair opposite his desk.

'What Mary did was—'

'Unforgivable!' The word came out with a harsh rasp.

'Surely that is for God to judge.' Ishbel's voice was quiet.

Her father's eyebrows rose at that, but he made no comment.

'It isn't up to us to punish Mary,' she continued. 'And it certainly isn't up to us to punish Mum.' She hoped that the word 'us' would help.

'Punish your mother?' His eyebrows had risen even higher now.

'Yes, Father – that's all this is doing. I can understand what you're going through,' she said carefully, 'but please try to imagine what this is doing to Mum. The family means the world to her.

'I'll soon be back in China, Mary's in America, Robbie will be on board a ship – what does she have left? It's breaking her heart.'

She could see from the expression on her father's face, from the deep, deep sadness in his eyes, that it was breaking his heart, too.

'Don't you feel Mary has been punished

sufficiently?' she asked quietly. 'I was lucky, I was able to spend some time with Gran before she died. Mary wasn't. Mary could have come home to visit if only you would have allowed it. Mary has lost her grandmother. Gran never saw her only great-grandchild. And Mum won't see her first grandchild.'

Her father remained silent, and Ishbel pushed her point home.

'You're not only punishing Mary, Father, you're punishing us all. You're punishing me – oh, yes, it hurts me to think of Mary without her family, and it hurts me to think of you and Mum living like this with all the – resentment between you. You're punishing Mum by keeping her away from Mary. You're even punishing your granddaughter. Think of little Alice Moira. What has she done to deserve this? Is she never to see her grandparents? Is she never to know a grandparent's love?'

Ishbel was shocked to see tears well up in her father's eyes. She rose to her feet.

'Please think about what I've said, Father,' she said gently, and walked out.

Chapter Thirteen

Jack wished now that they had stayed at home. Mary could say what she liked, but it was clear she wasn't well tonight.

'It's nothing, Jack,' she'd protested. 'Just a headache.'

But lately, her smile had lacked its usual brightness. This evening, it was very lack-lustre and forced.

Mary had enjoyed her first pregnancy. At the time, Jack had thought he'd never seen a woman look more beautiful. Her eyes had sparkled with vitality, and her face had shone with happiness.

This pregnancy, however, had been different from the start. Sickness had kept her in bed for days at a stretch. That had passed, thank goodness, but she still tired easily.

A nightclub wasn't the place for her, not tonight. Jack had thought it might cheer her up, but he could see now that he'd been wrong.

'Let's take you home,' he suggested, squeezing her hand. 'We'll have an–'

He didn't finish the sentence, for someone stopped at their table.

'So, Jack, this must be your lovely wife!'

Reluctantly, Jack rose to his feet. At the best of times, he hated mixing business with pleasure, and this wasn't the best of times.

He wasn't sure what to make of Al Capone. To look at, the man was nothing out of the ordinary – except for the scars on his face which Jack had heard were the result of an attack in a bar in Brooklyn.

He was a quick, intelligent man, there was no doubt about that, and he had a certain presence, but Jack couldn't quite bring himself to trust him.

'The prettiest name in all the world,' Al was telling Mary as he bent over her hand and kissed it.

'My wife's called Mary, too, you know. Everyone knows her as Mae, but she's a Mary. A beautiful Irish lass.'

As he charmed Mary with talk of his wife and six-year-old son, Jack watched him closely.

He was a contradiction – a strong man, known for his violent temper, yet equally so for his generosity and fairness.

'And how do you like Chicago?' he was asking Mary. 'I've been here for five years now and, after New York, it takes some getting used to.'

'It takes some getting used to after Scotland, too, Mr Capone,' Mary answered with a wry smile.

'May I join you?' Al Capone looked to Jack

for an invitation.

'Of course,' Mary replied.

'We were just leaving,' Jack said at the same time.

Al Capone looked at them both, glanced at their untouched coffees, and laughed.

'In that case, I'll have coffee with you before you leave...'

The man was charm personified. Whether Jack liked him or not was irrelevant – you didn't have to like men you did business with.

Not that Jack would dream of telling Mary he did business with Al Capone. She was far too inquisitive for her own good, always asking questions about how he knew people.

So far, he'd managed to keep his business interests away from Mary, and that was how he intended to go on. Prohibition was doing them all a favour, but Mary wouldn't necessarily see it like that...

'My dear, you're not well,' Al said with concern. 'Jack, I think–'

Jack was already on his feet. Mary was a breath away from fainting.

'The hospital,' he told her firmly.

'Jack, no,' she protested weakly. 'Don't make a fuss.'

'Make a fuss,' Al ordered as he helped Mary to her feet. 'There's nothing more important than our family's health.'

'I feel a little–' But Mary didn't have the

strength to tell them how she felt.

Thanks to Al Capone, who only had to click his fingers, a car was brought round.

Jack couldn't remember feeling more frightened in his life than during the seemingly endless journey to the hospital. Mary's head drooped on his shoulder. By the time they reached the hospital, she was unconscious.

The doctors acted quickly. Mary was taken away and Jack was left to wait. Each second felt like an hour, each minute like a day...

He would never forgive himself if anything happened to Mary. Never!

From the moment he'd first seen her, he'd loved her.

Yet – what had he done for her?

He'd dragged her away from her family, brought her to Chicago, despite knowing how desperately she missed her family and friends.

At the time, it had seemed the right thing to do. But why Chicago? So that he could accumulate even more money?

What use was money? Oh, he could give Mary the best of everything – as soon as this child was born, he'd planned a surprise trip to Shanghai to see her sister.

Yes, he could give her anything she wanted. But he'd give it all away right now, if only Mary could walk through those doors and take him in her gentle, loving arms...

Eventually, after what seemed like days, a doctor came through the doors and walked slowly towards Jack.

'Well?' Jack could see from the expression on the young man's face that the news wasn't good.

'I don't know for sure,' the doctor said. 'At the moment, she's holding her own, but I'm afraid it could be a long night.

'And the baby–'

'Well?' Jack snapped again. 'Will it live?'

He loved his little Alice, the brightest, prettiest two-year-old in the world, with all his heart. But the baby Mary was carrying now – the one who'd made her ill – suddenly meant nothing to Jack.

'I think you should prepare yourself for the worst, Mr Keller.' The doctor wasn't offended by Jack's rudeness. He was kind, and very softly spoken.

'Our main concern is for your wife.'

'Yes. Thank you.' Jack could hardly bear to ask. 'Will she–?'

'We can't say at the moment. I'm sorry. The next twenty-four hours will tell us more.'

'Thank you.'

If he'd tried to say more, Jack would have broken down.

The doctor patted his arm, turned and walked away.

Alice, their joy, had just celebrated her second birthday. She'd be asleep now, lying in her bed with her thumb in her mouth, in the safe hands of the nanny she loved. So innocent – ignorant of what was happening to her mother.

All Jack wanted was Mary. Without Mary, he had no life...

It was rare that Ishbel could spend a whole afternoon with Liang, but when she did, it was a delight. In the four years they'd known each other, Liang hadn't changed at all.

Marriage to Han hadn't changed her, and becoming mother to Zhang hadn't changed her. She still had that shy serenity, that bright, quick mind, and that gentle inner beauty.

'Is Zhang with your mother?' Ishbel was disappointed that the little boy was nowhere in sight.

'I think she's trying to make up for lost time,' Liang said. 'Because he was so ill, she feels–'

Liang didn't need to complete the sentence.

'She's taken Zhang to see her friends today,' Liang went on.

'He's won everyone's heart.' Ishbel smiled. 'I've never seen a man so proud as Han was when Zhang had his first birthday!'

'I'm lucky to have a son.' Smiling, Liang nodded. 'Lucky to have such a good husband, too,' she added quickly.

'Mm.' Ishbel hesitated. To marry a man chosen by your parents – well, Ishbel couldn't imagine a marriage built around such circumstances.

Liang seemed happy, though – as far as she could tell, it wasn't simply that she was grateful to have a kind, considerate and thoughtful husband.

'You and Han–' She didn't want to pry, but she was curious. 'You really are happy, aren't you?'

'Yes.' Liang didn't hesitate. Her smile told her friend it was the truth.

As they sipped the green tea Ishbel had learned to like, much to her surprise, Liang carried on the conversation.

'It isn't the love story of the century, and it never will be, but Han and I get along well. He treats me as an equal. I can talk to him, exchange ideas. We have endless discussions on all sorts of subjects.'

'That's good.'

Ishbel wasn't sure that would suit her, though. Oh, she wanted a man who treated her as an equal, and a companion for the exchange of ideas.

Yes, she wanted trust, respect and friendship. She wanted more, though.

She wanted love. She wanted passion. She wanted Gordon...

'Yet when I say it isn't the love story of the century,' Liang continued, 'I may not be right. I do love Han, in my own way.'

She frowned suddenly.

'I'm worried though, Ishbel.'

'Worried? Why, Liang?'

'Han is having to travel south.'

Ishbel grimaced. Shanghai itself was far from safe at the moment, with the continuing civil war, but conditions in the south were much worse. Only last month, two missionaries had been killed there.

'Do you remember me telling you about the fortune bird?' Liang asked.

'Of course.' Ishbel's eyebrows rose. 'And do you remember me telling you that it was all nonsense?'

'Yes.' Liang flushed. 'So it may be all right, but–'

'But?' Ishbel prompted.

'Twice I've consulted the fortune bird, and twice–'

Ishbel tried to hide her impatience. Liang had such a bright mind, and yet these old superstitions never died.

'Apparently, the time isn't right for making a journey,' Liang told her. 'Twice I've been told that. Twice.'

'Coincidence. Nothing more,' Ishbel said firmly, but Liang was clearly worried.

They talked about other things then, but Ishbel suspected they both had their minds on the dangers down south.

Ishbel was just going to ask more about

Han's trip when Liang's sister suddenly burst into the room.

'Mei Li! What are you doing here?' Liang asked in astonishment. 'No chaperone? Mother said you were at home–'

'Waiting to see our father?' her sister cried. 'Yes, I was. I've seen him all right. Oh, Liang, what am I going to do?'

'How would I know?' Liang asked, quietly and calmly. 'And where are your manners, Mei Li? I have a guest.'

'I know, and I'm sorry. I didn't mean to burst in on you both. I'm sorry, Ishbel.'

'Never mind, Mei Li.'

Whatever had upset her was serious – or serious to Mei Li, who could get upset over trivialities.

'I didn't know where else to go.' Mei Li sat down. 'I ran out of the house – Father will be furious! I had no idea of where I was going...'

'What's happened?' Liang's frown suddenly deepened. 'Oh, no! He's found you a husband, hasn't he?'

Liang's sister nodded.

'There was the most dreadful commotion. Father told me he'd found me a husband and I told him I would rather die. And I would! I told him I'm going to marry Robbie and no-one's going to stop me!'

'Robbie?' Liang asked.

For a moment, Ishbel shared her confusion. She remembered her grandmother telling her how close Robbie and Mei Li had become…

'My brother?' she whispered.

'Yes,' Mei's lively face was a changing tide of emotions. 'Hasn't he said anything to you?'

'No.'

But Ishbel knew she should have guessed. Every single letter she'd had from Robbie had mentioned Mei Li.

'But you can't marry Robbie!' Ishbel said in astonishment. 'I mean, Rob isn't the type—'

'Are you mad?' Liang whispered. 'Father won't allow you to marry a foreigner. You know he won't! If you know nothing else about our father, you know that.'

'It's Robbie or no-one!' Her sister jumped to her feet. 'I have his letters, Ishbel. He's told me he loves me. He's promised to marry me.'

'Mei, do think about this logically.' Ishbel's head was spinning. 'You hardly know Rob, and he hardly knows you. Your father won't allow such a marriage – mine won't, either. You just have to forget about marrying my brother. It can't happen!'

'Ishbel's right,' Liang said gently.

'I knew I shouldn't have come here! I'll marry Robbie. Believe me, I'll marry him!'

Before either of them could argue, Liang's sister had left the room as quickly and noisily as she'd entered it.

'I'm terribly sorry, Ishbel.' Liang rose to her feet. 'I'll order more tea.'

Ishbel was grateful to be left alone for a few moments, to recover her composure.

Mei Li and Robbie? Whatever had Robbie said to her? Could Robbie actually be in love with this headstrong Chinese girl?

Ishbel hoped it was a fantasy dreamed up by a girl determined to shock her parents, and to rebel against everyone and everything.

Yet she knew that, as soon as she returned to the Mission, she would read all of Robbie's letters again, to see if she could find one that didn't mention Mei Li…

When Liang returned to the room, she looked her usual calm self. She was carrying a long bamboo case.

'Did you know about this?' she asked Ishbel.

'About Mei Li and my brother? Oh, no.' She hadn't known, and she couldn't believe it now. 'Except that, when I went home, my grandmother was laughing about how Ivy, the maid at the manse, was teasing Rob. I remember not being too surprised by their friendship at the time. They're very alike.'

'I knew nothing about it, either,' Liang said. 'That's not surprising, I suppose. My sister doesn't confide in me.' She smiled. 'Unless there's no-one else available, of course. And she certainly won't confide in me if she knows I'll disapprove.' The smile faded.

'I'm so sorry, Ishbel.'

'It's your sister I feel sorry for,' Ishbel said, with a sigh. 'Nothing can come of it. She must know that your father will make her marry the man he's chosen, just as he made you marry Han. We must pray that his choice for her is as acceptable.'

'Yes … but I know exactly how the poor girl feels. It is the most frightening feeling in the world, Ishbel. It's as if your life has been brought to an abrupt end. It's as if—'

But then Liang's maid brought their tea.

As soon as they were left alone, Ishbel nodded at the bamboo case Liang had placed on the table.

'What's that?'

'Kau Chime.' There was a sheepish expression on her face. 'Fortune sticks.'

'Liang!'

'I know. It's just that – with Han having to travel south, and then Mei Li – I just want some confirmation that everything will turn out well, I suppose.'

'Only God can decide the future, Liang,' Ishbel said softly. 'We must trust in God.'

Liang wasn't listening. She was shaking the bamboo case.

Inside were seventy-eight numbered sticks. As she shook it, one stick rose out of the case and fell on to the table.

The stick was cross-referenced to an old text. When Liang had found that, she could read her fortune.

Ishbel could see from the expression on her friend's face that it wasn't what she'd been hoping for.

'It's nonsense, Liang.' Ishbel was struggling to be patient, but she had to admit to a certain amount of curiosity. 'What does it say?'

'It talks of turbulent times ahead. Don't look like that, Ishbel. It's only a bit of fun. And anyway, it's not supposed to predict future events. It simply describes the conditions ahead. Here – see what yours is.'

'I'll do no such thing!'

'Where's the harm?'

'No, Liang!'

Liang had never argued, and the fact that she did now both amused and pleased Ishbel.

These days, they were so close that they were like sisters. It was like having Mary in the room, cajoling and pleading with Ishbel to join in the fun.

In the end, she laughed and gave in.

'Gordon would be horrified if he could see me now!' But she shook the bamboo case.

'It'll be the same as yours,' she said, as a stick began to rise. 'It will come from the centre…'

The stick dropped on to the table, and Ishbel waited while Liang found the appropriate text.

Liang read it, frowning.

'Well?' Ishbel asked.

'It's a bit confusing – they sometimes are. It says that, although you'll get a strange proposal from a strange man, you should pay it no heed. It will mean nothing. It says you must have patience, Ishbel, during the years ahead.'

'A strange proposal from a strange man?' Ishbel stifled her laughter. 'I thought it wasn't supposed to predict events!' She shook her head. 'It's all nonsense.'

'Yes.' Liang put the fortune sticks away.

They talked for almost an hour, but their thoughts were never far from Mei Li's startling news.

That was typical of Liang's sister – she burst into your life, dropped the current bombshell, and left again.

It was only now, as it gradually began to sink in, that Ishbel could think more clearly about all this. And the more she thought, the more she worried.

What would happen when Robert heard about Mei Li's wedding plans?

Ishbel would have to write to her brother. She had to know how Robbie felt, and she had to persuade him to convince Mei Li that they had no future…

Gordon couldn't settle. He'd been looking at his newspaper cuttings about Eric Liddell.

The Scottish papers, naturally enough,

had made a hero of the young Scottish rugby star and runner who'd brought the country glory at the Paris Olympics.

Gordon was fascinated by the story of the young man, born in China as the son of missionary parents.

It must have taken courage for Liddell to stand by his Christian beliefs and withdraw from the Olympic heats held on a Sunday.

His twin sister had sent him the cuttings, but Gordon couldn't concentrate on them. He'd made up his mind now to speak to Ishbel, and he wished that they could get it over with.

He loved Ishbel, truly. When she wasn't with him, he missed her. A smile on her face warmed his heart; a troubled frown saddened him.

Whenever he looked ahead, Ishbel was always by his side, and that was exactly how he wanted it. He wanted to face the challenges ahead with Ishbel.

Only his own stupidity had stopped him asking her to marry him – the memory of that moment from the past when Liang Chen had clung to him and wept like a child.

That moment had haunted him for almost three years. Gordon couldn't even say why it had had such an effect on him. He'd always considered himself a mature, level-headed, practical person – Ishbel would say too level-headed for his own good.

Gordon certainly wasn't foolish enough to believe himself in love with Liang. She had the power to touch his heart – that moment when she'd cried in his arms, the time she'd sent for him when Zhang had been so ill – but that wasn't love.

He barely knew her. They were worlds apart in their beliefs...

'Anyone here?' Ishbel's voice broke into his thoughts, and as always when she came home, Gordon was relieved.

He hated Ishbel being out of the mission at the moment. Shanghai had been fairly safe till now, but last month, the civil war, three years old now, seemed to reach boiling point.

The collapse of the Northern faction's headquarters had left the road to Shanghai open. Thousands of leaderless troops were far too close to the city for safety.

Gordon met Ishbel in the hall. She stood on tiptoe and brushed her ice-cold lips against his cheek.

'Gosh, it's cold out there.' She was shivering. 'Tea?'

'Yes. Thank you.' He followed her to the kitchen. 'How are Liang and the family?'

'Liang is fine, although she's worrying about Han. Apparently, he has to travel to the south on business.'

'That's not good news.'

Gordon could understand the poor girl's concerns only too well. Apart from the political problems, severe floods had also caused devastation. Up to two million people had lost their homes...

'Zhang was with Helen,' Ishbel went on, smiling, 'So I didn't see him. But then Mei Li arrived...'

The more she told him about Mr Chen's plans, the more difficult he found it to believe.

'I can only assume that Robbie really has promised to marry her,' Ishbel finished. 'She wouldn't invent something like that.'

'But surely he knows what your father would say to that?'

'Don't!' Ishbel groaned. 'After Mary and Jack Keller, I can't begin to imagine what it would do to my father. Or Mr Chen, come to that.'

'Indeed.'

'But apart from that, Liang and her family are fine. And Liang sends her regards.'

'Thank you.' He couldn't think about Liang, not now. Gordon found he was actually nervous.

Ishbel stood by the stove and cradled her tea in her hands. She hadn't even taken her coat off.

'You're supposed to be a hardy Scot,' Gordon murmured, amused.

'Here.' He took the cup from her hands, and unfastened the buttons of her thick woollen coat. 'It's not that cold.'

'It's not that warm, either.'

Her laughter touched him. He loved the sparkle that danced in her eyes.

'Ishbel, may we talk?'

'Of course. Is something wrong, Gordon?'

'On the contrary. Ishbel, I'm not one for fancy speeches, but–'

Patience wasn't Ishbel's strongest point.

'I don't want fancy speeches!'

It was just as well. Every carefully rehearsed word was gone from Gordon's mind.

'Ishbel, will you please marry me?'

'Oh!' A hand flew to her mouth, then she was laughing and crying at the same time.

'Yes. Oh, yes!' She threw her arms around him, hugged him tight, then pulled back to look at him again.

'Do you truly love me, Gordon?'

'Yes,' he said at once. 'I truly love you.'

Their kiss was long and sweet.

The manse in Edinburgh was a hive of activity. November always brought preparations for the Christmas bazaar.

It never failed to amaze Donald Montrose that, bearing in mind every unnecessary item in the manse had been donated last year, there could still be so much to sort out.

There was, though. From the sanctuary of his study, Donald could hear his wife and Ruth McKinlay moving things around in the bedroom above him.

At breakfast that morning, Veronica had mentioned sorting out the children's toys.

'Ruth's coming to help me,' she'd said.

'Our youngest child will be nineteen in March,' Donald pointed out, bemused. 'We've donated toys to the church bazaar every year! I can't believe there are any left.'

His wife had given him an icy glare.

'We've plenty. All put by for our grand-children!' She slammed out of the kitchen, almost taking the door off its hinges...

This was impossible. Donald left his sermon notes on the desk and stood by the window, looking out at the bleak garden.

Their only grandchild was two years old now, and not a day passed that Donald didn't picture her.

He'd seen a photograph, one Ishbel had left on her first furlough, but that had told him nothing of young Alice's temperament. It might be as fiery as her mother's ... but Mary was no longer the daughter he remembered.

In the eyes of everyone – except Donald's, and those of the church – she was a married woman with a husband and a daughter. For all he knew, she might have another child by now.

Veronica would know. Mother and daughter had kept in touch by letter ever since Ishbel's visit.

Ishbel's wise words had touched a nerve.

Donald had no right to punish an innocent child.

For all that, Donald couldn't accept what his daughter had done, and he never would be able to.

Donald and Veronica didn't discuss their younger daughter. In fact, Donald acknowledged sadly, they discussed very little these days.

Last night, he'd dreamed of Mary, as he often did. The shame she had brought to the family was usually on his mind as he eventually drifted off to sleep, so perhaps it was only natural.

In last night's dream, she had been no more than five years old. He'd seen her coat, a beige, fur-trimmed one that was probably still somewhere in the manse, as clearly as if she were standing in front of him now, wearing it.

She'd been lying on her back, sliding down a steep snow-covered hill, and she'd been calling out to him. Donald had woken with tears on his face...

This wouldn't do. What he needed was company.

Just watching Veronica and Ruth sorting things out for the bazaar would help. Any sign that life was carrying on as normal would help.

Besides, he liked Ruth McKinlay. He could still remember the day she'd arrived at the manse with her two hungry bairns.

He could remember, too, the flash of anger in Mary's eyes as she'd told him that Ruth was going to clean what they both knew to be an already spotless scullery.

Mary again. His daughter refused to leave his thoughts today...

As he climbed the stairs, he could hear Veronica and Ruth laughing about something. How long had it been since he'd heard his wife laugh? Laughter no longer had a place in his home...

On the landing, he stopped in his tracks. There, standing in the doorway, was a very old, battered, much-loved push-along horse.

It had been Mary's most cherished possession for many years. She'd pushed it round the manse, round the streets–

She'd worn that coat then, the coat from his dream.

They'd walked together, Mary pushing her horse, Donald walking behind, towards her grandmother's house.

It had been wintertime and the snow had been thick. Mary had slipped, and her precious horse had careered into a wall at the bottom of the hill.

Donald had had to scoop her up into his arms, dry her tears, kiss her better and carry her down the hill to where Toby, her precious horse, would be waiting for her.

Fortunately, it had been, and Mary brightened immediately.

'I love you, Daddy!' she'd declared, her arms tight around his neck as she kissed him...

Someone was hammering on the front door. Donald spun around in case Veronica came out of the bedroom and found him with tears pouring down his face.

He met Ivy in the hall, by which time he'd managed to dry his eyes.

'A telegram for Mrs Montrose?' Ivy held it uncertainly, overawed by such a thing.

'Thank you, Ivy.' Donald took it from her hands. 'I'll give it to her.'

He strode upstairs to where Veronica and Ruth were still laughing. The laughter stopped abruptly as he pushed past the old horse and walked into the room.

'There's a telegram for you, Veronica.'

'A telegram?' She took it from him with hands that shook, read it once, and the colour drained from her face.

'Mary ill. Come at once. Fare telegraphed. Jack,' she read aloud.

'No! Oh, no!' Donald hardly recognised the cry that escaped him, but the pain was immeasurable.

Veronica was in his arms in an instant.

'You must go,' Donald told her, his voice hoarse with emotion as he held her close. 'You must go at once, Veronica. Our daughter needs you...'

Chapter Fourteen

'If you had nothing to worry about, Veronica,' Moira Kerr once told her daughter, 'you'd worry about that!' Veronica could hear dear Mum's voice now, and she might have been right, too. But any mother would worry, given these circumstances.

It was no time at all since she'd been on board ship for America, worried out of her mind about her youngest daughter. Jack's telegram had frightened her to death. Her first sight of Mary, a frail echo of the girl who'd driven them all mad at the manse, had frightened her even more. Mary had seemed so frail that Veronica had been frightened to hug her too tightly.

They had hugged, though, and as soon as Mary's health had started to improve, far too slowly for Veronica's liking, it had been wonderful to be together again.

Without the worry of Mary's health hanging over her, it had been a joy to get to know little Alice, the youngest member of the family...

And her journey home had been a pleasure. Veronica had thought she could finally stop worrying.

But now, here she was, in September, 1925, on a train bound for Southampton, to board yet another ship, this time for Shanghai. And she was still worrying!

This should have been a time of great excitement. Not only would she be seeing both her daughters again, but she would also watch her husband conduct Ishbel and Gordon's marriage.

It should have been one of the happiest occasions of her life.

Oh, she was very grateful for the inheritance from her mother that was paying for this trip. They'd all missed Mary's wedding, and it was wonderful to be at Ishbel's.

But – Shanghai! The very mention of the city still made Veronica shudder. How she wished she could persuade Ishbel to come home!

No-one would convince Veronica that it was safe. Only a few days ago they'd heard that anti-British rioters had been shot in the city.

Donald broke into her thoughts.

'It's impossible to open a newspaper these days without seeing Noël Coward's face staring back at you,' he grumbled. 'Whatever's this country coming to?'

Veronica knew he didn't want an answer. Mr Coward's plays, degrading or not, were the last thing on her mind. How Donald could even think about such things at a time like this was beyond her!

He'd be complaining about that Charleston dance next. Any craze that started in America was sure to make its way to Britain, and Donald hated it.

If he knew that Mary was an expert at it he'd be horrified!

And that was another worry. How would Donald be when he met his younger daughter again?

He'd been quick to make sure Veronica caught the first boat to America to be by Mary's side. If anything had happened to his girl, he would never have recovered from it.

But would he be able to unbend enough to show Mary that she was forgiven?

And how would he be with Jack? Would he even speak to the man?

Veronica herself didn't approve of the marriage. How could she? But for all that, she knew without doubt that it was happy. A good, strong marriage that would survive any problems put in its way.

She smiled to herself. Jack's fussing had almost driven her and Mary mad during that visit. He doted on Mary. She was his whole life.

No, Veronica couldn't approve of the way they'd gone about things, but Mary was married to a man who couldn't love her more, which had to be good.

And as for Alice ... to hear Jack talk, you'd think a brighter, prettier girl had never been born, and Veronica was inclined to agree with him. Alice would steal anyone's heart.

She gave a sideways glance at Donald, still engrossed in his newspaper and tutting to himself about Mr Coward's latest interview. Alice would especially steal her grandfather's heart.

'Not much longer now.' He was folding his paper. 'You're becoming a seasoned sailor, my dear.'

'I don't know about that.' She gave him a wan smile. 'I wish it were Ishbel and Gordon making this journey – if only they were being married in Edinburgh! Shanghai's so unsettled at the moment.'

'All the more reason for them both to be there.' Donald gave her hand a reassuring squeeze.

She knew all that, but it didn't stop her wishing Ishbel home.

At least things were better between herself and Donald, though. For the first time since Mary had eloped, they were growing close again.

In fact, she thought with some surprise, they were getting on better than they ever had...

Robbie Montrose sat on the quayside in the blistering Bombay heat and took Betty's letter from his pocket. He'd read it so often he knew it by heart, but it still made him smile.

It was almost six months now since he'd visited Newcastle-upon-Tyne. A twenty-four hour pass had given him time to see the family who had once made him so welcome.

How he'd changed from that young boy who had run away from home!

Everyone had changed, though. His friend Vic, even bigger and taller than Robert remembered, was courting a pretty red-haired Irish lass.

Vic's sister had changed, too. The last time he'd seen Betty, she'd been about to go into service.

These days, she was well thought of at the 'big house', as they called it. She was still as pretty as he remembered, and still had that wicked sense of humour. For all that, she seemed much more grown up.

She'd been courting, too. As far as Robbie could make out, Tom, the gardener's son, had asked her to marry him. For some reason no-one other than Betty seemed to know, she'd stopped seeing him.

According to Vic, their mother had tried to get Betty to talk about it, but his sister was very tight-lipped on the subject. It was unlike Betty...

'You must get lonely on those ships,' she'd said to Robbie. 'I'll write to you now and again if you like.'

'Thanks. I'd like that, Betty.'

They'd been exchanging letters ever since. This one was full of amusing stories about life below stairs, and Robbie felt as if he knew all the household staff in person.

'The next time you visit,' she ended, 'I'll cook you another apple pie. Even better than Ma's, isn't it?'

When they'd sat down to lunch that day, Robbie hadn't been able to believe the apple pie he'd been eating had been made by Betty. She'd been quite insulted.

Funny how he seemed to have a knack for upsetting Betty. He still hadn't forgotten the way she slapped his face that time Vic had inveigled him into kissing her...

He returned the letter to his pocket and sat staring at the horizon. All that time ago, he'd been desperate to get to Shanghai – to Ishbel.

Now, he was even more desperate to get there. He needed to see Mei Li.

When the letter had arrived saying that her father had chosen a husband for her, he hadn't been able to believe it. The concept was completely foreign to Robbie.

The letter had been so typical of Mei Li. Her English was perfect, yet her letter had been so garbled that it made little sense in places. She'd obviously dashed it off in the heat of the moment.

He'd written back immediately, of course,

telling her not to worry. Until he reached Shanghai, she must try to make her father understand that she wouldn't marry the man he'd chosen.

Typically, her reply to that had been downright rude in places. Mei Li had expected him to rush to her side and claim her for his own. She couldn't – or wouldn't – understand that these things took time.

He hated to think of her going through all this on her own, but getting a passage to Shanghai had been far from easy.

After Bombay, he should have been going back home, but he'd managed to wangle a transfer to another ship, bound for China.

He'd had to play on the Captain's compassionate nature by telling him about his sister's illness. Fortunately, the captain, a firm but fair man, had trusted him.

There were times, Robbie thought ruefully, when being a minister's son had its benefits…

But Robbie's ship had been held up in Bombay. Any hopes he'd had of making Ishbel's wedding had been dashed.

Because he'd changed ships, he hadn't heard from Mei Li for a long time. She must have written, just as he'd written to her, but her letters must have missed him.

They would probably be waiting for him in Shanghai!

He felt awful, letting the girl he loved face

all this on her own. How could she persuade her father that her heart lay with a man that he'd never even met? And how would Mr Chen feel about Mei Li marrying a merchant seaman?

The one thing that gave Robbie hope was that Sun Chen had himself married for love…

Mei Li he knew, wanted them to marry immediately, but Robbie preferred to wait. He suspected her father would want that, too.

If Robbie were honest, marriage was the last thing he wanted at this moment. He wanted it in the future, of course, and he couldn't imagine marrying anyone other than Mei Li, but it was too soon.

What could he offer her? He'd be away at sea. What would she do?

The questions went round and round and, as always, no answers came to him. All he knew for sure was that he couldn't wait to get to Shanghai and the girl so close to his heart…

Donald had never felt so emotional in his life. He couldn't stop shaking, couldn't stop his heart racing.

Perhaps it was due to the Shanghai heat, or the change of diet – but he thought it was the way he was feeling.

He would have liked nothing more than to have conducted Ishbel's wedding ceremony in his own church, but the small church in Shanghai, packed to overflowing with the couple's friends and fellow missionaries, was the right place – he knew that now.

That sight alone, the knowledge that so many people had been intent on wishing his daughter and Gordon well, had shaken him.

As had those young Chinese pupils from the mission, marvelling at their teacher's white dress. In the children's eyes, red was the only possible colour for a wedding dress, and they hadn't known quite what to make of Ishbel's white one.

The expression on her face as he pronounced them husband and wife took his breath away, too. Dear Ishbel; he was so proud of her! She couldn't look more beautiful, or more sure of the future and of her faith.

But if the church had been fitting, Donald couldn't say the same for this reception. The King would have felt more at home here than Donald did. Outlandish was the word…

'It's not quite what you'll be used to,' Ishbel had confided to him. 'But it's such a kind gesture on Helen Chen's part that I haven't the heart to appear anything but excited about it…'

It was indeed kind, but a traditional twelve-course Chinese banquet, to Donald's mind, was unnecessary and a little tasteless…

He felt a gentle tug on his trousers and,

looking down, smiled into the eyes of the new light of his life. Together, Alice and her mother, Mary, were certainly responsible for making his heart beat a little faster than was good for him.

Taking Alice's hand in his, he turned. If she was there, her mother couldn't be far behind. Sure enough, Mary was walking towards him.

He felt again that strong urge to open his arms, hold her to him and never let her go. And yet he couldn't do it...

Oh, they'd hugged on first meeting, but the embrace had been stiff and restrained. Onlookers might not have noticed their awkwardness, but he and Mary had been fully aware of it.

It was his fault, he knew – there was a barrier that he couldn't knock down. The truth was, try as he might, he couldn't forgive her.

If Mary had shown any sign of remorse or regret, perhaps he would have been able to forgive her. But she couldn't or wouldn't.

He gave her an awkward smile. She looked tired and too pale, and he felt again that urge to hold her close. With every beat of his heart came the painful knowledge they had almost lost her...

'I'm so glad you were able to conduct the ceremony, Father.' She smiled warmly, if wearily. 'I know how much it means to Ishbel.'

'To me, too.' He tried to match her smile and failed.

Would they ever be able to behave normally with each other again?

Did Mary mean that it would have meant a lot to her if he had conducted her wedding ceremony? That had been her choice. The fact he hadn't married her to a decent, God-fearing lad had broken his heart – and Veronica's.

'Isn't this grand?' Mary was gazing at their opulent surroundings. 'No expense spared. A little out of place perhaps, given some of the sights on the Shanghai streets, but it's Ishbel's choice.' She smiled. 'Or if not Ishbel's, a kind friend's choice. Anyway, I think it will be wonderful for Ishbel to have all this to look back on. The photographs should be wonderful.'

'Yes,' Donald murmured. He was surprised, and gratified, to find that the daughter who'd given his gardening jacket to some needy person on the street was still there, beneath the chic American clothes and styled hair.

'Even Alice is speechless,' Mary went on, smiling indulgently at her daughter. 'And believe me, that is very rare! I'm afraid she takes after her mother in that respect.'

Donald was relieved to be able to focus his attention on the little girl, who couldn't take her eyes off the bride and groom.

'Gordon's very serious, isn't he?' Mary said thoughtfully.

'There's nothing wrong with that,' Donald retaliated, too sharply. 'Marriage is a serious business.'

'Indeed it is,' she agreed, in that dangerously sweet voice he knew of old. 'And I'm sure Ishbel and Gordon will be very happy together. Just as happy as Jack and I are.'

She reached for Alice's hand.

'Come along, sweetheart. Let's go and find Daddy...'

With a huge sadness in his heart, Donald watched them cross the hall.

Jack Keller's face lit up as the little girl was swept into his arms and held high above.

Donald had shaken hands with the man, even thanked him for sending for Veronica when Mary was so ill, but there had been no hint of remorse. In fact, if anything, he had seemed almost proud of himself.

'Good gracious, Donald Montrose!' Veronica appeared at his side. 'You look as if you're about to do battle with the devil himself. And on Ishbel's wedding day, too!'

'I've just been talking to Mary,' he said grimly. 'There's a lot of anger in that girl.'

'There's a lot of anger in you, too, Don. The two of you have always clashed, and I suspect you always will. You're too much alike.'

'But at least I would have managed some

form of apology!'

'I should hope you wouldn't!' Veronica looked around, and went on more quietly. 'I hope the day never comes when a daughter of mine has to apologise for falling in love. Look over there – would you expect Sun Chen or Helen to apologise? In the eyes of their families, what they did was just as bad as our Mary going off with Jack. And what about you? Hmmm? Have you ever apologised for falling in love with me?'

'Me?' He stared at her, startled. 'What on earth are you talking about?'

'If you recall, I was far from the ideal choice as far as your parents were concerned. "A flighty young thing", I think the expression was!'

Before Donald could argue, the flighty young thing had turned on her heel, in a cloud of new blue suit carefully carried all the way from Edinburgh. But then she stopped.

'And don't you dare wear a face like that and spoil Ishbel and Gordon's day! Especially when Mr Chen's hired this photographer!'

Watching her stride away, Donald didn't know whether to be angry or amused.

Flighty young thing, indeed! Those were the exact words his mother had used to describe Veronica before their marriage. The two of them had soon become friends, but Veronica had never forgotten those words.

That telegram from Jack, the worry about Mary, her trip to Chicago – all those things had changed her. These days Veronica was just as strong-willed as her mother had been.

Veronica believed in speaking her mind, and, when she believed she was right, there was no arguing with her.

Donald found himself a little in awe, but extremely proud, of his new wife...

Leaving Alice with Jack, Mary made her way through the guests towards her father. She shouldn't have waltzed off like that, just because she thought he'd been making a pointed remark about marriage. Nor should she have told him quite so sarcastically how blissfully happy she and Jack were.

He was still very upset by it all, understandably so. She should have explained more gently, with more thought for his feelings.

Halfway across the room she saw Flora, Gordon's sister, making her way towards her. Once, long ago, it seemed now, they'd been bosom friends back in Edinburgh.

Mary and Jack were staying in a Shanghai hotel, but she knew Flora and her husband were staying with friends of Ishbel and Gordon.

Since they arrived, Mary hadn't seen Flora, except in the church, and they hadn't spoken since Mary left home.

Flora gave her such a hesitant smile it brought a stinging sensation to Mary's eyes.

'It's nice to see how the posh folk marry,' Flora said. 'The guests at our wedding only had a sandwich at the hall!'

'Oh, Flora!'

Mary spluttered with laughter, then threw her arms around her old friend and hugged her tight.

They'd been such close friends, spending many a happy day working together and planning how to spend their free time. It had hurt Mary deeply when Flora's refusal to approve of her marriage had brought that friendship to an abrupt end.

But it was no use dwelling on the past.

'Flora, it's wonderful to see you.' She blinked back tears. 'I heard you were married – Mum told me – but who's the lucky man?' She was looking around her. 'I saw you in church standing next to...'

'Clive McArthur.' Flora spoke his name with love and pride. 'He's from Glasgow, but there, you can't hold that against him, can you?' She laughed softly. 'He came to work on the ships in Leith – in the offices, thank goodness.'

'There's no need to ask if you're happy,' Mary said. 'I can see you are.'

'I am.' Flora suddenly looked down at her shoes. 'Your mum told me about – well, you know,' she said awkwardly. 'I'm so sorry, Mary. It must have been heartbreaking for you.'

'It was. It is. But I sometimes think–' Mary added, with a brave attempt at humour '–that Alice is more than enough for any parent.'

'She's adorable.' Flora smiled. 'And your husband clearly dotes on her. On both of you, in fact.'

'Yes, he does.' Another bright smile. 'You'll soon be having children of your own, Flora.'

'Oh, I hope so,' Flora said. 'It's what we both want, more than anything.'

'You haven't been married long.' Mary was suddenly worried that she'd touched a nerve.

'Almost two years,' Flora murmured.

Mary was surprised, but then, for so long she'd had no news from home.

'Two years is nothing.' But she knew that if she'd still been waiting after two years, she'd be beginning to worry, too.

At least she had Alice. There could be no more children, but at least she had Alice...

'I'm sorry about how I behaved before you left Edinburgh, Mary,' Flora said quietly. 'It was awful of me, especially when you must have needed a friend so badly.'

'I did.' There was no point in lying. 'It was a lonely time for me. Frightening, too. But I had no choice.'

Mary had never apologised to anyone for loving Jack, and she wasn't about to start now.

'Given the circumstances,' she went on, 'there was nothing else Jack and I could do.

315

I knew there would never be another man for me – I love him desperately, Flora. I can't bear to think of the pain I've caused my family, but nor could I have borne a life without Jack.'

'I can understand that now.' Flora smiled at her. 'So tell me all about life in Chicago. Do you like it there?'

'I'm used to it,' Mary said carefully, 'but it's not Edinburgh. I miss my home.'

'I would, too. And what do you think of Shanghai?'

'It's certainly different! It's increased my admiration for Ishbel and Gordon no end, seeing what they have to cope with.'

'Me, too. And I always knew they'd get married,' Flora put in with a grin. 'What took them so long?'

'I can't imagine,' Mary laughed.

'Do you remember…?'

After that the 'do you remembers' came thick and fast until Clive joined them. He was a lovely man, and Mary took to him immediately.

Then Jack brought Alice over. The wee one was immediately the centre of attention, and Mary saw just how much Flora longed for a child of her own…

'Grandad!' Alice said, beaming.

Sure enough, Mary's father was coming over to them, a smile on his face.

To her surprise, he bent down and lifted

Alice into his arms. She was laughing.

'You can't keep her to yourself all day, you know,' he told Mary. 'Well, Flora, Clive – what do you think of my granddaughter? As pretty as a picture, isn't she?'

'She's lovely.'

'She's adorable.'

'Just as pretty as her mother,' Jack said gallantly.

'And probably just as temperamental.' Donald Montrose chuckled.

Mary turned to look at him and, in his eyes, she saw everything she longed to see. The bond was still there; it could never be broken.

There was no need for her to explain. Father knew exactly how she felt – he always had...

A spare evening at last! Ishbel had looked at her wedding photographs a hundred times, but she'd promised herself that as soon as she had time, she'd go through them at her leisure.

Since the wedding a month ago, this was the first chance she'd had. Apart from work, there had been lots of other functions to attend, including two more weddings.

It would have been far more enjoyable if Gordon had been with her, but her husband was still out and she wasn't expecting him back for another hour...

She still found it hard to believe the kindness shown by Helen and Sun Chen. That reception had been more suited to royalty, she thought with amusement. But the photographs were a lasting reminder of a perfect day.

Her favourite was one taken in church. It showed her father, looking serious, yet proud, standing with herself and Gordon, and all his feelings were in his smile.

Another favourite was of her mother, dabbing a quick tear from her eye. Yet another was of Jack and Mary, laughing, as they swung Alice between them.

Ishbel laughed at herself. They were all favourites!

The ones of Mary were especially precious, though. The first time the sisters had seen each other for five and a half years – gosh, they'd shed some tears between them!

Mary looked older than she should, too pale and a little tired, but it had been perfectly clear how happy she was with Jack, despite the loss of their second child.

She knew Mary grieved for the baby, but with Jack's help, she would get over it.

Ishbel still didn't know what to make of Jack Keller. She wasn't altogether sure that she would trust him on any business matter, but he doted on Mary and Alice. Every thought he had was for them.

For all her misgivings about the man himself, she had to admit Jack was the perfect husband for her sister. He supported her, he cherished her, he made her laugh.

Yes, he was perfect for Mary. Her sister thrived on his love...

When Gordon returned, almost an hour and a half later, she was still looking at the photographs, spotting tiny details she hadn't noticed before.

'Are you looking at those again?' He laughed at her.

'This is the first real chance I've had,' she said, sharing his amusement. 'Come and see this one of your mother. What was she scowling at? One thing's certain, she'll not be too pleased by the photograph!'

Another hour passed as, together, they remembered what had been a perfect day.

'Didn't Liang look stunning?' Ishbel said softly. 'Just look at the embroidery on her tunic!'

'Lovely,' Gordon agreed.

'And this one of the children,' Ishbel went on. 'Don't they look angelic?'

'Appearances can be deceptive,' Gordon remarked, and Ishbel laughed.

'Wasn't it the perfect day, Gordon?'

'It was, my dear.' Gordon took her hand in his. 'The best of my life.'

Lightly, he touched the narrow band of gold on her finger.

'Mrs Campbell,' he murmured, as if he

couldn't quite believe it.

Ishbel knew how he felt. Sometimes, it still felt a little unreal to her. She was happy, though – so very happy!

'Are you happy, Gordon?'

'You need to ask?' He laughed softly. 'Happier than you'll ever know. I love you so very much, Ishbel.'

'And I you,' she murmured, kissing him.

'We have such a bright future ahead of us,' Gordon promised.

Before Ishbel had a chance to think about that, someone knocked at the door.

'I'll go and see who it is.' Gordon rose to his feet.

With Shanghai so unsettled, Ishbel didn't take too kindly to late night visitors.

'Ishbel!' Gordon called. 'A visitor for you.'

Who on earth could be visiting her at this time?

She went into the hallway and stopped in her tracks, hardly able to believe what she saw.

There, in the hall, with a huge kitbag at his feet and an even bigger smile on his face, was her brother.

'Robbie! Oh!' She rushed to throw her arms around him. 'How on earth did you get here? Why didn't you let us know you were coming? Oh, this is wonderful. Come inside and tell us everything. Are you hungry? Don't tell me you've just stepped off a ship!'

'Ishbel!' Robbie laughed at his sister's chatter.

'Well, honestly! What a shock!' She had to laugh. 'So you've finally made it to Shanghai, little brother.'

She drew back and looked at him. He wasn't little any more. Robbie was a man now.

Without letting go of his arm, she made sandwiches and sat Robbie down at the kitchen table.

'For once, you can talk and eat at the same time,' she told him, laughing. 'I can't get over how grown up you look!'

'Take no notice of her,' Gordon put in. 'Eat your food in peace, Robbie.'

In the end, Ishbel let him do just that. She was happy to watch him eat. He looked well; strong, fit and healthy.

As soon as he'd swallowed the last mouthful, she was asking questions.

'Why didn't you let us know you were coming, Rob? What a pity you didn't make it a month earlier! It would have been wonderful if you'd been at the wedding.'

'I tried to, but I had a job getting a ship for Shanghai. Then, when I did, it was delayed in Bombay for five weeks. As for letters–' He pulled a face. 'None of mine seem to have got through, and I haven't received any for weeks. Of course, they might have gone to my old ship…'

They talked long into the night, until Ishbel was almost asleep on her feet.

'Let me show you your room,' she said. 'Don't worry what time you get up in the morning. I'm sure you'll appreciate a long rest. Someone will be here – me, Gordon or Jane Clements–'

'I'll be up early,' he assured her, and hesitated.

'I haven't heard from Mei Li for nearly three months now. I want to see her as soon as possible.'

Ishbel's heart skipped a sudden beat. She'd assumed, wrongly it seemed, that he and Mei Li Chen had forgotten all thoughts of being together.

Liang's sister hadn't mentioned Robbie to her again and – well, she'd assumed it had been nothing more than teenage madness.

'You don't know?' She gave Gordon a helpless glance.

'Know what?' Robbie frowned.

'Oh, Robbie.' Ishbel didn't quite know how to tell him. 'Mei Li was married last week.'

Chapter Fifteen

Robbie Montrose had always loved the festive season, but he wasn't looking forward to the Christmas of 1926. It was impossible not to think of Mei Li. If they'd been married by now, what joy he'd have taken in telling her of all the old traditions!

It made a pleasant change to be in Newcastle, though. Robbie was on leave until the New Year, and had sailed at once to spend three days with the family he'd come to love so well.

It was so long ago since he'd run away from home, trying to get to Ishbel in China. He shuddered to think what might have happened if Vic hadn't knocked that pie out of his hand.

'You must have webbed feet,' Betty said with a wry smile. 'The first thing you do when you're given leave is get yourself on another ship!'

Robbie laughed as he shifted her packages in his arms. Vic's sister had begged his help, and he'd happily gone shopping with her.

He hadn't realised that 'buying a few provisions' could be so tiring or time-consuming. He was hoping they could soon head back to the house, and yet she showed no sign of finishing.

She stopped to look at some clementines. They seemed perfect to Robbie but, as they didn't pass Betty's inspection, the two of them carried on walking.

Wearing a thick blue coat he hadn't seen before, and a matching hat, she looked prettier than ever. Robbie had noticed several young men cast admiring glances in her direction.

'Let's stop for a cup of tea,' he suggested as the café came into view.

'Good idea,' she agreed. 'I'm parched.'

With a sigh of relief, he pushed open the door.

The café was decorated for Christmas, with sprigs of holly around the door and over the counter. The tablecloths were red and green, and each table had fir cones arranged in the centre.

'So,' Betty said, when their cups of tea were put in front of them, 'you've had Mam telling you all our news. What's yours?'

'I don't really have any,' Robbie demurred.

'You must have.' She shook her head in frustration. 'Honestly, it's like getting blood from a stone. How's Ishbel getting on?'

'Oh, fine,' he replied easily. 'We had letters the day before I left. Did I tell you she was expecting a baby?'

'No!' Her eyes widened in amazement.

'Honestly, you are the limit! No news, he says! But it's wonderful – your mam and dad must be thrilled to bits.'

'They are.' Smiling, he nodded. 'Of course, Mum would have been a lot happier if the baby was due to be born in Edinburgh.'

'Do they have good doctors and things out in China?' Betty asked curiously.

'Of course they do.' He laughed. 'Just as good as ours. Ishbel's doctor is actually a Scotswoman.'

'Does Ishbel want a boy or a girl?'

'She didn't say. I don't suppose they're bothered.'

Betty stirred a spoonful of sugar into her tea.

'And how's that other girl you told me about?' she asked. 'The one Ishbel met on the boat to Shanghai, and took to work at the mission? She had a baby...'

'Jane. Yes.'

'She married the baby's dad, didn't she?'

'Yes. I told you.' It amused Robbie that Betty should be so fascinated by the lives of folk she didn't even know.

'How are they getting on?'

'Fine. They've got another two children now – both girls. Teddy's quite big – Ishbel sends photographs sometimes.'

'That's a real fairy story, isn't it?' Betty murmured dreamily.

'Hardly. But all's well that ends well, I suppose.'

Betty gave him a quizzical look. 'Did you enjoy your visit to Shanghai last year?' she asked him thoughtfully. 'You've never said more than two words about it.'

'It was OK.' He took a sip of tea, but it was too hot for comfort. 'I wanted to see Mei Li – I've mentioned her to you?'

'A few times.' Something in Betty's voice made him look up sharply. 'So did you see her?'

'No.'

The last thing he wanted to talk about was his only trip to Shanghai. Mei Li had been married for over a year now, and he'd had no word from her. Not that he'd been expecting any, not now, but it hurt more than he could believe.

Mei Li married! Every time he thought about it, that dull ache settled in the pit of his stomach. At least it was a dull ache now. This time last year, it had been a raw, constant pain...

'Why not?' Betty asked.

'What?' Robbie shook himself. 'Because she got married just before I arrived.'

'Married? That's nice.' Her voice changed, and Robbie scowled at her.

'I didn't think so!' He took another sip of his tea; it was cooler now.

'We'd had an understanding,' he tried to

326

explain. 'I knew her father had chosen a husband for her, but I'd told Mei Li to wait until I got to Shanghai. Then we were going to be married.'

'Married?' Betty's voice was little more than a whisper. 'You and her? Married?'

'Yes.'

'I see!'

Betty didn't say another word. Few people had known of his plans to marry Mei Li, but now that he had told Betty, he expected some understanding or sympathy...

She drank her tea and banged down her cup.

'Are you ready, then?' she demanded.

'Yes.' Robbie quickly finished his tea and got to his feet.

The shopping expedition that had looked set to last all day was soon over. Once Betty had bought two dozen clementines – the same ones she'd rejected earlier – they began walking back to the house at a cracking pace.

'Is everything all right?' Robbie was puzzled by her behaviour.

'Of course. Why shouldn't it be?'

He wasn't going to argue when she spoke in that tone of voice.

It wasn't until they were almost back at the house that he wondered if his talk of marrying Mei Li had reminded Betty of the time she'd turned down the gardener's son at the big house where she worked.

'What about you?' he ventured hesitantly. 'I heard you were courting – the gardener's son, wasn't it?'

'It was.' If anything, her pace only quickened.

'What went wrong?'

'Nothing went wrong,' she retorted. 'He asked me to marry him and I said no. Quite simple.'

'Why?'

'Because I didn't want to!' she snapped. 'Good grief, I'd have thought even a numbskull like you could have worked that one out.'

Betty wasn't upset, he realised – she was angry. In fact, she was furious.

'Do you regret it, Betty?' He was still in the dark. She flashed him a quick sideways scowl without slowing her pace.

'There are times when I regret it more than anything!'

She sounded positively bitter now, and Robbie decided to let it go. Whatever he said seemed to be making things worse.

He didn't like to have an atmosphere between them, though. This time tomorrow, he'd be on his way back to Leith, and he wanted things to be right.

Betty's letters always cheered him up and he'd hate to lose that contact. Oh, her mother wrote to him, so he'd be up to date with the family's news, but Betty's letters were long, full of amusing stories.

She wrote often, too. Many a time, he'd have three or four letters to reply to once he got round to it...

'Your mum said you'd got Christmas Day off.' He changed the subject.

'Yes.'

'That'll be nice. I'll be thinking of you all sitting down to dinner together.'

'I expect you'll be too busy thinking about your Chinese girl!' Before he could make any response to that, she turned on him. 'And be careful with those apples! They'll be worse than useless if you drop them!'

That was it, Robbie vowed. He wouldn't say another word.

He'd been fourteen, coming up to fifteen, when he'd first met Betty. He hadn't understood her then, and he understood her even less now that he was twenty.

Robbie couldn't help thinking the gardener's son had had a lucky escape!

Ishbel couldn't believe the time was racing by so quickly. It seemed no time at all since they'd been telling the children the nativity story, and now they were almost into March!

'The time will really drag now that you're pregnant,' Mary had told her.

'Each day will feel like a month,' Jane Clements had agreed.

Ishbel found the opposite to be true. As usual, there were never enough hours in the day.

Even with their baby due in three months, she found it hard to believe. And Gordon was just as excited.

Would it be a boy or a girl? So long as it was healthy, she didn't mind either way, yet she kept imagining herself with a wee girl.

Gordon swore he didn't mind either, yet she suspected he would rather like a son. Boy or girl, he was already planning to teach it to play the fiddle...

She dragged her mind to the task in hand. It was their colleague Lizzie McKie's last night in Shanghai, and they'd invited her to the mission this evening for a farewell get-together.

Tomorrow, Lizzie would go home. Ishbel would miss her terribly but, thank goodness, Lizzie was a good letter writer. She was a good friend, too, and had already promised Ishbel that she'd call at the manse to see her parents.

Her reason for leaving had come as a surprise. After a whirlwind romance, Lizzie was getting married.

The romance itself might have been brief, but Lizzie and Archie had known each other since their schooldays.

She was about to remark on that when she spotted the faraway look on Jane's face.

'Anything wrong?'

Jane had been quiet all morning – unlike her, especially as they were so busy.

Perhaps she was simply tired. She and Edward had three children now; Sarah was three and Margaret two.

Teddy, a sturdy seven-year-old, which just proved how the time flew by, had been hoping for a brother, and had been bitterly disappointed on being presented with sisters instead. Fortunately, his disappointment had been short-lived – he adored his sisters.

Three children, though, added to the hours that Jane spent at the mission, would tire anyone.

'This trip to England,' Jane said with a heavy sigh.

'I thought you were excited!' Ishbel was amazed to see her friend wearing such a long face at the prospect of going 'home' to England. Edward was making one of his regular business trips, and Jane had been thrilled to learn she could go with him.

'I was,' Jane admitted. 'But – last night, Edward told me that he'd arranged to see Claire while he was there.'

'Claire?' Realisation dawned. It seemed a long, long time ago that Edward had been engaged to Claire. 'His ex-fiancée?'

'Exactly!' Jane's lips tightened into a thin line. 'I can't see there's any need for that, can you? I mean – well, for heaven's sake.'

'Do they keep in touch?' Ishbel was intrigued.

'No. I've kept in touch with her.' Jane pulled a rueful face. 'She sent us such a lovely message when we got married – I felt obliged to thank her. Then, because she seemed so nice and interested, and because I felt a bit guilty, I suppose, I kept in touch. I've told her about the children and everything – she's got a husband and young daughter of her own now. It's just that I can't see any need for Edward to go and see her.'

'Is he going alone?'

'We're all going with him.'

'Then what's the problem?' Ishbel asked.

'He was in love with her. She was once the woman he wanted to marry.' Jane covered some sandwiches with a cloth and then burst out, 'Oh, Ishbel, what if he sees her again and regrets marrying me?'

Ishbel's eyes widened in astonishment.

'Jane! That is the most ridiculous thing I've ever heard, and you know it. I can think of a dozen reasons why he might want to see her. For one thing, it will clear the air – I'm sure he still feels guilty about breaking off their engagement. For another thing, he wants to show you off. He has eyes only for you, Jane, and his greatest joy in life is introducing you and the children to anyone he comes across.'

Jane had the grace to blush.

'To the point of tedium,' Ishbel added,

with a chuckle.

Jane laughed, too, and for a while, they concentrated on preparations for the evening ahead. It was almost an hour later when Jane brought up the subject again.

'She's very pretty. Claire, I mean. Edward told me.'

'So are you!'

'But what if she's prettier?'

Ishbel gave her a mock scowl.

'I know,' Jane murmured. 'And I agree that looks aren't everything, but I'm still dreading it.'

'If Edward knew that,' Ishbel pointed out, 'I'm sure he wouldn't have suggested visiting her.'

'I shan't tell him! I wouldn't give him the satisfaction of knowing I was jealous. And please, Ishbel, don't breathe a word to him.'

'My lips are sealed,' Ishbel promised with amusement.

Ishbel's thoughts drifted back to the day she first met Jane. The young girl who had been convinced she would die before they set foot on dry land had changed beyond all recognition.

But Ishbel had changed, too. She hadn't known what to expect from China then. Now, six years later, she finally felt at home. She'd made so many friends over the years...

'I'm starving!' Gordon came into the kitchen, gave Ishbel a quick peck on the cheek and Jane a broad smile, then helped himself to a sandwich.

'The first of our guests will be here in about half an hour,' he told Ishbel, between mouthfuls. 'I bumped into Adam Butler, so I told him to come early.'

'Lovely,' Ishbel murmured.

She wasn't so sure, though. Adam, the Chens' American accountant, must be feeling very strange today.

She'd been convinced Adam was in love with Lizzie. Come to that, she'd been equally convinced that Lizzie was in love with Adam. She'd certainly got that one wrong!

'I'd stay and help,' Gordon went on, 'but I've got a mass of letters to write...'

'That's a poor excuse!' Laughing, Ishbel shooed him out of the kitchen.

'Oh, Gordon,' she called after him, 'you will play a few tunes for Lizzie tonight, won't you?'

Smiling, he put his head round the kitchen door.

'When have you known me refuse? There won't be a dry eye in the house.'

Nor was there. Ishbel lasted until Gordon's fiddle began on 'My Ain Folk,' but as they sang that anthem for Scots exiles everywhere, she glanced at Lizzie.

The tears were running unchecked down her cheeks – Lizzie, rarely known to show emotion!

'It's not the end of the world,' she told her friends. 'I'll keep in touch, and I'll expect long letters from you all.' She looked at Adam and laughed.

'Except you, Adam.'

'I might surprise you, Lizzie McKie.' He laughed back at her.

Ishbel was relieved to see his laughter seemed quite natural. He'd miss Lizzie, as they all would, but he was as keen to wish her well in her new life as everyone else.

'We'll expect to see the wedding photographs,' Ishbel reminded her friend.

'You will!' Lizzie promised happily.

In the past, whenever anyone had been visiting Scotland, Ishbel had been sick with longing, but this time, the homesickness just wasn't there.

She was still a missionary, but now she was a wife, and soon to be a mother. This was her home now.

Shanghai was stifling in the May heat, and that was what was making her tired, Ishbel suspected. Everyone was complaining it sapped their energy.

She was pleased to reach Liang's house. Inside, it was deliciously cool.

Liang, as was often the case, was doing two things at once, reading to Zhang and embroidering a jacket.

How she could concentrate on such intricate needlework and amuse her little boy at the same time was beyond Ishbel.

It was a heartwarming scene. Zhang, almost four now, was a picture of good health. It was difficult to remember they had once feared for his life.

As he bowed to her in his customary way, Ishbel thought again he was a little too serious for his age. Zhang needed brothers and sisters.

He had a quick, lively mind, and his parents couldn't teach him enough, but there should be more fun in his life, and less learning.

Not that she could criticise. Only now, with her own baby due next month, did she realise just how little she knew about parenting.

It was a frightening thought, but then Jane, Liang, Helen Chen – they would all be ready to help and advise.

Liang looked tired, and no wonder. Last month, her father had suffered a heart attack, something that had taken everyone by surprise.

He was making a good recovery, and he had the best doctors in attendance, but it had shocked everyone, including Sun Chen himself.

Ishbel didn't like to ask about him, not when Zhang was happily chatting away in his usual mix of English and Chinese.

'Is this your tiger's hat?' Ishbel asked, picking up a beautifully embroidered hat.

'Yes.' He nodded proudly.

'And who did all this?' She pointed to the delicate embroidery.

Laughing, Zhang threw his arms around Liang's neck and hugged her.

The boy was a delight, and Ishbel was disappointed when Liang's maid came to take him away for his lunch.

'He's a picture of health, Liang,' Ishbel said happily. 'Who would believe he was so ill as a baby?'

'He is. I marvel at him every day.' Liang smiled, but the weariness still shadowed her eyes.

'I saw your mother yesterday,' Ishbel remarked. 'She said your father is much improved.'

'Yes, he is.' Liang managed another smile.

'He'll be fine, Liang. Try not to worry too much.' As soon as the words were out, Ishbel realised how inadequate they were. How could the poor girl not worry? Ishbel would, if it were her own father...

'I'm not too worried. Not about my father.' But Liang's gentle eyes were clouded with concern.

'So it must be Han?' Ishbel guessed.

Liang's husband was making another trip to Nanning, in the south, and Liang always worried.

China was a country immensely proud of its past, and yet the future promised nothing but uncertainty. The situation in Shanghai itself was volatile. The general unrest, and the disturbing presence of the Japanese, meant businesses were changing hands all the time.

'I've had no word from him,' Liang said quietly.

'That means nothing,' Ishbel assured her. 'You know it doesn't. He's often struggled to contact you in the past, but he always has. You must have patience.'

'He had a difficult journey to Nanning.' Liang got to her feet and walked over to look out at the shady courtyard. 'I'm not even sure he's there yet. The river was blocked, so—'

'Blocked? Why?'

'More battles between the warlords,' Liang said with a heavy sigh. 'What is happening to my country, Ishbel?'

'I wish I knew.' Ishbel was sympathetic.

Liang sighed again. China's future was in the hands of God.

'Because the river was blocked, Han had to go to Hong Kong. From there he took the French coastal steamer to Haiphong.'

'Where's that?'

'In French Indo-China.'

Ishbel tried to seem calm.

'From Haiphong, he was planning to take the railway up to the frontier, use the bus to Lungchow and then take the river steamer downstream to Nanning.'

She took a long shuddering breath.

'I haven't heard from him since.'

With warlords vying for power, and bandits lurking everywhere, the thought of that journey filled Ishbel with dread.

'I'm not surprised,' she said gently. 'It's a long, difficult journey, Liang. And with the river blocked – well, anyone will struggle to get word out. You'll hear from him soon – you must try not to worry.'

But Ishbel knew that if Gordon were making the same journey, she would be at her wits' end...

Over tea, they talked of more general things, but it was clear that Liang had a lot on her mind.

'Is anything else worrying you?' Ishbel asked quietly.

There was a long pause before Liang answered.

'Yes,' she admitted at last. 'It's Mei Li, Ishbel, I've done a terrible thing. It's so awful that I'm not even sure I can tell you.'

Ishbel doubted anything Liang did would be awful, but she hated to see her friend so troubled.

What with Han's journey, and her father's health, poor Liang had more than her fair share of worries. It was wrong of her sister to add to them.

'Of course you can tell me,' Ishbel said. 'Isn't that what friends are for?'

'But this is – this concerns you.' Liang rushed on. 'Three months ago, I visited Mei Li in her new home. I know she's not happy in her marriage, but–' She shrugged. 'Only she can solve that problem.'

On that point, Ishbel was in full agreement. To have a husband chosen by your father must be a frightening experience.

But Liang had gone into her marriage with the intention of making the best of it. She had been determined to make it work, and the result was a strong and happy marriage.

Mei Li, on the other hand, had married full of stubborn defiance. It was as if she refused to be happy, and was determined to make sure everyone knew it.

Helen was very worried about her young daughter, Ishbel knew, and Sun Chen was bitterly disappointed...

'Mei Li had written a letter to your brother.' Liang's eyes were on her prettily embroidered slippers. 'She begged me to take it, so that her husband wouldn't see it. She didn't think she would be able to send it to Robbie without him discovering it.'

'Oh, dear!' Ishbel couldn't begin to imagine the contents of the letter.

'I took it,' Liang continued, 'but–' Her pale face flushed with sudden colour. 'I opened it.'

When there was no reaction from Ishbel, she went on. 'I read it.'

'I see.'

'It was a terrible letter, Ishbel. She was explaining why she'd had to marry instead of waiting as they'd planned. She went on to say that she couldn't bear her marriage and that – she wanted to get to Robbie and be with him.'

'Oh, no.' What would Robbie do if he got a letter like that? Her brother was head-strong, and just as stubborn as Mei Li.

'Did you send the letter, Liang?'

'No.' Liang spoke very quietly. 'No, I didn't.'

'Thank goodness,' Ishbel said, from the bottom of her heart.

'It was a terrible letter, Ishbel,' Liang repeated. 'The damage it might have done!'

'I know.' If Mei Li ran away from home, from her husband – well, the consequences were unthinkable. Her father would be devastated, for a start. 'I think you did the right thing, Liang. We must talk to her – make her see–'

'It's impossible,' Liang said simply.

Ishbel walked home that afternoon with a heavy heart.

'Liang! Come in, come in. Your servant, too. Why are you out, for heaven's sake? You know the streets aren't safe.'

Gordon shut and barred the mission door.

'We'd just finished our evening meal.'

Ishbel looked up as her friend came into the sitting-room. 'It's good to see you – but you shouldn't have risked it.'

'I'm sorry to intrude.' Liang always said that; she couldn't accept that they were delighted to see her, no matter what hour of the day or night.

This evening, though, she looked distressed.

Ishbel had just persuaded her to sit down when they had another visitor – Mrs Cheng, the mother of one of Ishbel's pupils. Ishbel had to leave Liang and Gordon alone.

Mrs Cheng's English was non-existent and Ishbel found herself struggling to understand her particular dialect.

Finally, she grasped that the poor woman was too frightened to let her child come to school any longer. Sadly, she wasn't alone.

Ishbel promised to call at Mrs Cheng's and give her son some work to do at home. She'd discovered that when parents saw that she wasn't too frightened to visit their homes, they gradually began to send their children back to the mission again.

'I'll bring Li some work tomorrow,' she promised.

Whether or not Mrs Cheng understood was debatable, but she left looking a lot happier than when she'd arrived.

When Ishbel returned to the sitting-room she found Liang, sitting, exhausted, nursing a bowl of tea.

'Sit down,' Gordon said. 'Liang has heard about Han, and I'm afraid it's not good news, Ishbel. She doesn't like to worry her parents, especially her father, so she came to us for help.'

'What news?' Ishbel's heart was pounding with dread.

'Han has been captured by bandits.'

'No!' Ishbel was on her feet in an instant. It was their worst fear – Han's life was in grave danger.

'Oh, no,' she said again. 'What can we do, Gordon?'

Gordon came to take her hands in his.

'I've told Liang that I'll go and talk to them.'

'No!' Ishbel clung to the lapels of his jacket. 'Gordon, no. They won't listen, you know they won't.'

'They must listen.' Gordon held her close. 'I must make them listen.'

'Let me come with you,' she begged.

'No, Ishbel. You must stay here. Stay here and be brave. Be strong.'

'But the baby–' she whispered.

'I'll be back before our child is born.' Smiling, he laid a gentle hand on her swollen stomach. 'God will be with me. With both of us, Ishbel. Never forget that.'

'Can't someone else–'

'No,' Gordon answered quietly, just as

she'd known he would. 'I have to go, you know that. Besides, I've given Liang my word. I must do what I can to bring Han home.'

She knew he was right, and she knew there was to be no argument.

'I am so grateful,' came Liang's soft voice.

'I'll take Tian with me. It'll be fine,' Gordon said.

Tian, the English-speaking Chinese guide, seemed to know every inch of China. He was honest, always willing to help, and completely devoted to Gordon. Within a couple of months of meeting Gordon, Tian and his family had converted to Christianity...

'Oh, Gordon.' Ishbel looked into his face. 'I love you so very much.'

'I know, my darling.' He stroked her face. 'Just as I love you.'

He kissed her forehead.

'You must try not to worry.'

It was too late for that. For Gordon's sake, and for the sake of their unborn child, she had to be strong – but, for the first time in her life, Ishbel knew real fear.

Chapter Sixteen

Ishbel gazed down at the perfect little miracle in her arms, and laughed to herself. Every time she looked at her son, her eyes filled with tears of joy, so that she couldn't see him properly.

'Wait till your father sees you,' she murmured softly, brushing the soft covering of hair on his head. 'He'll be so proud.'

What would they call their son? They'd considered dozens of names, and laughingly dismissed many more, but they had more or less settled on James Donald – James after Gordon's father, and Donald after Ishbel's.

Nothing had been definite, though, and she couldn't give their child a name until Gordon came home.

'James,' she murmured, trying it out. 'Yes, you look like a James.'

He was a plump, strong, healthy-looking baby, and Ishbel delighted in the way his tiny hands clenched into fat fists. His nose was small and stubby, and his mouth was in a permanent pout.

Added to which, she'd soon discovered, he had an extremely strong pair of lungs.

She loved to hold him, loved to feel his

rhythmic breathing as he slept. Warm and fed, he didn't have a care in the world.

'James.' Yes, she liked the name. There was the King James Bible, which her father had taught her to love. And there had been seven Kings called James.

Of course, she knew why she was concentrating all her thoughts on her son's name. It was to stop worrying about Gordon.

For all her calm outward appearance, she felt as unsettled as Shanghai itself, which was in chaos.

Ever since March, when General Chiang Kai-shek had gained control of the city, there had been trouble. Street fighting was commonplace...

She ran a finger down her son's rosy cheek.

'I wish I could have you christened tomorrow,' she said softly, 'but it won't be long. Your father will be home soon.'

She chanted those words like a prayer.

When Liang called at the mission earlier that morning, Ishbel silently sympathised with the anxiety in her friend's eyes.

Neither had mentioned Gordon or Han – there had been no point. Each knew exactly how the other felt. Instead, they'd talked of their children...

'I've brought you a cup of tea.' Jane Clements came into the room. 'Here – let me have him while you drink it.'

Smiling to herself, Ishbel handed over the sleeping bundle.

'Gordon will be so thrilled when he gets home.' Jane gazed down at the tiny baby in her arms. 'What a homecoming present!'

'I just wish he'd hurry up,' Ishbel murmured.

'Yes, you'll be feeling a little lonely.'

'It's not that,' Ishbel answered thoughtfully. 'I miss Gordon desperately, of course, but I can't in all honesty say that I'm lonely.' She laughed softly.

'I haven't had the chance – I've rarely had a minute to myself.'

'That's how it should be.' Jane gently rocked Ishbel's son in her arms. 'Left alone, you'd only worry. And what's the point in that? Worrying won't bring him home any quicker. Besides, there's nothing to worry about,' she added firmly. 'Gordon's got the best guide in China with him.'

That was true enough, and Ishbel took comfort from it. All the same, it was impossible not to worry...

'Adam Butler's sure to call in later,' Jane said, changing the subject, 'so I think I'll get him to help me move those desks around. Are you sure it's all right to move them?'

'Of course.' Ishbel nodded, glad to be able to put her mind to the schoolroom. While repair work was being done to the windows at the back, they planned to divide the room

347

in half so that the children wouldn't be so distracted by the work. 'I think it's an excellent idea.'

'Good.' Jane grinned. 'I bet Adam won't turn up now.'

Ishbel suspected he would. The Chens' American accountant had called at the mission every day since Gordon had left. There was very little he could do, but Ishbel had been touched by his visits.

With Sun Chen still recovering from his heart attack, Adam had been kept busy enough as it was, yet he hadn't missed a day – and he always managed to make her smile.

'You'd better rest now,' Jane said as Ishbel put down her cup. 'You know what the doctors said.'

'I know what the doctors said,' Ishbel replied dryly, 'and it's easy for them to say. Enough's enough, Jane. It's time to get back to work.'

'But the doctors–'

'Apart from being a little tired,' Ishbel cut her off, 'which is only to be expected, I feel wonderfully fit and well. Besides, if I don't work, I'll only fret about Gordon...'

Jane had no answer to that.

It wasn't Chicago itself that was making her restless, Mary Keller decided.

At this time of year, the humid heat was almost unbearable and, in winter, the cold winds and the sub zero temperatures were hard to bear, but it wasn't the weather, either.

In fact, she liked the city. It was lively and modern.

She had her own car, mainly to please Jack, but Chicago was so flat that it was just as easy to walk through the city and parks. In any case, she'd always enjoyed walking.

It was difficult to pinpoint the reason for her restlessness. And equally difficult to ignore it...

Alice would begin school soon, and that didn't sit comfortably with Mary. Her daughter, a bright, inquisitive child, needed the mental stimulation, but Mary had no idea how she might fill her days without her. Voluntary work, she supposed.

And how would Jack feel about that?

Dear Jack. She couldn't have a more thoughtful, considerate, loving husband – yet he'd almost developed apoplexy when she told him she'd helped distribute food to the hungry last Christmas!

'You took Alice there?' he'd demanded in astonishment.

'I had no choice,' Mary explained. 'It was a spur of the moment thing, Jack. I'd taken a few bags of old clothes down, and they were short-handed. There are a lot of hungry people in Chicago, and I only stayed for a couple of hours...'

It hadn't been handing out soup to the

needy that had upset him, Mary knew that. Jack knew as well as she did about city poverty, and he was more than generous in his donations.

It had been the thought of his wife and, more especially, his innocent daughter associating with these people!

Not that Mary had associated with them. They had been so cold and hungry, they wouldn't have cared if the President himself had been handing out soup and blankets.

She knew she would have to tread carefully when mentioning voluntary work to him…

'It's too hot, Mummy,' Alice complained, fanning herself with her hand.

'You're right.' Mary laughed at her pouting daughter. 'But there's nothing I can do about the weather. It is July, you know. Let's go home through the park – it might be cooler there.'

It wasn't.

'When I grow up,' Alice declared importantly as they walked, 'I'm going to be a missionary like Auntie Ishbel.'

'Are you, indeed?'

Alice had seen Auntie Ishbel once, and she'd been quite convinced that her lavish wedding reception was everyday life for missionaries.

Mary had to smile, but a small doubt niggled at the back of her mind. Alice already loved beautiful dresses, hats and shoes, and because she loved them, she and Jack indulged her a little more than was good for her, perhaps.

She would have a word with Jack later...

'It's very hard work,' Mary told her daughter.

'Yes, but didn't the Chinese ladies look pretty?'

'They did,' Mary agreed, 'but that was a very special day for Auntie Ishbel and Uncle Gordon. Everyone dresses up for weddings. Usually–'

But there was no point trying to explain reality to Alice. How could Mary tell her of the problems in China and the dangers foreigners faced there?

How could Alice even begin to understand what it was like to share your bed with rats, as Ishbel once had?

'I thought you were going to be an actress,' she said instead.

'I might.' Alice thought for a moment. 'Or I might be a princess. A real one.'

'Now that's a good idea,' Mary said, laughing to herself.

That evening when Alice was tucked up in bed, and she and Jack were enjoying a rare evening at home alone, Mary carefully brought up the subject.

'Do you think we spoil her, Jack?' she asked.

'Yes.' There was fond amusement in his

351

expression. 'We can have no more children, Mary, and our daughter couldn't be more precious to us. The love we share is very, very precious and Alice is the result of that love. Added to which, she's the most wonderful child ever born. You name me a couple who wouldn't spoil her!'

Mary had to smile.

'You don't think you're a little biased?' she ventured with a wry smile.

'Not in the least.' But he was laughing.

'Seriously, though, Jack,' Mary went on, 'I'm not sure it's good for her. She said today that she wants to be a missionary like Ishbel when she grows up!'

Jack laughed all the louder.

'Do you know why that is?' Mary asked. 'It's because of that wedding reception. Alice thinks that's how missionaries live!'

'She's only a child,' Jack reminded her gently. 'She still has a lot to learn about life. Who knows? Maybe she will be a missionary. But she'll be grown by then, Mary. She'll know what it means.'

'I suppose so.' Mary wasn't convinced. 'I still don't think we should spoil her so much, though.'

'She knows the difference between right and wrong, good and bad,' Jack said firmly. 'At her age, it's enough.'

He clasped Mary's hand tightly in his own.

'What's the matter, sweetheart?' he asked

softly. 'It's not Alice, is it? Not really.'

Mary flushed.

'I don't know, Jack,' she confessed. 'I just feel – restless. That's the only word that describes it. I don't know why.'

'I think I do.' Jack walked over to the dresser and picked up a letter that had arrived a few days ago.

'I think,' he said, waving it in the air, 'that you're homesick.'

'A little, perhaps,' she admitted.

As soon as the letter had arrived from her mother, reminding her of her parents' thirtieth wedding anniversary, Mary had known a strong longing for home. Presumably, Ishbel must feel the same.

What sort of celebration could it be when the family weren't together? Robbie might be home, of course, if he wasn't on a ship sailing distant seas, but neither Ishbel nor Mary could be there.

'It upsets me that I won't be in Edinburgh for their wedding anniversary,' Mary admitted quietly.

'I know it does…'

Mary went to bed early, leaving Jack to deal with some paperwork. She lay awake for some time; she never slept well without him beside her.

In the end, with sleep an impossibility, she got out of bed and went into his study.

'Can't you sleep?' He looked up from his

papers and smiled the smile he always reserved for her.

'No.' She sat on the edge of his desk. 'How much longer will you be?'

He snapped a ledger shut.

'I've about finished.' He rose to his feet and reached for her hand. 'Come on, sweetheart. You need some sleep.'

An hour later, lying beside him and listening to the rhythmic beating of his heart, sleep was no nearer.

'Are you awake, Jack?' Mary whispered.

'No,' he whispered back.

'Me neither.' She snuggled up closer to him.

'If I tell you a secret,' he said quietly, 'will you promise to go straight to sleep?'

'Of course.'

That was what he always said to Alice.

'I'm taking you home to Edinburgh, Mary.'

For a moment, Mary couldn't believe her ears. Then she sat up.

'For my parents' wedding anniversary? Oh, Jack!' Tears filled her eyes. 'Thank you, my darling. I did think of asking you, but I know how busy you are, and I didn't think you'd be able to spare the time.'

'You know perfectly well that I've always got time for you.'

'How long can we stay, Jack?'

'For good.'

It took a few moments for the enormity of

those softly-spoken words to sink in.

'For good? What – you mean–'

'I mean we're going home, love. There will be talk, of course, and things might be difficult, but I think we can deal with that. Your parents have accepted our marriage – more or less – and that's the important thing. Other folk will have to make up their own minds.'

Mary's mind was in a whirl. How did he expect her to sleep now?

'Of course, we'll have to make sure that none of the unkind talk reaches Alice,' Jack went on. 'I don't think it will, though. A child will usually win people round, no matter how hardened their views. Yes, I'm sure we can go back to Edinburgh.'

'Oh!' Mary leaned against him. How would people react? Her parents had come round, true enough, and Flora Cameron, her old friend, had finally accepted Mary's marriage, but people had long memories.

'Where will we live, Jack?' Mary was already imagining walking through Princes Street Gardens with Alice.

'My old home's still there,' he reminded her. 'Mabel's still taking care of it.'

'Oh, I'll be able to see Ruth almost every day!'

Ruth McKinlay had been the truest friend Mary could have wished for. She'd written long, long letters during all the years Mary had been in America, and Mary missed her and the children terribly.

'I'm not sure that's a good idea,' Jack said with mock severity. 'I still remember the day you accused me of putting that good woman and her children out on the street to starve!'

'If it hadn't been for me, Jack Keller,' Mary retorted with a giggle, 'that's exactly what the poor woman would have done. Although you did put a lot of needlework her way. Just think, I'll be able to see her posh new shop!'

'Indeed you will, always assuming you're not too overcome with exhaustion to travel. Sleep, Mary!'

With a huge smile on her face, Mary slipped down into the bed again. She could almost feel the fresh wind of home on her cheeks....

'Jack, are you asleep?' she whispered an hour or so later.

'Yes,' he said patiently, and she smiled.

'Can we surprise them? My parents, I mean?'

'If that's what you want,' he murmured, pulling her closer.

'It is,' she said firmly. 'Just think what a wonderful surprise it would be if their granddaughter arrived in time for their wedding anniversary!'

On that exciting thought, Mary finally slept.

The train was late. Robbie had been at Waverley for what seemed like hours, but now, it was officially late. He'd been pacing up and down ever since he'd walked on to the platform.

When Betty had told him she had a week's holiday, it had felt like the most natural thing in the world to invite her to the manse, but now it seemed little short of madness.

His mind raced with questions.

What would Betty think of Edinburgh? What would she think of the manse? What would she make of his parents – what would they make of her?

More importantly, could he manage four whole days without doing or saying something to upset her?

She would love Edinburgh; who couldn't? He tried to reassure himself.

As for the manse, he'd try to make her realise that it wasn't usually as chaotic as this. The anniversary party was so out of character for his father – Robbie suspected he'd been too surprised to argue!

The anniversary was weeks away yet, but his mother had decided it was 'high time the manse was smartened up'.

Everywhere Robbie looked, another cupboard was being emptied, another room being turned upside down.

Betty would like his parents, he knew.

Father might take a little getting used to, perhaps, but–

At last! A whistle, a chuff, a cloud of steam, and the train pulled into the station.

Robbie spotted her immediately, and she looked wonderful. Each time he saw her, she seemed more attractive.

In her last letter, Betty had said she was thinking of having her hair cut short, in the new fashion, but he was pleased to see that she hadn't. She wouldn't look the same without those blonde curls!

'Sorry I'm late,' she greeted him. 'The train kept stopping for no reason I could understand.'

'You're here now. That's all that matters.'

He took her small suitcase from her, and wished he could tell her how lovely she looked. But he couldn't think of anything that didn't sound stupid...

'It's a bit chaotic at home,' he warned her. 'Mum's decided to have a party to celebrate their wedding anniversary. It's not for weeks yet, but she's giving the manse a good going over.'

'Oh! Then she won't want me here,' Betty said anxiously.

'Of course she does. She's looking forward to meeting you.'

Robbie worried again about how the two women would get on ... you could never tell.

'Perhaps I'll be able to help,' Betty said hopefully.

'You're supposed to be on holiday,' he reminded her with a smile.

When he pushed open the door to the manse, he could hear his mother singing to herself in the sitting-room. The sound cheered him; it always did.

Mum must have been waiting for them, because she was in the hall before he'd had a chance to close the door.

'Betty! It's lovely to meet you at long last.' Veronica took her hands. 'Good journey? You must be tired out. Here, lass – come with me. I'll show you your room, give you a chance to freshen up, and then we'll have tea…'

They left Robbie standing in the hall, feeling redundant. And confused.

What puzzled him was that nagging worry that Betty and his mother might not get on. He'd no idea why it suddenly mattered so much.

It looked as if he needn't have worried after all. Far from it.

Betty and his mother talked the rest of the day away, as if they'd known each other all their lives. To Robbie, watching them, it was as if Mum was talking and laughing with Ishbel or Mary.

It helped, of course, that Betty had such a fascination with his family, and indeed, with people she didn't know from Adam.

Robbie could think of nothing more tedious than poring over wedding or baby photographs when you didn't know the people concerned – it was bad enough when you did know them!

Betty, however, found it fascinating, and it wasn't that she was being polite. She was genuinely interested.

Ishbel's wedding photographs were examined in minute detail, the surroundings, the people, the dresses – everything. Then the photographs of his young niece, Alice, were given the same close scrutiny.

'What a pretty dress she's wearing!' Betty said of one photograph. 'And doesn't she look exactly like her mother in this one?'

'She does,' Veronica agreed, 'but – here, look at this one where Jack's holding her. Isn't her smile like his?' She gazed fondly at the photograph.

'Jack's a lovely man. Devoted to our Mary and little Alice...'

Robbie had to smile to himself. 'A lovely man' wasn't quite how Jack Keller had been described at the manse in the past. Robbie still wouldn't trust the man as far as he could spit.

It had to be said, though, that he seemed to be a good husband and father, so Robbie kept his feelings to himself.

The following day, Robbie had assumed

that he'd have Betty to himself, but she and his mother had other ideas.

Over breakfast, they were busy making plans for a shopping trip.

Of course, Robbie could have gone with them, but as they were buying curtains for the manse sitting-room, he gave it a miss. That would be even more boring than looking at wedding photographs...

Then, that evening, Betty actually asked his father if he'd have time to show her round his church.

Donald Montrose couldn't have been more delighted. Betty had found a friend for life, and again, she wasn't just being polite.

The visit was highly enjoyable, but it was over far too quickly.

To Robbie, it seemed no time at all since he'd met Betty off the train and now, here they were, with half an hour to spare, waiting for the train that would take her back to Newcastle-upon-Tyne.

'I've had a smashing time, Rob,' Betty said happily, 'and your parents are lovely people. I was expecting them to be – oh, I don't know – a cut above, I suppose. But they couldn't have been nicer to me.'

'They liked you,' Robbie told her, smiling.

'I liked them, too.' She gave him one of her long, thoughtful looks. 'I haven't seen much of you, though.'

'I know.' He was glad she'd noticed.

'Have you heard from that Chinese girl of yours?' she asked, taking him completely by surprise.

'Mei Li? Heavens, no. I haven't spared her a thought for ages.'

'She's very pretty. I saw her on Ishbel's wedding photographs.'

Robbie had seen her too, but what he'd said was true. He didn't think of Mei Li often these days.

Perhaps it was because he knew, deep down, that marrying Mei Li had been an impossible dream. Or perhaps they simply hadn't loved each other enough. Or perhaps, and he was beginning to think this was more likely, he spent too much time thinking about Betty these days...

He looked at Betty, for so long that she began to fidget.

'Mei Li is pretty,' he agreed. But, suddenly, he found himself thinking how pretty Betty looked, and had to change the subject.

'I hope your train isn't too late,' he said.

'Are you trying to get rid of me?' She smiled at him.

'Far from it!' He wasn't looking forward to watching her leave one little bit.

'Good.' She seemed pleased about that.

All too soon, her train arrived.

'This is it, then,' he murmured.

'Yes.' She gazed at him. 'Well, aren't you going to kiss me or something?'

362

'What? Well–' He was completely taken aback. 'I remember the last time I tried that!'

'Oh, that.' She laughed softly at the memory of the day she'd slapped him across the face.

'You deserved everything you got! For one thing, it was very forward of you. For another, we were only kids.

'And for another–' Her eyes filled with a soft appeal he hadn't seen before. 'That was years ago, for heaven's sake! If you want to kiss me now, I'd like it. Very much.'

Robbie didn't need asking twice. As he gathered her into his arms, it was the most wonderful feeling ever...

In full view of everyone on the station platform, Betty linked her arms round his neck, and responded to his kiss with a warmth and a passion he'd never imagined possible.

When she drew away, her expression made every nerve in his body tingle.

'I'll miss the train,' she said, laughing.

'I think I'm in love with you.'

'You'd better make up your mind whether you are or not, Robbie Montrose.' She stepped on to the train and turned to face him. 'I've already turned down one marriage proposal because of you!'

And then she was gone.

Robbie raced along the platform as the train pulled out of the station, but there was no sign of her. When he reached the end of the platform, he stopped and watched the train disappear from view.

Then, with a spring in his step and an absurdly large grin on his face, he set off for home...

Ishbel returned from the prayer meeting in a far more positive frame of mind. She always did.

Gordon had run the meetings so well that, at first, she'd been a little anxious about taking over.

Her fears had soon been dispelled, though, and it was a wonderfully uplifting experience to feel the strength of friends praying for Gordon, Han and Tian, their guide.

One day soon, Gordon would be home, and until then, she had to be strong and brave. She had to trust in God to bring him home safely.

Tomorrow morning, she decided, she would pay Liang a visit. Her friend was in need of that kind of strength at the moment.

Ishbel knew exactly how the poor girl was feeling, because she felt exactly the same. At times, it would be all too easy to sink into despair.

She knew how it felt to toss and turn all night, longing for your husband's reassuring embrace – to wake in the morning and pray for his safety.

How it felt to long for the clasp of his hand, to see his smile, to hear his voice...

She also knew how difficult it was to hear of the fighting and the hatred raging in this country, and not worry yourself into a panic.

Ishbel was luckier than Liang. Her faith kept her going. She knew that God was with her, and with Gordon. She knew, without any doubt whatsoever, that He would give her all the strength and courage she needed.

Sometimes, Ishbel felt as if she'd been born with faith. Certainly, she couldn't remember a time when she hadn't had it. That was thanks to her father...

Oh, how she wished she could talk to Father right now. What had he said when she'd been leaving Scotland on her way to Shanghai?

'Never forget that God's aye by your side.'

She could remember the way he'd taken her in his arms and held her so close.

'I'm more proud of you than I can say,' he'd told her. 'God bless you.'

These words were a great comfort in times of trouble. Father was right; she was never alone.

Ishbel walked on quickly, eager to get home to James. To her, he was a person already, growing into his name – James Donald Campbell.

Jane Clements was at the mission looking after him, so he was in safe hands, but

Ishbel wanted her baby in her own arms.

She longed to feel his soft skin, to look into those pure, innocent eyes and see his father gazing back at her...

She had no sooner pushed open the door than Jane was at her side, guiding her towards the sitting-room.

'You have visitors, Ishbel. I'm sorry.'

Ishbel smiled at the apology. Jane would know how she longed to see her son before any visitors. The mission gave everyone a welcome, though, and she could wait a while for James.

She stopped in the sitting-room doorway as Liang, her husband, Han, and Tian, who'd guided Gordon south, rose to their feet.

Nothing seemed quite real. Ishbel's eyes were fixed on Han. He was home, he was safe! She wanted to cry with relief, but found that she couldn't utter a word.

Liang had been crying. No wonder, Ishbel thought, with a vagueness she couldn't shake off.

Then, finally, she looked at Tian.

'Ishbel, your husband saved my life,' Han said brokenly, but still Ishbel couldn't look away from Tian.

'Gordon?' She was surprised that her voice made any sound at all.

'He saved Han Hsien's life, Mrs Campbell,' Tian said in his gentle voice. 'He talked to those barbarians. He won Han's freedom.

366

Then, when we were returning – bandits–'
Tian took a long time to gather himself. 'We thought we had escaped, but they opened fire. We two–' He nodded towards Han, but then changed his mind about whatever it was he'd planned to say.

'Mr Campbell–'

Tian could say no more. Tears were pouring down his cheeks.

Chapter Seventeen

When Ishbel awoke that morning, she felt different. Tired, certainly, but that was only because she'd spent far too long last night reading through her diaries when she should have been sleeping.

It wasn't that, though. No, she felt brighter this morning.

She sat up in bed, and smiled to herself as she picked up the diary and pen that were lying on the table.

Saturday, February 16, 1929, she wrote. *Robert and Betty's wedding day. My little brother getting married. What do you think of that, Gran?*

It was nine years now since Gran had given her that first diary, yet Ishbel still wrote as if she was talking to her.

There was no need to ask the question, though – Gran would have been as thrilled as they all were. Betty was a lovely girl, and the family adored her.

Mum was convinced something was sure to go wrong, but Ishbel knew without doubt that it would be a perfect day.

'Your mother's a born worrier, Ishbel,' her gran used to say with fond amusement. 'All you can do is let her worry.'

Ishbel pulled back the curtains and looked out. At least it wasn't raining...

In his cot in the corner, James was still sleeping soundly.

Everyone, Ishbel included, marvelled at her son's quiet, placid nature. He took after his father.

Gordon had been quiet and easy-going, too, yet he'd had a stubborn streak, fighting hard for what he believed to be right...

How she wished Gordon could be with her today! Not a day passed when she didn't wish that, but today was special...

In a way, she wished she'd come home earlier. She'd had the chance, but she'd felt it important to cope with her loss on the spot, in Shanghai. She'd thought that her work would help.

It hadn't. She'd stayed in Shanghai for over a year after Gordon's death, but really, she'd contributed very little.

Her friends had been wonderfully supportive, and for that she was grateful, but her heart hadn't been in her work. It just ached for her husband.

What had started the healing process had been coming home, to Edinburgh – to her parents, to her sister and brother.

She'd arrived just before Christmas, and the timing couldn't have been better. Surrounded, once again, by all that was dear to her at the manse, the thought of returning to Shanghai grew more distasteful by the day.

But tomorrow would be soon enough to think of that. Today, she was going to do nothing more than enjoy her wee brother's wedding in her father's kirk.

A soft wail from the cot brought her out of bed. James was still half asleep, but she picked him up and held him close.

'And you, my boy, will behave yourself today,' she whispered. 'No crying during the ceremony, or you'll have Betty after you...'

He rubbed his eyes and smiled back at her, a picture of innocence. Then he was struggling to be put down.

How she wished Gordon could have seen that smile! But there was no point in wishing. She had lost her beloved Gordon – her closest friend, her staunchest ally, colleague and husband – but God had left her with the most precious gift of all, and she thanked Him, as she did every day.

Robbie's bride had been living on her

nerves for the last week, but now, standing beside him in his father's church as they repeated their wedding vows, Betty knew a great sense of calm.

To be Robbie's wife was what she had wanted almost from the day they'd first met.

For the last few days, she'd been thinking about Mei Li Chen, in Shanghai – more accurately, she'd been wondering if Robbie had been thinking of her.

Worst of all, she'd wondered if he'd wished the pretty Chinese girl had been standing beside him now.

It was nonsense, though; she knew that for sure now. A touch of last-minute nerves, that was all.

Whatever Robbie had felt for Mei Li was over. When he'd turned to look at Betty as she walked up the aisle on her father's arm, she'd wondered how she could have thought such a thing.

There was more love in his eyes than a girl could dream of. Love, pride, happiness, faith in the future…

Everyone in the church was pleased for them, and Betty could feel their love wrapping itself around her.

This was, by far, the happiest day of her life. Whatever problems lay ahead, she would keep the memory of this day close to help her through.

At first, her mother had been a little put

out. Not at Betty's decision to marry Robbie – she couldn't have been happier about that – but that the ceremony would take place in Edinburgh.

Mam had expected her only daughter to marry in the same church she had, the same church in which Betty and Vic had been christened. She'd soon come round, though.

Vic hadn't been too thrilled about it, either.

'We've got to go all the way to Edinburgh?' he'd asked in amazement.

'If you're going to be my best man – yes,' Robbie had told him.

At the thought of being best man, Vic had been too touched to argue...

Robbie's family had given her such a warm welcome, right from the start, that Betty had felt like a Montrose already. She was proud to take their name, Robbie's name.

And what a thrill, after seeing so many photographs and hearing so much about them, to meet his sisters at last!

Mary was nothing like Betty had imagined. She'd expected Robbie's rich sister to consider herself a bit better than the rest of them. Nothing could have been further from the truth.

On first meeting, Jack and Mary appeared to be an odd couple.

It was impossible to miss the fact that Jack was very wealthy, but, it was also clear that, millionaire or pauper, Mary would have sold her soul for him.

Sometimes, Betty thought, Mary must have felt as if she'd done just that. But she and Jack were devoted to each other, and equally devoted to their beautiful daughter.

At the thought of young Alice, Betty glowed. One day soon, she and Robbie would have children of their own. A beautiful daughter like Alice, perhaps, or a sturdy son like James.

Meeting Ishbel was something else again. Betty had always known Robbie adored his eldest sister, but that hadn't stopped her expecting the missionary to be a slightly stern, austere woman.

Ishbel was nothing of the sort. She was lovely, someone people from all walks of life were instantly drawn to. There was a quiet inner strength to her that Betty admired greatly. She was strong, yet fun-loving.

Robbie's mum had told Betty that when Emmeline Pankhurst had died last year, Ishbel had written home.

Mrs Pankhurst was a very special lady. She will be greatly missed, she'd written.

Mrs Pankhurst's views must have differed greatly from Ishbel's own, yet Ishbel clearly admired the older woman's strength of character.

Betty wondered if Ishbel knew just how people admired her – if she knew that, like

Emmeline Pankhurst, she was a very special lady.

Even on a day like today, when reminders of Ishbel's own wedding day, and of Gordon, must be almost too painful to bear, her warm smile hadn't faltered...

Robbie squeezed Betty's hand tightly, lifted her left hand and kissed it. They were husband and wife.

'You're looking a little lost, Jack.' Ishbel came to stand by Jack Keller's side.

'I'm just enjoying being spectator.' He gave her a quick smile.

'Are you thinking about Mary?' She laughed softly. 'Silly question. You're always thinking about Mary. You must wish, though, that she'd had all this.' She gestured round the church hall. 'The service in her own kirk, her parents' blessing, her family with her...'

'I don't wish it for me,' he said. 'For my own part, I really couldn't give a–' He stopped short. The last thing he wanted was to upset Ishbel.

'For Mary, yes, I wish she could have had all this. I know just how much it would have meant to her.'

'Less than you think, I suspect,' Ishbel said softly. 'I had it all, Jack. Not here in Edinburgh, of course, but my father conducted the ceremony, and I had my parents' blessing. My family and friends were there to wish us well.'

Yet now she was alone. A shiver ran along Jack's spine. He couldn't even begin to imagine how Ishbel must feel. He'd come dangerously close to losing Mary, and he knew he couldn't have coped...

'Mary and I are very lucky,' he answered simply.

'You are.' Ishbel nodded. 'Don't torture yourself with thoughts of anything else, Jack. Besides,' she added thoughtfully, 'I'm beginning to think that, now you're home for good, my father would rather like to have some sort of service in the kirk – so that your marriage is blessed before God.'

Jack's eyebrows rose.

'Perhaps I'll have a word with him,' Ishbel said softly, and Jack knew those weren't idle words. There was a strength about his sister-in-law that never failed to surprise him.

'These things have to be done carefully.' There was a sparkle of humour in her eyes. 'So that he thinks the idea was his all along.'

Jack laughed.

'It would mean a lot to Mary,' he said.

'I know it would.'

At that moment, Mary's laughter reached them. She couldn't have looked happier as she chatted with the bride and groom, Ishbel thought.

'Tell me something, Jack,' Ishbel said suddenly. 'Mary says she met this Mr Capone man, the one involved in those dreadful killings in Chicago last Thursday?'

'She did once.' Jack nodded. 'Mary met him at a night-club in Chicago. It was the night she was taken to hospital.'

'It was a sad affair,' Ishbel said quietly. 'You must be relieved to be away from trouble like that.'

There was very little that missed Ishbel, Jack realised. She was right, though – he was more relieved than she would ever know.

He knew no more than he'd read in the newspapers, but it was enough. Seven men had been killed in cold blood at Al Capone's orders.

Jack wanted no part of it... Ishbel's eyes were fixed on him, he realised.

'Do you know Mr Capone well?'

'No,' Jack answered immediately. He'd done a couple of business deals with him, and you couldn't know a man like Capone from that.

'Chicago is going through difficult times. When half the police force is under investigation for alleged corruption, there seems little hope,' he said.

'There's always hope, Jack.' She took him by the arm. 'Which is why we have to appreciate all that is good in life. And there is a lot that's good.'

'Indeed.' He was pleased to be away from a delicate subject. 'No-one knows that better than me, and if I ever need reminding, all I have to do is look at my wife and daughter.'

She smiled at him.

'So will you be joining the dancing, Ishbel?' he asked lightening the mood.

'Of course.'

'Really?' Once again, she'd surprised him. 'I've never imagined you to be overly fond of dancing.'

'I might surprise you, Jack,' she replied, laughing. 'Would you care to partner me?'

'You always do, Ishbel! And of course I will.'

A week later, Veronica's mind was still on the wedding.

'Get some sleep, love.' There was amusement in Donald's voice. The room was dark, but her mind was racing.

Veronica rolled over so that she lay on her side, facing him.

'I'm not sleepy. Tired, but not particularly sleepy. I was just thinking about our Rob. Remember when he was a lad, always getting into mischief? Remember when the little devil ran away, thinking he could find Ishbel?'

'I certainly do,' Donald replied grimly.

'And now look at him!' Veronica was smiling in the darkness. 'We couldn't have chosen a better wife for him, could we? Isn't Betty perfect? You couldn't wish to meet a lovelier girl.'

'She's grand.'

'Things have turned out well, haven't they, Don?'

'They have.'

Veronica heard the echo of her own satisfaction in his voice.

'Better than we'd dared hope.'

'And to have our Mary almost on the doorstep. And little Alice!' Veronica went on.

'Not so little now,' Donald pointed out.

'No, she's growing up fast.' And it was wonderful to be able to watch her. Whatever they thought of Jack – and Veronica never knew quite what to think of him – there was no denying he was a wonderful husband and father.

He might be a dubious character when it came to business matters, but he knew fine that his wife and daughter were all important.

'And what about our Ishbel?' Veronica murmured. 'She'll be fine, won't she?'

'Aye, she'll be fine.'

It still hurt Veronica terribly to think of her daughter being a widow at such a young age. It didn't seem right, or fair.

But then, Veronica thought with a soft sigh, life often wasn't. Sadly, there were plenty of women in Ishbel's shoes. Their friend Ruth McKinlay knew only too well what it was like to be left alone with bairns to care for.

'Do you think Ishbel will stay here now?'

Veronica asked quietly.

Donald was a long time answering.

'No,' he replied at last. 'I don't think she will, love.'

'But why?' Veronica demanded. 'What's the point in going back to China now? Of all the places in the world–'

'That's exactly the point,' Donald said quietly. 'That's where she's needed, and if I know Ishbel as well as I think I do, she'll return to Shanghai to carry on her work.'

'It's no place for a wee lad like James,' Veronica said shortly, and Donald reached for her hand and gave it a squeeze. 'We can't live Ishbel's life for her,' he said gently. 'If she stayed, she'd only regret it.'

Deep in her heart, Veronica knew he was right, and she should be grateful – which she was.

Mary, Jack and Alice lived nearby, and Betty and Robbie would be based at the manse for the time being.

It was much more than Veronica had once dared to dream of.

She had to smile to herself. For the last ten years, it seemed as if life had been a constant series of worries. Now, for the first time, she had little to worry about...

'I love you, Donald Montrose,' she whispered into the darkness.

The only answer was a tiny snore.

Veronica put her arms round him and

finally went to sleep.

Ishbel didn't recognise the handwriting on the envelope. All she knew was that the letter had come from Shanghai.

She put it in her coat pocket, pulled James's scarf a little tighter and checked that he hadn't taken his mittens off, then stepped outdoors.

It was bitterly cold; the ice was still thick on the small pond. Ishbel could still remember her father making that pond. He loved the garden with a passion, and enjoyed nothing more than working in it.

'Think how wonderful it will be to sit by water in the summer,' he'd said.

It was a delight in the summer, but now, just looking at the pond made Ishbel shiver.

James had no such qualms. He never seemed aware of the cold.

While her son went on his usual search for treasures, Ishbel sat on the old wooden seat. A blackbird landed on the lawn nearby, pecked at the ground, gave Ishbel a scowl and flew off again.

Apart from the occasional little cry from James, all was quiet. The garden had always been a haven. It was no wonder her father was so often drawn to it when wrestling with problems.

'Mummy!' James stood in front of her, holding a small pebble in his hands.

'It's lovely, sweetheart.' She wondered what made that particular pebble so much better than all the others. 'A very special pebble.'

He laughed, and ran off again.

If she were on her own, Ishbel doubted she would think twice about returning to Shanghai. But it was hard to take James away from his family – it didn't seem fair on him.

He deserved the childhood Ishbel had had, the childhood Gordon had had. How could she give him that, in a city torn apart by constant fighting?

Her thoughts went round and round. Memories of her childhood intermingled with memories of Gordon...

While James banged his pebble on the path, Ishbel took the letter from her pocket.

She was surprised to discover it was from Adam, and even more surprised to see that it covered three whole pages.

Three pages! She must pay their friend Lizzie a visit later, and see if that was a record. Usually you were lucky to get one, from Adam.

News of her friends in Shanghai was always welcome, but she soon discovered that this letter was unlike any of the others he'd sent.

No-one knows when you're coming back, or even if you're coming back. Your friends seem almost frightened to ask.

A few days ago, I saw Liang and Han, and

they told me that Liang is expecting another child.

When I said how pleased you would be on hearing the news, Liang said that she couldn't bring herself to tell you. She thought the news would hurt you. She couldn't understand how, given the circumstances, you could be happy for them...

Ishbel's heart was pounding as she read his words. How could Liang think such a thing? Her pregnancy was the best news Ishbel could have had!

She was a little envious, yes, but she couldn't have been more thrilled for Liang and Han...

Perhaps I'm wrong to tell you, but I know, without any doubt whatsoever, that the news will only make you happy.

But that's how it is here, Ishbel. Where you're concerned, people are choosing their words carefully. No-one will ask when you're coming back, yet everyone misses you desperately. I miss you desperately...

Ishbel smiled. She missed him, too – she missed all her friends in Shanghai.

You belong here, Ishbel, and deep in your heart, I know you believe that, too...

Silly tears smarted in her eyes. Adam was right; she did belong there.

She was no longer the naïve twenty-year-old who'd been so scared on that first long sea voyage to a foreign land.

Life would never be easy in Shanghai, but Ishbel had never wanted an easy life. She wanted a rewarding one, a life that was satisfying and useful.

She could no more stay in Edinburgh and take the easy option than she could reach out and touch the moon.

She owed it to herself, and to Gordon, to go back. What would he have thought if she simply gave up?

No, she must return to Shanghai and carry on the work that had meant so much to him.

Carefully, she folded Adam's letter and returned it to her coat pocket.

'Come along, James.' She rose to her feet and reached for her son's hand. 'Let's go inside, sweetheart. There's a lot to be done.' She knelt to hug him. 'We're going home, you and I.'

With her son's trusting hand in hers, Ishbel took one last look around. The sun peeped out from behind a cloud and began to warm the frozen ground.

Spring was on its way, bringing with it the promise of new life, and new hope for the future.

The publishers hope that this book has given you enjoyable reading. Large Print Books are especially designed to be as easy to see and hold as possible. If you wish a complete list of our books please ask at your local library or write directly to:

Dales Large Print Books
Magna House, Long Preston,
Skipton, North Yorkshire.
BD23 4ND

This Large Print Book, for people
who cannot read normal print,
is published under the auspices of

THE ULVERSCROFT FOUNDATION